The Rancher's Convenient Pregnant Bride

Sweet inspirational
contemporary cowboy romance

Book 3 in
the Bear Creek Saddle Series

by *NY Times* & *USA Today* bestselling author
Shoshanna Evers
writing as
Shoshanna Gabriel

Stand-alone 3rd book in the Bear Creek Saddle Series by Shoshanna Evers writing as Shoshanna Gabriel

About the book:

The handsome rancher has an offer for a modern marriage of convenience this city girl just can't refuse… for her baby's sake.

Eric Hunt, a handsome young rancher in the **small mountain town** of Bear Creek Saddle, Idaho, learns **he can't have children of his own.** His desperate prayers to God for healing are answered with **a crystal-clear vision**: a beautiful woman with warm brown eyes—his future wife?—and she's holding a baby. *But how…and who?*

Across the country, Lindsay Moore's glamorous Manhattan lifestyle is ripped out from under her when she falls victim to an investment scam, loses her job as an executive at the bank…and finds out **she's pregnant** by a man who wants nothing to do with her, or her baby. Abandoned and heartbroken, Lindsay is **done with love.**

When Lindsay's sister asks her to come out to Bear Creek Saddle Ranch to be her maid of honor and help plan her upcoming wedding, **Lindsay has nowhere else to go.** But she's completely out of place in the mountains, and without the sense of importance and identity her career and money used to give her, she feels lost. She's no longer sure of her value, and she never imagined she'd be in this predicament… **single, broke, and raising her baby without a father.**

Eric is the groom's best man, and when the bride-to-be's beautiful sister Lindsay arrives, they find themselves drawn to each other, despite all of their differences. With those warm brown eyes, **could Lindsay be** the one from his vision? When Eric discovers Lindsay is pregnant, **he knows God sent Lindsay to him for a reason.** Eric wants to marry her and be a father to her baby, **even if they're not in love yet**—she's beautiful inside and out, and he feels called by God to make the proposal. For Lindsay, it's a way out of the mess she's made of her life—**an offer for a modern marriage of convenience** that she just can't refuse.

But can a man and a woman with nothing in common, find common ground...and maybe even love...before their child is born?

The Rancher's Convenient Pregnant Bride
Book 3 in the Bear Creek Saddle Series
by Shoshanna Gabriel

Shoshanna's Testimony

"But he was pierced for our transgressions, he was crushed for our iniquities; the punishment that brought us peace was on him, and by his wounds we are healed." Isaiah 53:5 (NIV)

I USED TO BE known as Shoshanna Evers, a *New York Times* and *USA Today* bestselling author of steamy romance, from 2009-2015. Why did that end in 2015? In short, I came out in a public blog post as a Christian, and explained why I could no longer write sexy books. My career immediately crumbled.

Everything changed—my writing career, my religion, and my name. In 2014 (while still writing as Evers) I had a "road to Damascus" experience, and I started to think seriously about Jesus as the Messiah, and what that meant for me. I'm Jewish, so that was something I had *literally never* thought about before.

The seeds had been planted as early back as December 2012, after the horrific Newtown shooting, when I turned to the *Tanach* (Old Testament) for comfort. For the first time, the Messianic prophecies seemed to jump out at me. I noticed something I'd never seen or heard before: *Isaiah 53*. At my Jewish synagogues, from Reform to Conservative to Orthodox, from the time I was an infant through till adulthood, *I'd never heard Isaiah 53 read*. It was always skipped over in the weekly Haftorah readings, presumably because it just didn't correlate with any of the Torah (Pentateuch) portions or any festivals. Reading it shocked me. Even after looking into what the rabbis and Jewish philosophers teach about this chapter (they don't believe it's about the Messiah, but about Israel), I *still* couldn't shake the effect Isaiah 53 had on me.

I can't quote all 12 verses here, so please… check it out for yourself, and you'll see why this Jewish girl nearly fainted while reading it for the first time.

I barely knew anything about Jesus. What little I did know came from the musicals *Godspell* and *Jesus Christ Superstar*. That's all I knew, but I could see the Prophet Isaiah was telling me all about Jesus long before Jesus came to Earth, and I'd never even known it. This started over a year of questioning and researching to find out if Jesus was actually the Messiah I had been looking for all along.

A year later, at the end of 2013, my family and I left Los Angeles and settled in a small mountain town in north Idaho. I attended church weekly for the first time in my life, and I loved it. It felt so right, even if I wasn't ready yet to fully give myself to Jesus. I loved praying in English instead of Hebrew, and I loved the church family.

In 2014, I had gone from writing erotic romance to less-explicit but still very steamy romance (books that came out that year had been written the year before). In 2015 when I bit the bullet and got baptized (despite the extreme disapproval of my secular Jewish family), things started changing for me very fast, from the moment I came out of the water.

I had been getting more and more successful as Shoshanna Evers. Writing sexy stories was very good to me, but it wasn't good *for* me, personally—not when it was keeping me from writing the stories I truly wanted to tell. I found myself writing faith elements into my storylines, only to have to remove them because they weren't part of the Evers "brand." I didn't want to freak out my readership, who hadn't signed on for anything having to do with God. Most importantly, I started feeling weird about what I was doing with my writing. I wanted to use the gift He had given me in a way that would be for His glory.

I'd never felt ashamed or weird about writing sexually explicit stories before—and I won't judge those who do. Who am I to throw stones? But something had changed in me. Writing love scenes was no longer my thing, which—considering I had written and had been editor of the 2011 non-fiction book *How to Write Hot Sex*—was going to mean *a major overhaul* in my life.

When I wrote *I Am Not Your Melody*, which I called "a Bear Creek Saddle short novel" and prequel to an upcoming series, I was already tired of writing sex scenes (after writing them in every book since 2010, I had essentially burned myself out). And my hero, Bill, was clearly (to me) having a faith crisis, but I couldn't articulate that. When the book came out, it wasn't the book I had really wanted to write in the first place. Despite that, I knew the book was good and that it fulfilled the promise I'd made to my readers as Shoshanna Evers: *Sexily *Evers* After*. It sold fifteen thousand copies in the first week as part of the *Cowboy 12-Pack* book bundle, and kept on selling. The follow-up series was bought by a big publisher.

But ultimately, I realized I couldn't sign the contract. I was just…*done* writing secular romance. There was no way I'd be able to write the series the way the publisher wanted me to. Instead, I wanted to write inspirational romance. They were very gracious and let me out of the contract. My agent—who was also very gracious—and I parted ways because she didn't represent Christian fiction. In one fell swoop I had lost a six-book contract and my agent, and though it felt as if I were pressing the career-self-destruct-button, I wrote that blog post entitled "Saying Goodbye to Erotic Romance" (http://bit.ly/GoodbyeErotica) in November 2015, where I came out as a Christian and told my readership what was happening.

The response from readers and many authors was overwhelmingly wonderful, despite the negative effect the move had on my publishing career. A percentage of my most loyal readers assured me they loved the way I tell stories, so they'd still read my books, and the Christian romance author community was so kind and welcoming. For some reason, I'd expected them to keep their distance, since I was "that kind" of author who had written "those kind" of books, and I didn't belong over in the squeaky-clean section of the cafeteria. But just the opposite happened—the inspirational authors welcomed me with open arms. Those ladies really walk the talk, friends.

There have been, of course, some readers who are upset. They've told me they're done reading my books. The day after the blog post went out, I had to step down as the Erotica Captain for a big annual book convention. I had created panels and topics, and I was going to be speaking on them as well. The panels went forward, but without me on them. The decision hurt my pride a bit, but it made sense. I needed a clean break in order to move forward.

Shoshanna Gabriel is my new name for my new genre. No more *Sexily *Evers* After*, now my promise is a *Faithfully Ever After*. Originally, I'd wanted to keep the name Shoshanna Evers, since I'd

spent nearly six years building it up and had my "letters" (*NYT &
USAT*)—but I have too many sexy books out as Evers, and I didn't
want my future readers to accidentally pick up a backlist book and
have a heart attack. Giving up my bestseller status to start all over
again wasn't an easy decision, but it's one I made after a lot of
prayer, and it feels right.

Now that the publishing contract for my new series was gone,
I was able to revise the opening book to be how I'd originally
intended it to be, as a sweet inspirational romance. I re-titled it
Second Chances for Trampled Hearts (Book 1 in the Bear Creek Saddle
Series) and wrote it under the name Shoshanna Gabriel.

I'm thrilled to have the opportunity to share the rest of the Bear
Creek Saddle Series with you in a personal, very real way that I never
would have been able to if I'd gone against that little voice
whispering inside of me, a voice that said, *God has a different path for
you than the one you are on.*

All I want now is to write for His glory, and to do His will. It's
not easy. But it's worth it.

Please pray for me, friends, and I'll be praying for you. Happy
reading!

All my best wishes,

Shoshanna Gabriel

Chapter One

"For you created my inmost being; you knit me together in my mother's womb. I praise you because I am fearfully and wonderfully made; your works are wonderful, I know that full well. My frame was not hidden from you when I was made in the secret place, when I was woven together in the depths of the earth. Your eyes saw my unformed body; all the days ordained for me were written in your book before one of them came to be." *Psalm 139:13-16 (NIV)*

LINDSAY MOORE PRESSED into the seatback of the yellow taxicab and stared out the window at the pedestrians weaving their way down the overcrowded New York City sidewalks. At least the cab driver hadn't given her the side-eye when she'd told him her destination…not that she'd have blamed him if he had.

Her sister didn't even know anything that had happened to her, since Megan had left Manhattan and moved all the way out to the small mountain town of Bear Creek Saddle, Idaho.

Megan didn't know the very worst part of it all. The stupidest mistake Lindsay ever could have made…and now, here she was.

God, I need You. What do I do now?

Just…help a girl out. Please, help me now.

As if on cue, her phone rang—the upbeat country music she'd programmed to play whenever her sister called. The cheery guitar strums seemed out of place in the dreary cab interior.

Thank You.

Lindsay accepted the call, barely able to control her emotions. "Meg! How are you?"

"I just had this urge to call you," Megan said, her voice bright and clear as day, even though she was on the other side of the country. "And I thought, 'you know who's good at planning events?' You! What do you think? Will you help me?"

Lindsay laughed and blinked back the tears that threatened to escape her eyes. "I don't know anything about planning a wedding outside of Manhattan. I get shaky on the details if I stray too far from the Upper West Side, even."

"I'm positive you have tons of vacation days and sick days stored up that you never take. Come on out to Idaho. You can stay with me. Who better to plan my wedding than you?"

"You'll get sick of me if I come out an entire month before your wedding. That's a long time."

Megan's voice sobered. "I miss you, and I'm excited for you to get to know Zach before we get married. There's plenty of room at the ranch for you."

"I don't have…" Lindsay paused. What could she say at a time like this? "…a dress yet."

"It's Idaho, not Mars. You can buy anything you need here. And it's not like Amazon doesn't ship here if you can't find what you want. You don't even need to pack a toothbrush, much less your fancy-pants shampoo." Megan laughed into the phone, and Lindsay could just imagine her younger sister's big smile.

"Let me think on it, and I'll get back to you," Lindsay said. "Love you."

"Love you more."

Ending the call brought Lindsay back to reality—to the chilly, dark cab, to the steadily increasing cab fare, and the final destination she never, ever had wanted to go to in the first place.

"Wait—" she called to the driver through the plastic partition.

The driver slid the partition open. "What?"

She thought about the money Grant had given her this morning, nonchalantly handing over the bills as if they'd had George Washington's face on them instead of Benjamin Franklin's.

"I can't—I don't want to go to the women's clinic after all."

"You want to get out here?" The driver tapped the meter. "You still pay."

Lindsay took a deep breath. "Drive me to JFK, instead, please."

He groaned. "The airport, now? I'll have to turn around."

As if that minor inconvenience was going to change her mind now.

"Thank you," she said, and sank back in her seat once more, this time with a sigh of relief.

Her sister had no idea what a huge impact her invitation had. The timing couldn't be a coincidence. That *had* to be God.

If only she'd asked Him for help sooner—before she'd even gotten into this mess.

While Megan probably wasn't expecting Lindsay to show up on her doorstep so soon after their conversation, there was no way Lindsay could risk going back to Grant's place—where her few remaining personal items were—unless she'd "taken care of things." His words.

As if it were so easy. No big deal.

If she went back, he'd convince her all over again to do the one thing she did not want to do. At least at her sister's house, Lindsay could expect some love and support. There was no going back now. Only forward—to Idaho.

What was a born-and-bred Manhattan girl going to do in the mountains with a bunch of cow ranchers?

A small voice spoke inside of her: *You'll live… You both will.*

Lindsay laughed out loud, the sound breaking the silence in the cab. This was happening. It was really happening.

She gently placed her hand on her abdomen, even though there was nothing to see or feel just yet.

We're going to be okay, Little One.

* * *

Eric Hunt took in a deep breath of the clear mountain air, and looked toward the rising sun over the evergreen trees. The rays filtered through the woods, glinting off a small puddle of water on a rock near his boots. He tipped his brown Stetson lower over his eyes.

It was a good hat. He'd bought it—a better version of the old cowboy hat he'd had—the same week he'd become an official co-owner of the ranch he'd been working on as a wrangler, since he'd been a teenager.

'Cause now, he wouldn't be all hat, no cattle.

"Thanks for coming with me." Eric glanced at his brother, Ryan, who walked next to him. "Barely see you anymore these days, feels like."

"Wait till you fall in love and get married." Ryan chuckled. "You won't want to be away from your wife for too long, either."

Whatever. Love was fickle. Love couldn't be trusted to be there any longer than it had been for him in the past.

Values, common goals, now *that* had staying power—like what his brother and sister-in-law had.

Whether or not he fell in love, Eric had always assumed he'd get married at some point, so he could have a partner in life, and have children.

Now that assumption was off the table.

Eric wanted to be with a woman who wanted to be a mom and raise a family—but from now on, he was only going to be able to date women who didn't want kids at all.

That right there was a conundrum.

"I was thinking about that last night," Eric admitted. He'd been silently praying, from the moment his head hit the pillow, as he always did before he fell asleep. "Picture popped in my head, clear as can be. Like a movie. Man, it was so clear…it felt like…"

What was the right word?

"…like a vision," Eric said.

That was it. There was no better way to explain it.

"You mean a dream? Never known you to have…*visions*." Ryan, his elder by three years, said the word cautiously—like he didn't believe him.

"Not visions, plural." Eric raised his index finger to clarify. "Just one. One in my whole life. Ain't so crazy for me to have just one little picture in my head from God, is it?"

Ryan shrugged.

"It happened to folks in the Bible, right?" Eric asked.

Maybe it shouldn't matter as much as it did—but he wanted Ryan to understand how important it was to him, for what he'd seen to be from God—for it to be *real*.

"I guess it don't matter if it was a vision or a dream either way," Ryan conceded. "What'd you see?" He paused, as if unsure of his wording. "Or… um…what were you dreaming about?"

"It was me, and a girl—I mean, a *woman*—and she was holding a little baby. And the girl was looking at me with these warm, brown eyes. Best thing I've ever seen." Eric smiled.

Maybe he'd fallen asleep sooner than he'd thought, and it was just a dream, after all.

But it had felt so real. It felt…*true*. As if God had answered his desperate prayers for healing with this vision, to comfort him.

"Well, a wife and a baby." Ryan looked relieved. "That's doable. At least you weren't having visions about winning the Kentucky Derby or something. I thought you were gonna say something crazy."

"It *is* crazy," Eric muttered.

Ryan didn't know, and it wasn't his fault for not knowing—it was Eric's.

"Why do you want me to get married so bad, anyway?" Eric kept a steady pace to their hike, keeping up with his brother.

Ryan shrugged, and Eric dropped it. He was happy for him. Ryan had found himself a good woman, and they lived just a few miles from Bear Creek Saddle Ranch, which Eric co-owned with his best friends. But he saw his friends at the ranch a lot more often than he saw his own brother.

"I got some good news," Ryan said suddenly, interrupting Eric's thoughts. "Maybe it even has something to do with your, um…vision." He laughed.

"What's up?"

Ryan grinned. "Tiff's pregnant."

"Oh, wow, man, that's awesome," Eric exclaimed. He patted Ryan's back with a hearty thud, and grinned back at him. "You're gonna be a dad. That's crazy."

A tiny slip of jealousy crossed Eric's mind before he shoved it away, clearing his mind of anything other than happy thoughts. What if the baby in his vision was meant to symbolize Ryan's child, not his own?

Couldn't be.

Eric knew what God had shown him. It was his own wife and baby.

"And you're gonna be an uncle," Ryan added.

"Wow. That's nuts."

An uncle… Maybe being an uncle would be enough for him. He could be a really good uncle, take his nephew (or niece) out camping and teach him (or her) how to fish, that kind of thing.

Would that be enough?

Sure…maybe. For a while.

"When's she due?" Eric asked.

"It's still early. We haven't told everyone yet, 'cause she's still in the first trimester. We'll have a Christmas baby." Ryan couldn't seem to stop smiling.

God, let me be purely happy for him, without being sad for myself. It ain't right. Take that feeling away, Lord, if You can.

Well—of course God could. The question Eric had to answer for himself was, was he ready to stop the pity-party?

Maybe not quite yet. Ryan didn't even know.

Man.

"Sooner you get married," Ryan was saying, "sooner you can get to work on bringin' a little cousin into the world for my kid. Just like what you saw, man. They can grow up together, like we did."

"Yeah."

They hiked in silence for a few long minutes.

"I didn't mean to push you," Ryan said, breaking the silence. "I get it. Just 'cause I married Tiff when I was your age, doesn't mean *you're* ready to settle down."

"Ain't any girls in town who'd want to marry me, anyhow." Eric tried to keep his voice casual. As if it didn't matter.

Even though it did.

Ryan stopped in his tracks. "Are you kidding me, bro? You're all set, man—you got the ranch, built your own home, an' we can't go anywhere together without girls looking at you more'n once."

"You look just like me." Eric shook his head and gestured to his brother's thick head of dark hair, year-round natural tan, and even the same blue eyes.

"Nah—you look just like *me*." Ryan laughed. "I was here first, remember?"

"Can't forget. Big shoes to fill." But Eric smiled.

They'd gone almost an entire mile farther before they stopped to drink some water and enjoy the view for a minute.

"So." Eric took his hat off and wiped the sweat off his brow before setting it back on his head. "I got something to tell you, too."

"What's up?" Ryan was drinking from his canteen, and a bit of water spilled on his shirt when he spoke. He wiped his mouth with the back of his hand.

"I went to the doctor a few weeks ago," Eric said carefully. Felt good to finally bring it up. Now was as good a time as any.

"You all right?"

Eric could sense the concern in his brother's voice. Their mother was a breast cancer survivor, and knowing cancer ran in their family put them both on edge whenever anyone brought up the subject of doctors.

"No cancer," Eric said quickly. May as well lead with the good news. "But I can't have kids, anyways. That's why the vision shook me up, I guess."

"What?" Ryan looked shocked. "How would you even know that?"

"I thought everything seemed fine. Everything in working order. But the doctor found internal scar tissue. He thinks it's from a real old injury when I was kid. I can think of more than one that could've done me in."

"Scar tissue." Ryan frowned. They started walking again, but he'd slowed his pace.

"Yup. Inside, blocking…um…man, I don't want to get all detailed and medical, all right? But I ain't got no swimmers."

"Nothing comes out when—"

Eric bit the inside of his cheek to keep from growling at his brother. Zach, his best friend who owned the ranch with him, had asked him nearly the exact same question.

"How many other ways can I say *I thought everything was fine?*" Eric said in exasperation. "No issues I would've known about without a doggone microscope, all right? It's a problem you can't see with your eyes. Either way—it don't matter how long I'm married for, I ain't gonna get my wife pregnant. You got it now?"

Ryan was silent. "I'm sorry, man. How'd you, uh…find out?"

"Doc found the scar tissue, thought it might be something cancer or whatnot 'cause of Mom's medical history, and when they did the imaging he figured it out. So he tested um…you know, with the microscope. This…this ain't a problem that's going away. Surgery's kinda a risky option."

"But it's an option?"

"If I'm willing to risk losing my ability to have marital relations at all, I guess," Eric explained. "And I ain't willing."

"Don't blame ya." Ryan shuddered as if the mere thought had given him the chills. "Maybe you can adopt."

"Yeah, maybe…"

It wasn't a bad idea. Not that a guy could compare kids to dogs, but if Eric could love Boomer as much as he did, and Boomer was a whole different species, how much more would he love a kid, even if they weren't related by blood?

"Maybe," Eric repeated, brighter this time. "Yeah."

"Maybe you'll even find a woman with kids of her own already. They're not all off the market, you know."

"That's true." Eric gave his brother a quick smile. Ryan was good at saying the right thing to make him feel better. Always had been.

There could still be the right girl for him out there, somewhere. *Lord, please drop her right in my lap where I can't miss her.*

* * *

Two crammed flights later, with a short layover in Denver, Lindsay found herself in Spokane, Washington—only a couple of hours' drive over the border into Bear Creek Saddle, Idaho. There wasn't even an airport in north Idaho for her to go to, as she'd discovered when she got to JFK and rushed to the counter with the crumpled hundred-dollar bills in her hand.

She hadn't texted her sister, which was at best, dumb, and at worst, rude; but what if her sister told her she wasn't ready for guests just yet, and that the invite was really meant to be for a few days or a week from now? In this case, it would be better to ask for forgiveness rather than permission.

Finally, she got the courage to text her sister, even though it was after ten p.m. Either way, Lindsay would be hanging around the airport for a while. That was fine. She could spend the night there if she had to.

Wasn't like she had anywhere else to spend the night.

It was entirely possible Megan wouldn't see the text until the morning. At some point, Megan would have to come over and pick her up from the airport. The cost for a cab all the way to Bear Creek Saddle from Spokane would be more than she had left after buying the plane ticket.

"*Surprise!*" she texted to Megan's cell. "*I'm here, at Spokane International. I know it's late and last minute.*"

It took a few minutes as Lindsay stared at her texts, waiting for a response, but then her phone rang instead.

"Lindsay?" her sister asked when Lindsay picked up the phone. "Are you really in Spokane?"

"Yup! I…have a lot to talk to you about."

"Everything okay?"

Well, she had her health, even if that health included an unplanned pregnancy.

"Yes," Lindsay replied. It almost sounded convincing. "I just need a ride to your place."

Her sister half-laughed, half-groaned. "Hang on."

Lindsay waited until Megan came back on the line.

"You're in luck," Megan said. "Zach's friend, Eric, is out in Liberty Lake at the vet with his dog. He can swing by and pick you up when he's done."

"He's at the vet at this hour? Is his dog all right?"

"I hope so," Megan said. "Zach said he got into a scuffle with a goat. The dog—not Eric."

"As one does," Lindsay murmured. "I mean—that's great. Not great about the dog, of course. Great about the ride. Can you give him my number? I'll wait in the baggage terminal for him. Tell him to take his time and make sure his dog's okay—I'm in no rush."

"Will do, Linds. Can't believe you're actually here! I'll make up a bed for you."

Baggage claim was nearly empty after the people from her flight got their bags and left. She checked on her phone to see how far Liberty Lake was from Spokane. Not too far. They were both in Washington State, for one thing. That was lucky.

Thank You, Lord.

She hoped this guy Eric wasn't too put-out by picking her up. He was probably worried about his pet, to have driven hours to an emergency vet in the middle of the night. His name seemed very familiar.

Best man.

That was it. Eric would be Zach's best man in the wedding. Lindsay remembered now. She would walk down the aisle with him, since she was going to be the maid of honor.

Well, this would be a strange way to meet him, but they would have met eventually at the wedding, anyway.

It was only an hour later when her phone buzzed with a new message alert.

"This is Eric—Zach and Megan's friend. I'm here for you."

Hallelujah. It had been a long, difficult day, and she couldn't wait to sit back and ride to her sister's place.

Lindsay stood, hefting her purse over her shoulder—her only bag.

Across the terminal stood a tall, handsome man with broad shoulders and a brown cowboy hat. Seemed about the same age as Zach. Could that be him?

He caught her staring and touched the rim of his hat, as if to say "hello." Or maybe to say, "I see you looking at me."

"Are you Eric—"

"Lindsay?" the man asked at the same time.

"Yes." She smiled as he walked over to her.

"Wow. You really do look just like her," Eric said. "Shorter, and shorter hair, like she said…are you her twin or something?"

Lindsay laughed. It was a compliment, as far as she was concerned. "Her big sister. I'm here early to help plan the wedding."

"That's great," Eric said, his face breaking into a smile that looked completely genuine. "She talks about you all the time. Are you the big-time banking exec from New York City?"

"That's me," Lindsay said, with a lighthearted laugh. "Um, well…actually, I'm not working at the moment. So I've got plenty of time to help her out with the wedding and everything. I'll probably be here for a while."

"I'll grab your bags," he offered, looking behind her.

"Um, no bags. Just me." She shrugged, as if that was totally not weird at all. "I can borrow Megan's clothes. We're the same size, she's just a few inches taller. Not fair, I know, especially since I'm supposed to be the big sister."

Ugh. She was rambling. She couldn't help it—he was too good-looking. Those blue eyes of his contrasting against his olive skin and dark hair. Amazing.

It was making her nervous.

"Okay." He nodded, but she could've sworn he'd looked at her strangely.

Which made sense, of course. Who travels across America without so much as a toothbrush or a change of socks?

"Is your dog going to be okay?"

"Boomer's all right." Eric slowed his long strides, allowing her to keep up. "He won't be messing with the goats again anytime soon, that's for sure. Got a good long scrape on his side, got some stitches."

"Poor guy." Lindsay loved dogs, though she rarely had the chance to interact with any. Her building didn't allow pets, and none of her friends had dogs. The only ones she saw were when she walked in Central Park and visited the dog park. "What kind of dog is he?"

"Airedale Terrier. Big guy. Bark is much worse than his bite."

"Good to know."

"Good for the goats, too."

They got to Eric's truck, a big black pickup with what looked like a sad and sedated Boomer lying in the backseat.

Boomer barked when Eric opened the door for her.

"Go back to sleep," Eric said. "It's just Megan's sister."

That seemed to be good enough for the dog, who obeyed, promptly resting his big furry head on the bench seat.

"Let me help you up." Eric offered Lindsay his large, calloused hand, and she took it gratefully.

"Thanks." Normally she took the subway everywhere, and occasionally cabs or Uber. Not many people in New York City had big work trucks like Eric's.

He waited until she was settled and buckled in before he went around to the driver's side. How chivalrous.

Completely unlike Grant, who hadn't even offered to accompany her to the clinic for what could've been the biggest, most awful event of her life…even though it was his baby, too.

Well, not anymore, it wasn't. As far as she was concerned, Grant gave up his paternity the moment he'd paid her to permanently get rid of it.

There. Anger. That was better.

Much better than heartbreak. Grant wasn't worthy of heartbreak.

She'd gotten so, so very close to falling for him, too. Good thing he'd shown her his true colors.

It had only taken him five years…

"Wasn't expecting Megan's call tonight. This a surprise visit?" Eric asked, staring straight ahead at the road.

"Sort of. Megan invited me, but I didn't tell her I went to the airport immediately after she called." Lindsay laughed, as if it were all in fun.

There was no reason to tell more to this complete stranger, even if he was her brother-in-law-to-be's childhood best friend.

"You own the ranch with Zach, right?" she asked, to jog her memory.

"Yes indeed. Me, Zach, Chris and Jay." He didn't look at her as he spoke, but it seemed to be more a result of keeping his eyes on the road and less about shyness.

She couldn't imagine such a big, good-looking guy being shy. He'd taken his hat off in the truck and set it on the console between them. Dark tendrils swept across his forehead, and he ran his fingers through them to push his hair back.

She didn't know what exactly to ask, or what to say. What did she have in common with this guy, anyway, other than her sister? Country life was vastly different from her life in New York. Ranching and banking were worlds apart. And from what she knew of the group of ranchers at Bear Creek Saddle Ranch, they were good guys who went to church every week and walked the talk.

Not like her. A hypocrite who had essentially prostituted herself for a place to sleep.

But that was too much of a departure from how she liked to think of herself, so no wonder she'd clung to Grant like a life raft in open water. Hoping he'd love her and want to marry her…so she wouldn't see herself for who she was, or what she was doing.

God, what have I done? Please, please forgive me.

No matter how many times she'd asked God for forgiveness, she kept feeling the urge to ask one more time, as if maybe the first time hadn't stuck. Even knowing the extent of God's grace for those who repented, she was having a hard time with it. Was she good enough to forgive? Did she even deserve to be forgiven?

And now she was bringing an innocent child into this mess. A child who wouldn't have a father in his life. From everything she'd learned after researching online, having a father figure in the home was, statistically, really important for children. Those kids with the good luck to grow up with married parents at home led, in many cases, infinitely more privileged lives. She mourned that loss for her child's sake, if not for hers.

Of course, plenty of people grew up with a single mom as the head of the household, and did perfectly fine. She'd be okay. Her sister had said Zach had grown up without a dad, since he'd abandoned him and his mom when he was young. That was probably more traumatic for a kid than not knowing their father to begin with, right?

None of it was ideal.

Maybe it would be best if she gave her baby up for adoption to a nice married couple.

The thought hurt her heart.

Eric shifted his hands on the steering wheel, appearing to be as lost in thought as she was. A little conversation would help keep her out of her head.

"So, Eric—did you always want to be a rancher?"

"Yeah, I think I did."

He didn't expand on his reply. Not one for talking much, it seemed. Or maybe it was just with her.

Well, if there was one thing Lindsay was good at, it was getting people to talk and open up. It was one of her jobs at the bank, to make new clients feel like they were her best friend, so they'd trust her enough to put lots of money in the bank. Even if that was part of the job (people skills, as they said), she did genuinely like meeting new people; and by the end of their meetings, she usually had a real interest in them and hoped for their financial success, whatever that might mean to them.

"Tell me about your ranch," she pressed. "I know nothing about this stuff, and I'm going to be staying there with Megan, so I could really use a primer."

"Not much to say, I suppose," Eric said. "Used to be Bill's ranch, but after Melody passed—" He coughed, as if covering for a break in his voice. *Who was Melody?* "Well, Bill sold us the ranch."

"Did you know her well? I'm sorry for your loss."

"She was a good lady. Really threw Bill for a loop when she died. But he's back on the saddle again—he and Allie—that's his new wife—they own Freddy's Diner in town now. Us guys have been working on that ranch since we were kids ourselves."

"You, Zach, Chris and...?" She paused, prompting him to remind her of all the names. They were all going to be groomsmen. She should know this.

"Jay." Eric nodded and checked something on his dashboard. "Sorry, I gotta fill 'er up. You hungry or anything?"

Starved.

"Only if you are." Lindsay hoped the tone in her voice did not sound especially hungry.

She hadn't eaten since the cookies on the plane. And prior to that, she hadn't eaten in the morning before the cab ride. Too nervous, plus she might've needed major sedation.

"I know just the place—they get their beef from us. Burgers an' gas right over the Idaho state line."

They rode past a big green highway sign that said:

WELCOME TO IDAHO: *WELCOME CENTER 8 MILES*

Not too long after, he pulled off the exit ramp. It was so dark out at night compared to the city. Despite the street lamps, there were entire stretches of road bathed in darkness.

From the backseat, Boomer whined.

"Settle down." Eric pulled in by the fuel pump in front of a tiny diner/convenience store, and reached back toward the dog. "I'll get you one too when we get back."

Eric opened the driver's side door and turned to Lindsay. "Stay inside the truck till I get 'er fueled up."

"Yes, *sir*." She didn't bother to keep the sarcasm from her voice. Why was he ordering her around like she had to listen to him? Were all Idahoan men like that?

If Eric noticed her annoyance at his tone, he didn't act like it. He swung his long, muscular denim-clad legs out of the truck and jumped to the pavement.

The truck jostled as he put the fuel pump into her side of the vehicle, and for some reason, it felt personal. Like he was jostling her.

What is wrong with me? This guy was doing her a favor. A *big* favor, and on very short notice. She was probably just tired. Exhausted, even.

And famished.

He left the pump in the truck and grabbed the windshield washer, dripping in soapy water.

His thin white T-shirt stretched over his biceps as he reached in front of the truck to get to the windshield. With a jump that really rocked the truck, he hopped up onto the floorboard of the driver's side for easier access.

Lindsay didn't want to stare, but he was so intent on cleaning the bugs off his glass that he didn't seem to notice her at all. So there was no harm in just watching him work, right?

Don't lust. That wasn't even what had gotten her into her current predicament (what had? Pride? Or its opposite, shame?), but it could definitely get her into another bad situation.

At least she couldn't get pregnant twice at the same time. Small comfort.

It was strange—she'd spent her twenty-eight years as a virgin, then lost her virginity only a month ago. But the experience had her looking at men in a completely different way.

Or maybe it was just something about Eric. Any woman would agree he was easy on the eyes. If he wasn't such an Idaho cowboy type, he could've been a model in New York. Did he know that? Or was he completely unaware of his effect on women…on her?

She startled a bit when he got back in the truck. Could he tell she'd been thinking about him that way?

"Didn't mean to scare you," he said. "I gotta move the truck so we can grab some food."

When they parked, he came around to her door even as she was opening it for herself. That was nice. Gentlemanly, even.

"Thank you," she murmured, taking his hand to jump down. But as she did, her foot slipped off the running board on the side of the vehicle, and Eric wrapped his arm around her waist, holding her against him, her legs dangling in the air, a foot above the ground.

It had to be at least a foot, because the way he was holding her, their faces were even. She could see right into his eyes.

Blue eyes.

Amazing, deep blue eyes.

Lindsay turned her head away.

"Sorry 'bout that," he muttered, setting her down on the ground.

"No problem." Her cheeks flushed, and she ran her fingers through her dark brown hair.

"Looked like you were gonna slip, there," Eric said. "That's all."

"I get it." She looked over at the small diner, which also appeared to be a convenience store, based on the advertisements in the windows.

But Eric was already walking ahead of her. She ran to catch up. Behind her, in the truck, Boomer barked his disapproval.

"Boomer!" Eric yelled over his shoulder, and the dog quieted. "He still don't get that I'm bringing him back his favorite."

"Hamburger?"

"Yup." Eric held the door for her.

She could get used to this door-holding thing.

"Must be a wonderful vet, for you to travel so far," she noted.

"In a real emergency, if I have to, I take 'im down to Coeur d'Alene. But if there's time enough to drive, I'll take him to his regular vet in Liberty Lake. He knows Boomer, and the horses at the ranch, better than any of the other vets 'round here."

There was no hostess to seat them, so they seated themselves. Worn red vinyl booths filled the eating section of the storefront. Eric took the seat facing the door.

A pretty waitress in her early forties, with long blonde hair pulled back in a ponytail, greeted them. "Hi, Eric!" she said. To Lindsay, "and miss."

Was she still a "miss," and not a "ma'am," as she was so often called in New York? Soon she'd be a mother. Hopefully she would graduate to "ma'am" by then. People had told her she looked young for her age, which her mother used to say would bother her until it flattered her.

What would her mom think of her situation now?

Don't even think about it. If Lindsay hadn't known her mom was in heaven, then she'd assume she was rolling in her grave, as they say.

"What can I get for ya?" the waitress asked. Based on the flirtatious eyes she was giving Eric, she seemed to be completely infatuated with him.

Poor lady. He had no clue she was interested.

Eric flashed her a smile full of naturally straight, white teeth, and handed her the laminated menu that had been sitting on their table when they got there. "The usual."

"Burger, no pink, no cheese, all the toppings, and fries." She scribbled on her pad. "How 'bout for your girl here?"

His girl?

Eric didn't correct her assumption.

"I'll have a cheeseburger—medium—lettuce, ketchup and mayo, please," Lindsay said.

"Pink or no pink?" the waitress intoned.

Lindsay looked at Eric in confusion. What did she mean?

"A hamburger with cheese," she repeated to the woman.

"Some pink," Eric interrupted. "Thanks, darlin'."

That got a big smile from the waitress. *Darlin'.*

Maybe this friend of Megan's fiancé was a big flirt, himself. Maybe he was a player, like Grant. Someone who was happy to play the field with no cares, no love, and no conscience regarding the consequences.

Didn't matter how good-looking Eric was, or how close he was to her soon-to-be brother-in-law. Lindsay would have to be careful around him.

She couldn't afford to make any more life-changing mistakes

now. No flirting or falling for a man at the drop of a dime. Any decisions she made from here on out wouldn't only affect herself.

Without consciously thinking about it, she laid her hand to rest over her womb.

* * *

When the waitress set the food down in front of them, Eric bowed his head. It had been a long night, and he was hungry as a bear, but his burger wasn't going anywhere.

"You say grace, too?" Lindsay asked in apparent surprise. "Do you want to say grace for both of us?"

Why not. He reached his hand out across the table, the way his parents had done with him around the dinner table, and she took it.

Her hand was tiny compared to his, soft and white. It was clear she wasn't into vegetable gardening or anything more than typing, if that. But her skin was so soft, he had to physically restrain himself from running his thumb along her smooth knuckles.

When Megan had asked him to pick up her sister at the airport, she'd told him to look for a girl who looked just like her, but shorter, with shorter hair. The description was apt.

Unlike his friend's fiancée, though, Lindsay had brown eyes. *Warm* brown eyes. And…if possible…she was even more beautiful.

Not that it mattered. A trendy New Yorker who didn't know a cow from a potato wouldn't want anything to do with a guy like him.

And even if she did, the relationship would end before it could begin. Because he wasn't going to get married and ruin some poor girl's life with his own problems.

"Lord," Eric said, gripping Lindsay's hand, "thank You for this food. Please bless it to our bodies, and please fix Boomer up quick. Maybe keep him away from the goats, if that's Your will, Lord."

He paused, and added a silent prayer of his own: *Please God, if that vision was for real, let me know what to do with it. Why does this Lindsay girl have brown eyes?*

"In Jesus' name we pray," Lindsay added quietly. "Amen."

It had to be a coincidence, those beautiful brown eyes of hers. Or was it?

* * *

Lindsay turned off her cell phone—something she'd never done before. If she'd been at a movie or in a meeting, she'd just turn it to vibrate, instead. But the only person who mattered in the world was right in front of her now, in this rustic log cabin in the mountains of northern Idaho. Forget the distractions of social media, emails or texts.

She had her sister. And thank God for that.

"I know," Megan was saying as she placed two mugs of hot decaffeinated coffee in front of them, "Bear Creek Saddle was a bit of a culture shock for me, too, when I first left Manhattan. It's a different world out here." Megan smiled. "In a good way."

Lindsay nodded, running her hand along the smooth grain of the wooden dining table. Her fingers itched to move, to do something, without having a phone to fiddle with.

Would her sister ask her? Did she already know...was it written all over her face?

"I couldn't believe it when you called me last night from the airport," Megan said. "I mean, obviously I really wanted you to come out here, not just for my wedding, but so we can hang out.

But I figured it would be tough to get you away from that bank for more than a day and a half, much less an entire month before we tie the knot."

Lindsay winced. That was as good of an opening as any.

"The bank let me go," Lindsay said. "I mean, they didn't just let me go on this trip…they—they fired me."

"Oh no!" A few drops of coffee splashed over the edge of Megan's coffee cup as she moved it from her lips. "When was that? Yesterday? Tell me everything." She shook her head in disbelief. "You know what? Forget them. God has something better for you, He always does. Who needs them, am I right?"

"Yeah." Lindsay hoped her sister was right, that this was all just part of God's bigger plan for her…but if that was the case, then maybe His plan was to turn her into the female Job. Megan didn't even know the half of it yet.

"The silver lining is," Megan said, "you can stay with me as long as you want now. We'll stay here in Zach's house, and Zach will stay in the practice-cabin—I mean, guest cabin—out back."

"I can't kick a man out of his own home."

"Oh please, he'll be fine. We're not kicking him out. He's already been sleeping out there every night since my lease was up on the other place I was renting, and I've been staying here."

"Are you sure you want me staying with you for so long?" Lindsay didn't think of herself as a particularly awful housemate, but her other girlfriends hadn't let her stay nearly as long on their couches after she'd been evicted from her own place.

Megan rolled her eyes. "Come on. It's only four weeks till the wedding, at which point—"

"I'll have to leave, obviously." Lindsay took a sip of her coffee.

"I understand." What was different about it? Real cream, instead of artificially flavored creamer?

"Nooo, I was going to say, that's when you move into the guest cabin, and get on your feet again. You can stay as long as you need."

Tears unexpectedly welled in Lindsay's eyes, and she laughed in surprise.

"I have zero idea why I'm crying. Must be tired. That's really nice of you, Meg. You have no idea." She tilted her head back so the tears wouldn't fall, and smiled. "Thank you. I mean it."

Megan reached out and took Lindsay's hand. "Of course. Can you tell me what happened? That's really messed up of them to fire you after, what, five years with them? That's forever these days."

"I know. But they have a policy about not allowing banking executives in charge of people's accounts to have significant non-student-loan debt, and um…"

Do not cry. Do not cry.

"You don't have debt, though, right?" Megan asked.

"I do now." Lindsay laughed nervously, but it wasn't funny. Nothing about this was funny. "Kind of a crazy story."

Megan leaned forward across the table from her, as if to remind her they had all the time in the world. Lindsay wasn't going to be able to avoid telling her much longer. It had been hard enough keeping it from her since Megan had run off to Idaho.

"It's not like you to get into debt," Megan said. "Or to lose a job. What's going on?"

"Do you remember that story about Bernie Madoff that was in the news a while back?" Lindsay didn't wait for her sister to respond. Of course she didn't remember—it wouldn't have been on her radar back then. "He had this whole Ponzi scheme, where big money investors would invest in his hedge fund. But the hedge fund wasn't real...whenever his investors wanted to take out some of their money, Madoff would give them money from new investors. He got away with it for years, until—"

"I want to hear about *you*, Lindsay, not some scandal," Megan interrupted.

"This is about me," she said quietly. "I fell for the same thing. Not with Madoff, but a very similar scam. I didn't know. I lost all of my inheritance from Mom."

Megan gasped, then covered her mouth. "Please tell me you're joking. You're just trying to freak me out."

"When have I ever done that?" Lindsay sighed. "I had taken out money to supplement my income at the bank. But the money I took out wasn't really investment income, like I thought. It was some other poor guy's money. And now I have to pay that all back."

"Wait." Megan pushed her chair back and stood, pacing the hardwood floor. Everything was wood in the cabin, from the floors to the walls to the ceiling to the countertops, table and chairs. "So not only did you lose all your savings, but you owe money now, too? How much?"

Lindsay's stomach sank. She didn't want to tell her. But her sister had to know. Lindsay had kept her in the dark long enough, and sunlight was the best disinfectant.

"Twenty-five grand." Lindsay laughed weakly. "I didn't know. I thought it was mine. I didn't...know."

"You just had to have the designer clothes, those expensive purses and shoes," Megan shot back.

"Whoa, why are you angry with me? I'm the victim here."

"I'm sorry," Megan said. "But if you didn't have such an

expensive lifestyle, you wouldn't have taken out so much cash, and you wouldn't be in so much debt, and you wouldn't have lost your job."

Lindsay stared at the table. It wasn't fun getting a lecture from the same girl she had taught how to apply eye-shadow just ten years prior. "I suppose you're right. But the joke's on me, because I had to sell all that stuff to make rent. And now I don't even have the thrift-store clothes I bought to replace it all."

Megan took a deep breath and sat back down, pulling her chair to the table with a scraping sound across the floorboards. "You've been able to pay your extravagant rent just from selling your clothes?"

"And purses. And shoes. But only for one month. You know how much an apartment on the Upper West Side costs."

"So you're good till the end of this month?"

Lindsay shook her head. "This happened months ago. I've been sleeping on friends' couches ever since."

"You should have told me," Megan said. "Why didn't you? How could you keep this from me all this time?"

"I'm sorry," Lindsay said, for what felt like the hundredth time. "You were so far away, and dealing with your own issues. You didn't need to hear about mine."

"That's what sisters are for, though…"

Lindsay gave her sister a half-smile, her coffee all but forgotten on the tabletop. "I'm just so glad you're here for me now," she said. "Can I really stay here?"

"Of course."

"My friends ditched me." Lindsay didn't like the petulant sound in her words. She shook her head, and tried again. "I mean, I don't blame them. I couldn't go shopping with them anymore, or go out to lunch, or to the theater. None of the things we used to do together. They couldn't cover my lunch bill forever. I get it."

Megan scoffed. "No way, that's not right. What they should have done is started planning things to do that don't cost money. Whatever happened to meeting up in Central Park for a picnic? Or having coffee at someone's apartment? Or watching a movie on TV together?"

"They don't want to do stuff like that. And we did hang out a bit when I was at their places, sleeping over. After a week or so, they'd end up politely asking me when I was moving on." Lindsay swallowed hard, determined to keep her voice from cracking. "I went through all my friends, Megan. Every single girlfriend I had let me stay with them, until they didn't. I couldn't get a new job that would pay my bills. I was getting more money from my unemployment checks than I'd get from taking on any of the jobs that were available to me. And then that ran out. Obviously."

What she didn't say was that she'd tried to get an entry-level job, just something, anything, and had been rejected for being "overqualified." Three times. They didn't want to pay to train someone who would leave the moment something better came along, which, theoretically, it would.

"I'm so sorry," Megan said. "I don't know what to say, other than I still can't believe this happened to you."

Lindsay steeled herself for the final bit of truth she had to tell her sister. The one Big Thing she'd kept secret since she'd found out.

God, give me the words to say.

"I did something stupid," Lindsay said. "I went against

everything I was taught, everything I told you to do, even. I feel like a total hypocrite."

"What do you mean?"

Her sister was five years younger than her, and while Lindsay knew Megan wasn't going to be a virgin on her wedding night, thanks to a long live-in relationship prior to her moving out to Idaho, Megan had finally come around and was waiting with Zach for their wedding to consummate their relationship.

Lindsay, at twenty-eight years old, had maintained her virginity. All through high school, all through college, and through various boyfriends (who would usually dump her after she wouldn't sleep with them several months into the relationship). And yet, here she was.

God, give me the words, please. I need You.

"I didn't have any women friends left to stay with," Lindsay said slowly. "I was too proud to call you. I'm sorry. One of the guys I knew from work, you probably don't remember him from my birthday party a few years back—Grant Bowland—he offered to let me stay with him."

"I understand," Megan said. "I mean, I stayed in Zach's guest cabin when I first moved here. To be fair, you kinda freaked out on me when I told you I was taking a stranger up on his offer."

"Because *I knew* that when a man asks you to stay with him, ninety percent of the time, his motivations aren't pure. You lucked into a good guy. I didn't."

"Oh my goodness, did he hurt you?" Megan squeaked. Her knuckles, gripping her coffee mug, where white. Maybe the mug would shatter in her tight hold.

"No, no." Lindsay sighed. "It was my choice. I felt…indebted to him. He was letting me stay with him, buying all my food, taking me out to dinner and paying, offering to use his contacts in banking to find me another job. He even hinted that if it worked out with us, he'd pay off my debt. That we'd be together, a real couple. But it was all just a manipulation to get me to sleep with him. And...it worked."

Megan nodded. "I get it. Kinda reminds me of Todd." Todd was her ex-boyfriend, and a real piece of work.

Tell her.

"I got pregnant, Meg."

Megan cocked her head, her eyes wide. "I think I misheard you. Say that again?"

"Grant said he didn't want a relationship with me, not for real. That he definitely didn't want a baby now. I mean, he's thirty-five, so you'd think he'd be ready to settle down, but no. Seems like he wants to play the field for another decade or so, then find some young trophy wife to marry. He gave me five hundred dollars to...take care of things."

Megan stilled. "Did you?" Her face was blank, impassive. As if she was trying so hard not to judge, and yet was waiting for the worst answer.

"No."

Her sister exhaled. Lindsay hadn't even realized Megan had been holding her breath. "Thank God."

"You called me and invited me to come here when I was in the cab on the way to the women's clinic. I didn't want to risk going back to Grant's for my things, so I just went directly to the airport instead. I used the money he wanted me to use for the abortion, to fly here."

She almost expected Megan to chide her for taking his money, but instead, Megan leaned back in her chair with a smirk. "Good."

Lindsay grinned. "Thanks. I mean it, Meg. Thank you for understanding."

"What are your plans for the baby? Have you thought about it?"

"I've considered giving the baby up for adoption." Lindsay looked down at her hands. "But I don't think I have the strength to give him up. This baby already feels like my child."

Megan reached across the table to her. "You shouldn't give up your baby if you don't want to. It's not a decision you can take back."

Her sister was right.

"I don't want to give up my baby," Lindsay said. "Just the thought upsets me."

"So this means…I'm going to be an auntie?" Megan asked. "For real?"

"Yes!" Lindsay touched her belly. "I don't know if my baby is a boy or girl, but I keep getting nauseated, so I think it's healthy, either way."

"I heard lemonade is good for that. Do you want some?" Megan was already standing and on her way to the fridge.

"Sure!"

Lindsay's heart rate settled. She wasn't going to be kicked out for getting pregnant outside of marriage—it didn't even look like Megan was going to scold her about it. It was probably already clear to her sister that she'd already taken herself to the woodshed over it. Megan just seemed relieved Lindsay was keeping the baby.

"Hey, don't tell anyone about it just yet, okay?" Lindsay added.

"I'm not even at eight weeks. I want people here to get to know me before they find out I'm preggo."

Megan slid an icy glass of hand-squeezed lemonade in front of her. "You got it. I have to tell Zach, though. I tell him everything. But he knows how to keep a secret that's not his to tell."

Lindsay nodded. That made sense. Now that Megan was engaged to be married, she couldn't expect her to keep anything from her husband-to-be.

"Let's talk about your wedding," Lindsay said. Now that she'd confessed it all, she felt a burden had lifted.

Finally.

It hadn't been nearly as bad as she'd built it up in her mind to be.

"I'm going to plan the best wedding for you and Zach, ever."

As they sat across from each other, discussing color schemes, themes, and budgets, Lindsay finally let herself relax a bit. Yes, she was far away from the only home she'd ever known. Yes, she was going to have a difficult time being a single mother in a small, conservative town. But she had her family, and family mattered most of all.

"I have an idea…" Megan took a sip of her coffee and grinned.

"The last time you gave me that look, we both ended up getting grounded for two weeks."

"It's not *that* crazy, not really," Megan said, shrugging off the reference to the time they'd "borrowed" their mom's car as teenagers.

Lindsay smiled. "All right, lay it on me. What's it going to be? Destination wedding on a mountaintop? The bridesmaids all have to enter on horseback?"

"Nope. Much simpler. I want a double wedding," Megan said. "With *you* as the other bride. Let's get you hitched before this baby is born!"

Lindsay laughed and shook her head. "That's more impossible than getting me to climb to the top of a mountain for your vows."

"Nothing's impossible. I just so happen to know three very eligible, very handsome bachelors."

"Like…Eric Hunt?" Lindsay paused. The memory of his arm around her waist when she slipped out of his truck brought heat to her cheeks.

Megan smiled. "You might just be perfect for him."

"Not in my condition," Lindsay reminded her.

"*Exactly* in your condition." Megan grinned, and God help her, Lindsay couldn't help but to smile back, even though she had no idea why.

Chapter Two

T HE FOLLOWING DAY, Lindsay stepped outside the cabin and nearly ran directly into the chest of a tall, well-built man in a heather-gray T-shirt. She gasped and jumped back.

"I'm so sorry!" She looked up at his handsome, familiar face. "Eric—I was expecting you to be Zach for some reason."

"Not that lucky," the young man said with a grin. "I was hoping Zach was here, actually."

"No, sorry." Lindsay looked around her at the vast ranch, at the rolling hills of grass spotted with black cattle. A big horse grazed on the front lawn. Had it been there last night? It had been so dark when Eric had dropped her off, and she'd been so exhausted, she honestly couldn't remember.

Did horses sleep outside? "You know what? I think Zach's out at the stables with Megan," Lindsay remembered. "How's Boomer doing?"

"Zonked out at my place under my desk. No more chasing goats, least not for a few weeks, I bet."

"I've never seen a goat in real life," Lindsay said. "Are they…vicious?"

For some reason, Eric cracked up laughing, as if she'd told him a joke. "I'll tell you one thing. You can't buy happiness. But you can buy goats, and that's pretty close to the same thing."

Lindsay smiled and shrugged. "I really wouldn't know."

"What do you think of the place?" He opened his arms wide, as if to encompass the whole ranch. His wingspan was huge. "How you liking Idaho so far?"

The hesitant look that crossed her face must have been obvious to him. She quickly rearranged her expression into a smile. "The burgers are good, I know that much."

He laughed at the reference to their date.

Date? No. *Don't be silly.*

"I just got up a little while ago," she admitted, "and I haven't had a chance to look around yet. So far I'd say…it's pretty different from Manhattan."

"You can say that again." Eric seemed to take it as a compliment to his home state, though Lindsay wasn't sure she meant it that way. "You can ride with me over to the stable to find Zach, if you want. Sound good?"

Lindsay peered over his broad, muscular shoulder, looking for evidence of his truck. "What did you ride over here in?"

"*On*," he corrected her.

On…what?

Eric gestured to the tall black horse grazing on Zach's front lawn, its long tail swaying gently in the late morning breeze.

"Come on," Eric said and, before she could respond, took her hand as if they were old friends. "I'll introduce you to Smoky."

Lindsay followed him, her hand enveloped in his. He was acting a lot more friendly and talkative than he'd been the night before.

Maybe he'd just been really worried about Boomer last night. Or maybe he was a morning person.

Or was something different going on here—something like…flirting?

It was hard to tell if Megan had suggested Eric would be a good match for Lindsay because she wished it to be true, or if she had some sort of gut instinct on the matter.

Doesn't matter.

Not like he'd want a woman who was already pregnant with some other guy's child. And besides, she had no business being interested in any man at this point.

She had a baby to focus on.

Getting attached to someone wasn't worth the pain when it ended. Grant had taught her that.

Maybe this time she'd remember the lesson, instead of letting herself get hurt.

The horse raised his head at Eric's approach, but appeared completely uninterested in her.

"Hi, Smoky." Lindsay smiled to show Eric's horse she was friendly. Unless horses interpreted smiles as baring teeth? "Nice to meet you."

The horse was unimpressed with her introduction. Were horses supposed to wag their tails, like dogs, or at least sniff or…whinny or something?

Lindsay looked at Eric. "I don't think he likes me."

"Nah, he's just slow to warm up." Eric took her hand, the one he was holding, and lifted it up to gently pat the horse's flank.

"Umm…" This was weird. She didn't know a thing about horses, and it had to be obvious.

If she wanted to impress Eric, it would be much better if she could hop on a computer and showcase her organizational and financial skills, rather than hop on a horse.

Didn't look like that was going to happen anytime soon. Even if—for some strange reason—the situation arose, clearly this cowboy was the type who liked a girl comfortable on a ranch.

Riding a horse couldn't be that hard, could it?

"Come on." Eric swung up onto Smoky's back, leaving Lindsay on the ground. "I'll help you."

"I've never done this before." Lindsay hesitated, but he reached his arms down toward her.

"You can do it—grab my hands."

The closest she'd ever come to riding a horse was riding on a carousel…and this horse was much, much bigger. She craned her neck up to look at Eric, seated so casually on Smoky, as if it were no big deal. "I've never even *touched* a real horse before."

Eric grinned. "We'll go easy on ya. One step at a time."

Right. One step at a time.

He nodded toward the leather loop…a foothold thingie. "Lift your leg up to get your foot in there…nope, other leg." Eric laughed. "Sorry. I shoulda been more specific."

Now she had to get on that horse just to show him she could.

As she struggled, at the last moment, he hauled her up under her arms like a sack of potatoes.

"Straddle the horse, Lindsay—right in front of me—there ya go." He put his arm around her waist like a seatbelt, which definitely helped her feel more safe.

"I did it!" Lindsay held onto the horn-thing in front of her on the saddle for dear life, and turned her head to see him. "I can't believe I actually did it."

"Knew you could."

She looked down. "This is really high up." But his arm was wrapped around her waist, holding her close to him on the saddle.

"You okay?"

"I won't fall off, will I?"

"Not with me, not a chance."

Even though she barely knew the man, that made her feel better. Eric seemed very sure of himself, and his confidence was contagious.

"Okay. Let's do this."

Eric did something with his thighs (or reins?) that made the horse move, and soon the ground was moving beneath them at a steady rate.

Was it safe for the baby for her to ride on a horse? It was a bumpy ride.

Not that she'd dare ask him. The longer she had for people to get to know her, before discovering her situation, the better. Maybe then they'd be more supportive, like her sister had been.

"How ya doing?" Eric asked from behind her.

A bit nauseated from the motion. Seasick…horse-sick. Morning sickness?

"Fine."

Evergreen trees were everywhere. Like Christmas trees that hadn't been strung up with lights yet.

The image brought to mind the Christmas story. Lindsay would be fine to be pregnant on a horse, because Mary and Joseph rode a donkey for days through the desert when Mary was nine months pregnant, after all. Good.

You'll be fine, Little One.

"Is all this land part of your ranch?" she asked.

"Yup. Look up there, see the black dots? Those are our cattle."

Whoa. She'd never seen a cow in real life before. If she met one, would she ever be able to enjoy a hamburger again?

"Can we go see them?"

"Sure," he said. "But first I have to stop at the office."

Smoky took them to an old white farmhouse surrounded by a gravel drive with a couple of pickup trucks parked outside.

Eric dismounted, which left her up on the horse all by herself.

"Should I…wait out here with Smoky?" What if he ran off, with her on his back?

"Course not." He held his arms up to her so she could come down.

"Wait!" She pulled her iPhone out of her pocket and handed it to him. "Can you take a pic of me on the horse? No one will believe it."

Eric looked completely taken aback by the idea. "No one will believe you rode…on a horse?"

She shrugged and reached for her phone. "Never mind."

"No, no, I'll do it."

"No," she argued back. "Because now if you take the picture, it will only remind me of how I'm acting like a silly tourist and you got all weirded out by it."

Without asking her to pose, Eric snapped a quick picture. "Candid shot," he quipped. "I'm not weirded out. You're a New Yorker, and this is new for you. I get it. If I were in New York, I'd probably take a photo of me in front of a skyscraper or something."

Her defenses dropped. "Exactly! And I walk by skyscrapers all day, every day, and never even look up."

He held his arms up to her to help her get off the horse. "Did

I make you feel better about being a 'silly tourist'?"

She smiled, feeling shy for some reason. "Yes."

Eric lifted her body down as if she weighed nothing, and set her gently on the gravel, her shoes touching the pebbles with a satisfying crunch.

"I'd be happy to take a picture of you anytime you want," he added. "Just ask."

"No way. I'm not making that mistake again. I'm going to pretend this is all normal for me, until I start to believe it."

Eric shook his head. "Good luck with that."

She followed him up the steps into the old white farmhouse, blinking at the transition from the bright sunlight outside to the darker interior. The inside of her thighs hurt from the horse ride. She wasn't accustomed to using those muscles.

It only took a moment for her eyes to adjust to the inside of the farmhouse. Off to the side, in what she assumed had originally been a living room type area, was a front office setup. Straight ahead was a long, narrow corridor with doors leading into rooms. Their individual offices, perhaps?

A good-looking young man with light brown hair and golden stubble on his jaw stepped into the hallway, and did a double take when he saw her.

"I thought you were Megan for a second there." The man chuckled. "You must be Lindsay! I'm Zach, Megan's fiancé."

He grinned and stuck his hand out to shake hers, but she was already stepping past it and going for a hug and a peck on the cheek.

She backed up to go back for the handshake, but Zach put his arm around her shoulder, and he laughed. "I'll take a hug, sure."

Nice one. Not awkward of her at all (*ahem*).

"Well," she said, nervous laughter in her voice, "we're almost family now."

"Of course." Zach nodded to Eric. "Is he giving you the fifty-cent tour?"

"He's charging me twenty bucks," she deadpanned. "I didn't qualify for the discount, I guess."

It was a silly joke, but Eric rewarded her by actually chuckling for real. She smiled at him.

Thankyouverymuch.

"Looks like you've got quite the operation running here," Lindsay added. "I don't know if Megan told you, but I work in—I mean, *worked* in, previously—banking. I handled some pretty high-level accounts."

Did it sound like she was showing off, bragging about her skills? Ugh. "I didn't start out as an executive, of course," she added, to try to soften it. "I worked my way up, and got to learn a lot along the way."

"Yup," Zach said, "she's told me all about you. Megan really looks up to her big sis. You know more about the business aspect of this than any of us."

"Well, I do have my master's in business finance," she said. "I mean, not that that's such a big deal."

Stop talking. Why couldn't she shut up?

She always did this when she was nervous. Tried to make a good impression and failed miserably by overdoing it.

Forget about impressing Eric—or even her sister's fiancé—all she'd just accomplished was sounding like a stuck-up, overeducated braggart.

Don't keep talking. Don't try to fix it.

"If you ever have anything I can help with, business-wise," she added, "I'd be happy to take a look at your numbers."

Zach and Eric exchanged a look.

A long look—over her head, since she was about a foot shorter than them both. The two men just stared at each other, as if they were speaking to each other with a silent language only childhood best friends could speak, without words.

Oh no. She was weirding them out. They were probably plotting how to get her out of their offices before she set up shop, uninvited.

"Of course, I'm sure you all have that under control." Lindsay shrugged, as if she wasn't even a teensy bit interested in seeing the behind-the-scenes workings of a huge cattle ranch.

She was very interested, of course. Lindsay lived and breathed financial sheets, accounting, and data, when she wasn't enjoying the lifestyle her work afforded her.

Had *previously* afforded her.

"Never mind," she said again.

Why didn't her mouth listen when her brain told it to shut up?

Eric finally spoke, but he wasn't speaking to her, he spoke to Zach. "What if—"

A door down the hall opened with the slam of wood on wood, and Lindsay jumped at the echo of the sound in the old building.

A man stormed out of the office, ignoring her completely, and cut Eric off.

"No way," the man said.

Whoever that was, she'd totally ticked him off, and she wasn't even sure how.

Eric put his hand on her lower back in a protective, comforting way. As if to tell her not to worry. That he had it handled.

Eric glanced down at her and nodded his head toward the guy. "Lindsay Moore, this is Christopher Green. You'll love him once he stops being so scary."

Chris paused mid-step. "Sorry." He made a gesture as if to tip his hat in her direction, but he wasn't wearing a hat. Habit from muscle-memory?

"No—it's totally okay," she said quickly. This guy didn't seem like someone she wanted to have against her.

"I'm…ah, I'm Chris. Sorry 'bout that. Lots of business stuff going on. Ain't worth blabbing about and boring ya with it, that's all."

Lindsay nodded and smiled, her heart rate going back to normal. She certainly couldn't hold it against him for making a bad first impression, considering that's exactly what she'd just done.

"It's nice to meet you, Chris," she said. "I didn't mean to be nosy. I just miss talking shop, I guess."

She laughed like that was a joke, but it wasn't. There was something to be said for having her career, and for being respected for her opinion.

That was all gone now.

Now, to everyone in Bear Creek Saddle, she was just the sister of the bride, the city girl out of place in the mountains, and eventually, the broke single mother-to-be.

Her career days were over.

For now she had to focus on getting out from behind her mountain of new debt, and find a new job in this tiny town where she could work and still be able to take care of her baby.

Did something like that even exist? It certainly didn't feel like it based on her own work experience…sixty-hour work weeks, glued to her phone, even on the weekends, putting out clients' fires as they came up. Not exactly conducive to nurturing an infant on her own.

There were some moms where she used to work, but they would take only a few weeks off after their baby was born, and then the baby would essentially be raised by a nanny, or go to daycare for ten hours a day when the mom came back to work. The few women she knew who told her they were taking a year off to be with their baby, never came back. Not once in the five years she worked there.

It was either all or nothing, it seemed.

Would she even be happy as a stay-at-home mom? Would that be enough for someone like her, who was accustomed to high-stakes work and the dopamine rush of respect and accountability?

The three men were looking at each other again. Above her head.

Lindsay sighed. "I better get out of your hair."

Eric touched her arm. "Wait. I haven't given you your twenty bucks' worth, yet."

She grinned at his reference to her dumb joke about the cost of his "fifty-cent tour," as Zach had called it.

"That's all right," she conceded. "It's going to be tough for you boys to get any work done if you have to do it all by communicating solely through your eyes."

Eric winced. "Sorry 'bout that. Just work stuff. Why don't you check on Smoky, and I'll be right there."

Lindsay knew an exit line when she heard one, so she took his "suggestion"—which was phrased much more nicely than the order she'd have expected him to give (like "Go outside and I'll meet you there," maybe). She waved over her shoulder to Zach and Chris as she walked out. "Nice meeting you guys."

"You too," they called in unison.

Sure.

Outside the farmhouse office, the bright sunlight hit her eyes, and she furrowed her brow. Smoky was nibbling on a bush, and looked up at her guiltily when she came up to him, as if she'd caught him doing something he shouldn't be doing.

"I really don't care," she told him. "Munch away. I'll be the fun aunt, not your mom."

The voices inside the farmhouse were getting louder.

It wasn't right to eavesdrop. Curiosity killed the cat, right? And she loved cats.

But she couldn't help overhearing.

Especially Chris's voice. His deep baritone, combined with rising urgency, made it impossible for her to ignore. "This ain't a tour stop. Don't bring that girl in here again."

Ouch. Chris was one of Zach and Eric's best friends. And already he was done with her.

"She's family now," Zach responded to him. "You can't lay down that law."

Her future brother-in-law was a keeper. Praise God.

"Maybe she could actually help us." That was Eric's voice. Quieter. Calmer. "She's smart with this stuff, Megan's always said that. I bet Lindsay would be able to turn this all around."

Yes. *Thank you!*

In Manhattan, Lindsay's days had revolved around a packed schedule where she was in charge. She had control of millions of dollars and the ability to loan it out, to make a difference in people's lives and businesses.

Now, standing out in the gravel parking lot, alone with Smoky, she had zero idea what to do with herself…and it wasn't a feeling she was accustomed to.

Here in the mountains of north Idaho, she'd become the useless city girl who knew nothing—nothing about horses, or goats, or cows, or anything ranch-related.

But Eric saw past that…with his vote of confidence, he'd proven he knew she was more than what she seemed.

He'd stood up for her.

Lindsay's heart clenched, but just for a moment. That's all she wanted from a man—for someone to stand up for her, to protect her.

That was all Grant would've had to do. Stand up for her and their baby. Be there for her. Not shovel her into a cab with cash and orders to "take care of it."

She never should have let their relationship move from the realm of colleague and friend to something intimate.

That was her mistake, and she would never, ever make it again.

So she wouldn't let her heart respond to Eric looking out for her.

But what he'd done—especially considering he didn't even know she could overhear him—certainly said a lot about Eric, and she respected that.

Lindsay liked that about him…among other things. Like those shoulders…

Wait.

What were the guys arguing about in the first place?

The only thing she'd be able to help them with—that Megan

would've mentioned to them, anyway—would be finances or business profit and loss consultation, that sort of thing.

Was something going on with the ranch?

Chapter Three

ERIC STRODE OUT of the farmhouse office, his frustration grinding into the gravel beneath his boots.

Why did Chris have to be so wary and cynical all the time? The only people in the world who Chris trusted were him, Zach, and Jay. Maybe Megan now too, since Zach trusted her enough to marry the girl. Oh, and Bill, and his wife Allie. It was a small circle. Anyone outside the circle couldn't be let in, as far as his best friend was concerned.

Even if they really could use the help.

When Bill had sold them the ranch, they had already spent the better part of their lives working on it for Bill as ranch hands, but were never involved in the money aspect or handling clients. That was a new deal for all four of them, and to be honest…it wasn't as easy as it sounded.

Running a huge business didn't even sound that easy to begin with.

They could really use Lindsay's expertise, and Lindsay had said she'd be around for a long while. What if Lindsay could help them figure out just how much they were gaining or losing each month? Her organizational skills alone would be worth her weight in gold.

They couldn't even *find* half the numbers they needed to get together.

Part of it was they were all busy working on the ranch itself, growing and harvesting the grass, taking care of the cattle, and setting up transport for the livestock since they didn't have their own butchering facilities (thank God—because Eric didn't have the stomach for it, even though he loved to eat beef, and he cared deeply about that beef coming from a happy, well-cared-for cow). They had to set up shipment of the beef to their clients, from restaurants and supermarkets, to individuals who wanted to skip the middleman by prepaying for their beef.

And of course, there was taking care of their own log cabins, which they'd built themselves—each helping the other; their land and veggie gardens; and the chickens they kept for their eggs. He traded beef for chicken meat with a neighbor, since his chickens were egg-layers only.

Eric rarely had to buy groceries unless he wanted a specific spice or a processed product, because they grew their own groceries right on the ranch.

It was a good life. But they needed someone running that office full time, and none of them were up for the job.

They all wanted to be out on the ranch, riding their horses. Sitting in the office all day sounded like torture. So they did as little as possible, and split up the work as much as possible.

Which caused a big problem whenever bills had to be paid, and the money wasn't always there. It was a complete mess.

And now, they'd all acted like jerks around Megan's sister.

Not good.

Lindsay was talking to Smoky, who seemed to be warming up to her.

She was really cute. He liked the way she pushed her hair behind one ear when it got in her face, and how she laughed at his jokes. It was nice having someone who hadn't heard them all before.

He couldn't blame her for being so new to everything. Megan was kinda like that, too, when she first got to Bear Creek Saddle.

But Megan had really wanted to embrace country living, whereas Lindsay seemed to be totally confused as to how she ended up in Idaho when she was born and bred for the Big Apple.

Even though the sisters looked alike, they seemed pretty different with their personalities. Lindsay was like a more cautious yet more outgoing version of Megan, which was weird, because cautious and outgoing weren't words usually used to describe the same person.

And then of course…while her sister had blue eyes, Lindsay had eyes the color of chocolate.

Warm brown eyes.

Best thing he'd ever seen.

Just like in his vision.

Lord, did You send Lindsay to me? Where's the baby from my vision supposed to come from, if not from me? How's this supposed to work?

Was he supposed to marry her, this girl he'd just met? Would she even want him?

No. Of course not.

Eric shook his head. This was probably all in his imagination.

"Hey there," Lindsay said to him as he approached. "Smoky ate a little of that shrubbery, and I didn't stop him because I want him to like me."

"Did it work?"

"I think so…? He's looking at me now, at least." Lindsay smiled up at Eric, and his spirits lifted.

She didn't seem mad at him for walking her into the lion's den at the farmhouse, so that was a good thing.

"Sorry 'bout Chris," he said. "He'll warm up to you, just like Smoky. It just takes a bit of time to earn his trust."

"Maybe I should bring Chris out here and let him eat a little of that shrubbery, too."

Eric laughed at the visual imagery. "If it worked once, maybe it'll work again."

She grinned. "I get it, though, about Chris… I can be the same way, myself, sometimes. All it takes is getting burnt once, and it affects how you view new people."

Interesting.

"Did you get…burnt?" Eric rubbed Smoky's face, between his eyes and down to his nose, the way he liked. He paused. "Sorry, that's probably too personal."

"It's okay." She waved her hand as if to brush away his concern at overstepping bounds. "Pretty recently, actually. Someone—a guy I've known for five years at the bank and had considered a friend— turned out to be unworthy of my trust."

Eric wasn't sure how to respond. Had the guy hurt her? Physically, emotionally?

"I'm sorry that happened." What had that guy done to make her feel that way? "Do you need me to fly to New York and kick his butt for you?"

She grinned. "No, but thanks for offering. He's probably feeling a bit burnt himself—I never said goodbye. I just left and took a cab to…" She paused. "To the airport. And that's when you came and drove me here."

"Have you thought about calling him to let him know, at least, that you're not a missing person or something?"

Lindsay's eyes widened. "I hadn't thought about that. I probably should call him." She sighed. "I really don't want to. But I suppose it's only right… though, to be fair, he hasn't even tried contacting me. You'd think he'd do that, if he thought I was missing or something."

"Is he a jerk?"

She shrugged. "He doesn't think he is. He probably thinks I am, since I ran off with the money he gave me."

Wait—what?

Lindsay gasped and shook her head. "That sounds so bad. It's not like that. Well, not really."

Eric didn't say anything. She didn't seem like she was going to let that hang there, unexplained, and sometimes silence was the best response.

"Grant gave me—that's his name, Grant—well, he gave me a bunch of money for a doctor's appointment, but I used it on the plane ticket instead. It's not like he was expecting to get that money back."

He couldn't let that go. The mention of doctors, after everything both he and his mother had been through, raised red flags.

Didn't matter if the question was too personal…she didn't have to answer, but he had to ask.

"Why the doctor? Are you sick?"

She paused, as if repeating the question in her head, or figuring out how to answer it without revealing too many details.

"I'm not sick," she said finally. "The plane ticket was more important, and I have no money left at all, so it was kind of an either-or thing."

"Do you still need to go to the doctor?" he asked. "I have a great doctor in town you could see."

At first she glared at him. Maybe he was getting too personal, after all.

But then her expression changed, and she slowly nodded. "I probably should see a doctor, actually—just to get a checkup, make sure everything's fine."

Hopefully there wasn't anything wrong with her, the way there had been with him. His checkup hadn't gone the way he'd expected at all, and had life-altering results.

Please, heal me, God.

Surely it was His will to heal him, if that vision was real, right?

It had to be.

"You look pretty healthy to me," he said. "I'm not a doctor or anything, but you've got like a…glow."

Lindsay laughed and shook her head. "Thanks."

He mounted Smoky and held his hands down to help her up. "I take it you were surprised by the fact I'm not a doctor."

"Totally surprised."

She gave a little jump to help herself onto Smoky's saddle, with an "Oof!"

He felt more comfortable asking her questions with her facing the front, not looking at his face. "So…I know you're a big-time banking exec and everything, but are you really out of money?"

She didn't hesitate. "I haven't been working for months. Unfortunately."

When he didn't respond, she added, "That's one of the reasons

I'm here. I can live for free while I help plan Megan and Zach's wedding. You know how much New York costs."

"Guess it's pretty expensive."

"Put it this way…it's very possible you paid less for this whole ranch, all this land and everything, than some people pay for a one-bedroom condo in Manhattan."

Whoa.

They rode back out to the main driveway, and he steered Smoky toward a shortcut through the south field so he could check on the irrigation system there and make sure it had turned on.

"Do you want to work, or are you…taking a break, or something?

She turned around in the saddle and gave him a look. "Of *course* I want to work. My career was everything to me!" Lindsay turned back around, staring straight ahead. "They let me go, even though I was doing really well for them."

"Man. Why'd they fire you, then?"

"Long story."

She laughed, as if it were funny, but he could tell just from the stiffness in her spine that it wasn't funny at all to her.

"Short version," she said quickly, "I got scammed and got into debt, and the bank has a policy about not letting employees with lots of debt have access to accounts containing lots of money."

"Gotcha."

This conversation was the strangest thing.

Eric had never, in his entire life, had such a long, personal discussion with someone he'd just recently met. It took a couple of years of being friends with the guys—when they were kids—before they started telling each other deeply personal things, and there were still probably some things they didn't share with each other.

But after only knowing Lindsay for a short while, she'd already admitted to him that she'd gotten scammed, had major debt, been fired, been burnt by a guy who was untrustworthy, then took the guy's money and ran off with it without telling him, that she needed to go to a doctor for some unspecified health concern...what else?

She liked her burgers a bit pink on the inside.

It was crazy, but her being so open with him made Eric feel like he could trust her—even at this early stage—simply because he knew so much about her already.

It had all been a completely one-sided conversation, though. He hadn't told her much about himself at all. She'd seemed happy to do the talking, and he was happy to listen. Did she feel like he was being closed-off, and this was her way to get him to open up to her?

Was it possible she already knew about his sterility condition, and was waiting for him to tell her himself?

It was possible.

He'd told Zach. And while Zach wouldn't tell anyone but Megan, it was possible that Megan had told her sister.

The thought made him cringe.

Eric didn't want pity.

He didn't want her thinking that he was broken, or less of a man.

Especially since...he was starting to really like her.

He cleared his throat. "Wish I could offer you a job here. God knows we could use your experience. But Chris is just..."

"I get it." Lindsay reached over and patted his thigh casually, which was next to hers on the saddle.

She may have meant it as a nonchalant little pat, but her hand sent a tingle up his leg. Why was she having this effect on him?

Was it because of the vision, or was it just…something about Lindsay?

"If you need the money," he said, "I could really use some help at my house. If someone else did all the cleaning and cooking, I'd have more time to spend working things out at the office."

She was silent.

"Sorry—I didn't mean to imply…" Great. Now he'd ticked her off. "I mean, I know you've got a master's and you're used to wearing fancy clothes to work, and you probably got paid a fortune, but…I just figured I'd offer, that's all."

"That's okay," she said. "It's going to be a while before I'm able to pay down my debt and get back to my career—if my reputation survives, and that's a big 'if.' I'd much rather work on a computer with some spreadsheets than fold your laundry, but…it *would* be close to Megan's house, which is important, since I don't have a ride."

Was she considering it?

"It's real close," he added. "You could take a horse or one of the ATVs…and it would only be a few hours a day, so you'd have plenty of time to help plan the wedding, still. And then you'd have some money of your own."

Lindsay turned around on the saddle to face him, but he'd been leaning forward to speak in her ear as they rode, so her face was much closer to his than she'd probably expected.

"Sorry!" she squeaked. "Too close." Lindsay giggled as he pulled his head back. "You must've thought I was going to kiss you or something."

"Course not." He grinned. "I'm not that lucky."

Her cheeks pinked up. "I was going to ask what the going rate for a housekeeper and cook was around here."

"Sorry. Didn't mean to make you blush. It's an entry-level job, but since it involves so much trust—"

"How so?"

"Never got a housekeeper before, 'cause having a *stranger* go through my things…" He shook his head.

"What's changed, then? You're not worried I'll find the cookie crumbs in your bed and know what you're up to?"

He pretended to growl. "Who told you 'bout my cookie addiction?"

She laughed and put up her hands, as if to feign surrender, but Smoky chose that moment to drop his head to the grass—and Lindsay yelped as she started to fall off the saddle.

"Whoa!" Eric lunged for her, and in his exuberance to catch her before she fell, ended up falling off the saddle himself, his arms wrapped around her waist.

Instead of saving her, he brought her down with him.

"Tuck your head!" he yelled.

They tumbled to the uncut grass, and he rolled to land underneath her to cushion the blow.

Fortunately, Smoky knew enough not to step on them.

The fall knocked the breath out of him for a moment.

Owww.

"Oh my goodness, are you okay?" Lindsay rolled off of him, pulling up to her knees beside him in the tall grass. "I'm okay, I think. I'm so sorry."

He sat up and shook his arms out at his sides, a silly habit he'd done since he was a kid whenever he got hurt so he could "shake it off." For some reason actually shaking his arms seemed to help.

"I'm all right," he said, bringing his arms down quickly. "We were already half off the saddle when we dropped, so it wasn't as high of a fall as it coulda been."

"I can't believe I made you fall off a horse." She looked genuinely shaken up. "You probably never do that."

"Not usually, nope. Ain't your fault, though. I practically threw myself off. Wasn't thinking, just acting."

He pulled a piece of hay from her soft, dark hair.

"Thank you. You were…you were protecting me."

Well, he'd tried, anyhow. The fact that she was on the ground meant he hadn't done as good of a job as he'd intended.

But that look she gave him as she said it…she was treating him like a man who had earned her respect.

After months of having his manhood secretly in doubt because of his newly diagnosed sterility…fearing he'd never see that look on a woman's face ever again…Lindsay had just made him feel like a million bucks.

"Did ya tuck your head like I told you?" he asked. "You didn't hit your noggin, right?"

"I'm fine. Just…hurt my pride, that's all." She smiled and waved her hand, as if her pride didn't matter much anyway.

"Let's pretend this didn't happen, then," he suggested. "That'll help my pride, too. I was trying to save you, and look where that got us." He gestured to the hay around them, and this time she laughed for real.

"Thanks for trying, anyway," she said. "Can we…walk? I don't think I want to ride a horse again anytime soon."

Eric stood and helped her to her feet. "Nope. You gotta get

back on the saddle right away after a fall. It's important."

"Huh. I guess that's where the saying 'Get back on the saddle' comes from."

"Yup." He nodded toward Smoky, who was waiting patiently for them to get back on. "Lemme help you up first. And this time, keep your legs tight on the horse, face forward, and hold on."

"Yes, sir," she said, as if he were a drill sergeant.

Second time she'd said that to him. "You can call me Eric." He winked to soften his words.

He took a moment to check on Smoky, then jumped up onto the saddle behind her, wrapping his arms tightly around her waist.

Her breathing was still a bit fast.

"We're okay," he reminded her. "But now I feel terrible, 'cause I told you there wasn't a chance you'd fall off."

"I think...I have to go to the doctor," she said quietly. "Can you front me the money for that, and I'll start working for you tomorrow?"

"Of course—I'll just give it to you," he said. "Are you okay? Did you hurt something?"

"I think—I hope—everything's fine," she said, but her breath caught in her throat. "I want to be sure. Can you...give me a ride to town?"

Oh no.

Lord, let her be okay. Why was she suddenly so scared? She'd seemed fine before, even laughing.

"Yes. Hold on." He turned Smoky out of the field, keeping a tighter grip on his reins this time. "My truck is back at the farmhouse."

"Thanks."

Why was her voice shaking? What had he done to her with that fall?

"What aren't you telling me?" he demanded. "Are you injured?"

Lindsay shook her head. He wanted her to turn to face him again, more than anything, but he'd already scared her off from doing that. So he spoke to her back.

"Let me help you. Where are you injured?"

"I'm not injured," she said finally. "The fall didn't hurt me, but I realized when I got back on the horse—I-I've heard stories of women after a big fall, and I looked real quick just to see and there's a spot of blood now, and no way for me to know."

Spot of blood?

"I don't know if he's hurt or not—" Her voice cracked. "*What if I hurt my Little One?*"

"Wait—what are you talking about, Lindsay? Where are you bleeding?"

"I'm not really bleeding, it's just a tiny spot but—"

He ran his hands over her arms and back quickly, searching for any wounds, the way the EMT had done on him when he broke his arm, years ago. "Tell me what's going on!"

"I'm…oh, Eric, I didn't want to tell you this, not until I had to. God knows what you'll think of me now. I'm not this person, *this isn't like me.*"

He hugged her close to him, her back against his front in the saddle. "It's okay," he whispered.

He didn't know what else to say.

"Please don't hate me, Eric," she whispered back. "I'm pregnant."

Chapter Four

LINDSAY DESPERATELY WANTED to see Eric's face after she'd told him she was pregnant, but she didn't dare turn around in the saddle and risk falling off the horse again.

Eric pulled Smoky to a full stop. "No more riding."

"You're kicking me off?"

She had bigger things to worry about. While Eric had mounted the horse behind her, she'd taken a quick peek in her jeans. Just to be sure. It was only a tiny stain in her underwear, but it was brand new, right after the fall.

Was she having a miscarriage?

Please, God, don't let this be happening. Please save my Little One.

And then for Eric to just stop the horse, when she wanted to gallop as fast as they could to his truck.

Didn't he see the urgency in her situation?

He was probably disgusted by her now. Not only had she not told him she was pregnant, she'd basically lied by omission by telling him so much personal stuff…yet leaving that one huge fact out.

And Eric was, from everything she'd heard from Megan about the guys at Bear Creek Saddle Ranch, a church-going Christian who walked the talk.

She used to think of herself that way, too.

But now she was just a hypocrite. Telling her sister to save herself for marriage, while she gave it up so she could continue to stay at Grant's apartment. A man who wasn't worth half of the heartbreak he'd caused.

Unbelievable.

When all along, she could've just called her sister for help, and left Manhattan behind long before she'd lost all of her girlfriends, and long before she'd sold everything she owned, and long before she essentially sold herself for a nice place to sleep and the potential for Grant to stay with her.

It was basically prostitution, on many levels. No wonder Eric was kicking her off his horse. And no wonder he no longer wanted anything to do with her.

Eric hopped off and then carefully helped her dismount.

There they were, back on the grass.

Part of Lindsay expected Eric to get back on Smoky and ride away, but he pulled out his phone.

"Jay, where're you at?" Eric asked into his phone.

She couldn't hear Jay's answer.

"You on your tractor?" Eric pressed.

Lindsay tried not to listen as Eric talked more with Jay.

What could she do? Her situation and Eric's cold dismissal had her feeling helpless. And still scared. What had she been thinking, riding a horse while she was pregnant?

Eric turned to her and pocketed his phone. "Jay's gonna get my truck, drive it out here to pick us up, and then he'll ride Smoky back to the stables."

"Where does that leave me?"

"With me, of course. In my truck."

Thank God. He was still willing to be in close proximity to her, at least. That was a start.

"Are you going to drop me back off at my sister's? I understand. I really do."

"I'm gonna take you to the doctor," he said, looking at her strangely. "You need to get checked out, remember? You didn't hit your head, did you?"

"No." She took a deep breath. "I thought you were...done with me."

Eric shook his head forcefully, and lifted the brim of his hat, his gaze on her eyes.

"Just done riding, that's all. It ain't safe for you. If you'd have told me you were pregnant, I'd never've suggested we ride Smoky in the first place."

She turned away—couldn't look into those blue eyes of his. "You're angry with me," she said. "I don't blame you."

"Yeah—well. None of my business, I guess." He sighed. "I'm angry at myself for letting you fall in the first place. It ain't your fault."

"I should have told you. I'm sorry I didn't."

"An' there I was, like an idiot, making you get back on the horse, when that's the last thing you need in your...condition."

Jay pulled up, driving right over the grass, in Eric's big black pickup truck.

"What's going on?" Jay got out of Eric's truck and looked at Lindsay with concern. "Sorry—hey, I'm Jay. Wish we were meeting under better circumstances."

"Me too," Lindsay said quietly.

"I hope you weren't hurt in the fall. But Eric's right, if you're not sure, best to get checked out. Dr. Peterson is the best in Idaho, as far I'm concerned."

Lindsay looked at Eric. He hadn't told Jay she was pregnant.

That was nice of him, to keep her secret. Maybe he figured it wasn't his to tell. How had she not realized that, while he was talking on the phone with Jay? She'd just been so worked up.

Still was. Was she going to lose this baby? Had she brought this on herself, by taking Grant's money to have an abortion in the first place?

What if God was punishing her?

I didn't mean it, Lord. I didn't know how much I love this baby until I decided to keep him. Let me keep him, Lord. Please.

"Let's go," Eric said, slipping back into his dominant way of speaking.

She got into the passenger seat with his helping hand, not even annoyed at his tone. It didn't matter if he took the lead—she didn't want to think right now. She had too much else on her mind.

What if she'd hurt her baby?

Why was she so dumb as to not even *think* about her baby when she accepted the offer to ride Smoky?

The realization struck her like a bucket of ice water.

She'd been so interested in Eric, in how handsome and sweet he was, that even though she'd thought about having a bit of morning sickness, when it came down to spending more time with Eric, she just...forgot she was pregnant.

Just like that.

Forgot about her own baby.

What kind of mother did that?

God, am I going to be a horrible mother? She paused. *God, God, am I going to be a mother* at all?

Her breath hitched in her throat. Eric pulled her seatbelt across her shoulder and clicked it into place, as if she were a child. She didn't care.

At least someone was looking out for her, since she wasn't doing a good job of it on her own.

"Sorry," she mumbled.

"Don't worry about it. You've got a lot on your mind."

He drove them onto the main drive, and Jay waved to them from atop Smoky's back.

"Does Megan know?" he asked. "About the baby?"

"Yes," she said. At least she'd done that, scary as it had been to tell her in the first place. How awful would this have been, if she had told Eric and not her own sister?

"Do you want to call her, and let her know what's going on?"

Lindsay nodded, but Eric couldn't see her, because he was driving with his hands at ten and two, looking straight ahead, as he always did. A safe driver.

"I'll text her now."

When they pulled up into the parking lot at the medical building, Eric came around and helped her out of the car.

Was it just her, or was he treating her like she was a fragile flower now that he knew she was pregnant? Or maybe it was just the situation, her having fallen.

"I'm fine," she said, but she took his hand anyway. Because what if she wasn't fine?

They walked into the doctor's office, and Eric spoke to the woman at the front desk on her behalf. Normally that would annoy her, since she could certainly speak for herself, but in this instance, she was grateful. Maybe it even seemed as if Eric was her husband, and she was pregnant with his baby. Maybe.

Married to Eric?

If only. That would fix everything.

She'd have someone to take care of her and the baby when he was born, she wouldn't have to worry about working some crappy job just to get by. If they were married, Eric would probably even help her pay off her debt. And most importantly, she'd have a man in the house to help her raise her child.

To be a daddy to her son.

She didn't know for sure that her baby was a boy, but he sure *felt* like a boy. Not that she knew what a girl felt like. Just that, for whatever reason, she kept thinking of her baby as a "he."

Could be a girl, perhaps. But she'd be surprised if it was.

Don't get too attached.

She wasn't even at twelve weeks yet. And she may have just ruined everything, by falling off that horse.

Then again, getting pregnant out of wedlock was actually a huge problem in her life. She never wanted to kill her baby, but if it miscarried by accident, then would it really be so bad?

What if this was God's way of trying to help her out of the precarious situation she'd put herself into?

NO, God! No. That's not what I want!

She hadn't wanted to get pregnant, but now that she was, she definitely wanted her baby. She already was attached, for better or worse. There was no going back now. If she'd miscarried, she'd feel so…empty.

Thy will be done, I guess. And hopefully His will was for her to be holding a sweet baby in her arms in another seven months or so.

Please. I'm so sorry I forgot I was pregnant for a moment there. It will never happen again.

The door to the back office opened, and a short older woman in pink, cheery scrubs poked her head out. "Lindsay?"

Eric stood, offering Lindsay a hand, which she really didn't need. It's not like she had a huge belly yet, or anything. But she took his hand just the same.

It was chivalrous of him, and his touch was comforting.

He was taking care of her the way she'd been desperate for Grant to do.

"Thank you," she said softly.

He looked concerned. Really concerned. But he also looked so big and strong, and his hand on hers helped calm her rapid heartbeat.

"Eric," she whispered. "Can you come in with me?"

Eric looked surprised, but quickly composed himself. "Isn't Megan coming?"

"No, I told her I was fine and not to come. I didn't tell her about the spotting. She'd freak out, and I don't need that right now. And I didn't want her reading me the riot act for riding in the first place."

"Gotcha." He took his hat off and held it. "Of course I'll come in with you, if you want me."

Yes. She did want him.

How had she come to trust this man she barely knew, so quickly?

Lindsay smiled grimly at the medical assistant who called her name, and stepped on the scale as she told her to. Normally the idea of being weighed in front of anyone, much less a cute guy, would have her anxious, but she didn't care now. She was pregnant. She was supposed to gain weight, right?

In fact, she wasn't even going to look at the number on the scale. She'd let the doctor tell her if something was wrong with her weight, and leave it at that.

The thought released any lingering anxiety she had over stepping on the scale. "Don't tell me how much I weigh," she warned Eric. "I don't care."

He grinned at her. "Just know I'm gonna fatten you up. I make a mean chocolate chip cookie."

She smiled despite herself. It was good he was with her.

Eric joined her in the doctor's office, after she changed into the medical gown and sat on the table covered in crinkly white paper.

With him sitting in the chair beside her, he really did look like he was her husband, and he was there to help her with their baby. Grant would never, ever do anything like that.

Grant wanted nothing to do with their baby—*her* baby. He would never be a part of her child's life.

What would she give for a good man like Eric to have been the one to impregnate her, instead of a jerk like Grant?

There was no point wishing for that now. The past was done, and she couldn't change who was the biological father of her child.

But she could find someone to help her raise him. Maybe if Eric was in her life, maybe…just maybe, he'd be like an uncle to her child.

Maybe that would be enough.

He caught her staring at him and he gave her a supportive nod, as if to say, "you've got this."

Dr. Peterson, an older gentleman with a bald head, a trimmed, gray beard, and thin-rimmed glasses, knocked briefly and opened the office door.

She sat up straighter. Doctors weren't supposed to judge, right?

If only she could say Eric was the baby's father. That would make everything easier. Maybe the doctor would even just…assume. Although, Eric would probably be quick to say the baby wasn't his.

After Eric introduced her to Dr. Peterson, the doctor took a seat on a rolling stool and flipped open a notebook.

"So, what's going on today, dear?" the doctor asked.

"Well, I'm about eight weeks pregnant, I think. I actually haven't been to the doctor yet for my pregnancy, so I'm not entirely sure. But I took about half a dozen different pregnancy tests, and they're all positive, so…" she trailed off.

What if she wasn't even really pregnant?

No. There was no way for all of those pregnancy tests to be wrong. And she'd missed her period for two months in a row, now.

"Okay," the doctor said, noting down the date of her last cycle, and going through some more personal questions.

It didn't matter that Eric was hearing all of this. For whatever reason, he'd agreed to being there with her.

The doctor glanced at Eric, and if she hadn't been looking right at him at that moment, she would've missed the quick exchange. In a small town, this doctor probably was Eric's doctor as well, so they probably knew each other well, which would mean, if she was pregnant and Eric was taking her in, the doctor probably assumed that Eric had gotten her pregnant.

Eric didn't say a word to the contrary.

Interesting. That was amazing of him. It was as if he didn't care

Shoshanna Gabriel

what the doctor thought. And it seemed almost...protective of her.

"We were riding a horse this morning," Lindsay continued, "and we fell off."

"It was her first time riding," Eric cut in. "I wouldn't have let her if I'd known...how dangerous horseback riding can be for pregnant women."

Huh. It seemed like he'd almost said if he'd known she was pregnant. But he switched it at the last second... was he letting the doctor assume he was the father? And if so, why?

Also, thank You God, for making the whole situation less awkward, if that was indeed the case.

At least, for this appointment at least, she wouldn't be the girl who'd been abandoned by a man who knocked her up and left her like so much garbage.

Never thought that would be an apt description for her life, but here she was.

"I don't think I'm hurt from the fall," she added. "But when I got back on the horse, I got so worried—and I checked and saw I had some spotting. It wasn't there before the ride." She took a shaky breath, gritting her teeth. "I can't believe I went riding for the first time ever while pregnant."

"We're going to do another pregnancy test to check your HCG levels, to make sure they're at the level they should be at this stage in your pregnancy. And we'll do an ultrasound to see how your little one is doing."

Little One.

That's what she called her baby, too. Lindsay liked this doctor even more now.

"You have that here?" Lindsay couldn't hide her surprise.

"Oh yes," Dr. Peterson said, "I'm a Family Practice physician—a jack-of-all-trades. You have to be, in a small town, so people don't have to travel an hour for basic care I can provide here."

That made sense. She nodded.

"A Family Practice doctor's residency focuses on caring for the whole family, not just adults—kids, and OB/GYN, as well," he added. "But I can refer you to a specialist in Coeur d'Alene or Spokane, if you'd like. A female obstetrician, perhaps."

"Maybe that would be good, if something's not right." There was something about this doctor she really liked, though. "But can you tell me right now, today, if my baby's okay?"

"That's the plan." The doctor set everything up, and put a huge drape over her legs, urging her to scoot to the end of the table. This was so weird. And with Eric right there!

"I can leave, if you want privacy," Eric said.

"No," she said, a little too loudly. "I mean, unless you want to leave."

"I want whatever makes you more comfortable."

She glanced up at him in surprise. How did he know exactly what to say to make her feel better?

"Can you sit by my head and hold my hand? Everything's covered by the drape anyway, right, Dr. Peterson?"

"That's right. He won't see a thing. I can't do this on your belly because you're too early on for that. I'll get a better view internally." He spoke softly, as if only to her...and Eric, bless his heart, pretended not to hear.

He looked away from the doctor and just held her hand.

Within moments, the screen on the ultrasound came to life. She couldn't tell what she was seeing at first, but then she heard it.

Bah-dum bah-dum bah-dum

At the steady, rapid sound, Eric turned his head back around and stared at the screen with her in wonderment.

His heartbeat! Her Little One was alive!

"Your baby is doing fine," the doctor said.

She hadn't realized she'd been holding it all together until she let out a sob of relief.

Thank You. Thank You.

"Oh wow," Eric said, sounding even more relieved than she was, if that was possible. "Praise God…wow."

"What about the spotting?" she asked.

"That can happen in some pregnancies. Falling off the horse probably didn't help." The doctor turned to Eric. "No more riding for her."

Ha. Normally she'd be ticked off the doctor had told Eric *not to let her* ride—no one would dare say such a thing in Manhattan, instead of just telling *her* directly—but she was so relieved, she simply nodded in agreement with a huge smile. God bless Idaho, different as it was.

"So…I'm okay? The baby's okay?"

"Yes, ma'am," Dr. Peterson said.

Well, she'd graduated from "miss" to "ma'am," so that was a start.

The doctor closed his notebook and stood. "You should take the rest of the day off, and lie down with your feet up. If you're still spotting tomorrow, call the office and let me know. But I have a feeling it was just one tiny scare. I see it all the time."

"Thank you, doctor," Eric said. "Is she eight weeks along, like she thought?"

"Eight weeks, two days. Everything looks good so far, and we'll check again at twelve weeks, so make an appointment."

Was Eric happy she was pregnant?

Why?

Or was it just that he didn't want to deal with the mess she'd become if she'd lost her child?

"I'll take her back and get her into bed right away," Eric said, and then he winced.

Lindsay laughed out loud.

"I mean, you know," he muttered. "Bed rest. I'll tell Megan to help her."

The tips of Eric's ears were turning red. That was adorable. Guess she wasn't the only one who sometimes said ridiculous things by accident.

It made her like him even more. Although, after how wonderful he was with her just now, she didn't know how that was even possible.

If only she could go back in time, and meet Eric before she got pregnant. If she'd been able to meet him as a single woman, instead of a single mom.

Before she'd been soured to the concept of love entirely.

Maybe something would have blossomed between them.

But not now. She knew that. There was no reason for Eric to take on the responsibility of a woman's child from another man.

Some guys do, though. It happened all the time, right?

But probably not with such a young, handsome man, not someone who had a large, successful ranch and who could have any woman he wanted. Surely not.

There was no reason for him to choose her.

The door shut quietly behind Dr. Peterson, and Eric and Lindsay were left alone in the room.

He reached over to her and hugged her, pulling her in gently against his muscular chest.

It was so unexpected, and yet it wasn't. It felt completely natural and right to be in his arms, to take comfort in his strong embrace. She could feel his heart beating through his T-shirt.

Bah dum. Bah dum.

Much slower and heavier than her baby's. Eric had the heart of a man.

Chapter Five

ERIC DROVE THEM back to the ranch carefully, as always. But this time he was aware he had special cargo—not just Lindsay, but her baby as well.

"Thanks for taking me," Lindsay said. "And paying for it. Once I get insurance, and…well, you know."

"It's fine," he said, staring out the windshield at the road. "I'm glad you got checked out."

"It was amazing seeing my baby on that screen," she said. "It made this pregnancy so much more…real."

"It's real, all right."

She was silent. Had he sounded off-putting to her?

"I thought it was pretty amazing, too," he added. From his periphery, he could see a flash of her smile.

"I suppose you're wondering how a nice girl like me got knocked up in the first place."

He didn't respond. But yes.

That was exactly what he'd been wondering. Even if she'd had sex before, which happened before marriage more often than not these days, it seemed—for better or worse—

Worse. Look at the consequences.

Yeah. Well, even if she'd had sex before, and that wasn't his business, didn't she know to use birth control? How did something like that happen?

Unless she was raped. Could that be what she meant by being "burnt by a man before"?

"I truly did believe in saving myself for marriage," she finally said. "I did. But I let myself get into a bad situation, and after I'd stayed at all of my girlfriend's apartments for as long as I could, I ran out of friends who were willing to help me out."

Before he could say anything, she continued, as if she already knew what his response might be.

"Don't say that I could have stayed at a shelter." She paused, looking out the window. "Those shelters can be really scary."

While a shelter may have been Eric's second idea if he didn't have any friends in the area, his first thought would have been going to see family, wherever they may have been in the world.

But that cost money, too.

"I could see that," he said. "Shelters might be pretty rough."

"Yeah," she said. "And…well, I guess I was still thinking of myself as 'temporarily broke' instead of full-on 'poor.' I used to have a really nice place on the Upper West Side. I had a wardrobe to die for—"

"Really?" he asked. "Would you die for it?"

She huffed. "Don't be a jerk. It's only a saying."

"Just asking."

He hadn't meant to be a jerk, but the truth was, he probably held a little something against the rich Manhattanites, the people who didn't even know where Idaho was on a map because they just didn't care. The ones who called his beautiful hometown "flyover country." As if the only places that mattered where Los Angeles and NYC. Forget about everything in between.

"Doesn't matter now," she said. "It's all gone. Sold it all. And I ended up staying at a guy friend's house. I thought he was a safer, better bet than any shelter, anyway—I mean, I'd known him for almost five years from work."

"You don't have to explain yourself to me," Eric said. "You don't need to."

"I *do* need to," she insisted. "You know everything now, except this. You should know. *This isn't like me.* I wasn't sleeping around or anything like that."

He didn't respond. What could he say?

"We'd never dated or anything, so I figured I just wasn't on his radar that way, right?" she said. "But once I moved in, it became very clear that the only way I was going to stay there was to be his…" Her words trailed off, as if she didn't want to get more specific.

"Did that guy hurt you?"

Because if that guy did anything to harm one hair on Lindsay's head, Eric was ready to hop on a plane right that minute just to punch the guy in the nose.

"No, no," she said quickly. Maybe she sensed his testosterone rising. "He…convinced me, basically. Made me think we had something real together. And I said yes."

"None of my business, but aren't there ways to prevent unwanted pregnancy nowadays?" Eric grit his teeth.

He didn't mean to sound rude or sarcastic. It was just so hard to imagine how she'd gotten herself into this situation.

"Of course," she said sharply. "But I wasn't on birth control because I never intended to have sex. And I didn't ask for a condom, because—to be honest—I was just in shock that I was doing what I was doing to begin with."

Wow. Eric didn't know what to think. It was so much to take in, all at once, from a girl he'd only recently met in the first place.

She crossed her arms. "I've said way too much. That's probably the last visual you wanted in your head."

True. He didn't want to imagine her in some other guy's bed.

"It's all right," he said quietly.

"You know what I realized, while we were in the waiting room?" she asked. "I've been telling you every minute detail of my life, yet I barely know anything about you."

"Would it make you feel better, if you did?"

"Yes. Can you tell me something secret, something you don't want anyone to know, just like you know about me?" She laughed dryly. "That's probably the only way to make me feel less awful."

Should he tell her?

Could he?

Yes.

"I can't have kids of my own," Eric said. He cleared his throat. "It's called 'obstructive azoospermia.' Got internal scarring and so no swimmers in the semen. Sorry to get so gross, but you asked for it."

Lindsay gasped.

He wanted to face her, but ever since that car accident when he was seventeen, he never took his eyes off the road for a conversation. Never.

Did she think he was less of a man?

"Didn't find out until pretty recently," he added. "Not long before you got here."

"I'm…goodness, I'm…so sorry."

"Don't need your pity."

That came out sharper than he intended it to.

She paused. "I know."

The silence was thick with unsaid words. What was going through her mind at that moment? What did she think of him now?

"Did you want kids, before you found out?" she asked, finally.

"'Course I wanted kids!" He took a breath, and tried again, calmer this time. "But for whatever reason, this is the hand God dealt me."

They pulled up the long drive, under the large log entranceway that read BEAR CREEK SADDLE RANCH.

"I'm dreading telling Megan what happened," Lindsay admitted. "She's going to freak out."

"Might not even be home. Zach was saying they were heading to an expo in Spokane today to try and get new clients. Unless that was tomorrow."

Lindsay's thumbs ran across her phone, and a moment later, it buzzed in her hand. "You're right—they're out today." She breathed an exaggerated sigh of relief. "Guess I won't have to worry about that, after all."

"Wait—who's gonna bring you lunch, then?" he asked. "What if you need help? The doctor said to stay in bed with your feet up—"

"Well, he said I could go to and from the bathroom, so that's a plus."

He couldn't tell if she was being sarcastic or not.

"You should come to my place. I can help you out until Megan gets back. Seriously, you're probably starving. Last thing you need is to be on your feet cooking right now."

Lindsay hesitated.

Why? Did she not want his help?

Or did she think…

Oh.

"You won't owe me anything," he added softly. "I ain't like Grant."

"I know."

"Besides—I put you into this situation, so at least give me the comfort of helping you out of it."

"What?" she asked, sounding confused. "Grant put me into this mess—and I did as well. But not you."

"Grant didn't put you on a horse and then let you fall off it, though." He parked in front of his log cabin.

She took off her seatbelt, but didn't make a move for the handle.

"If you're really not comfortable, tell me, and I'll take you back to Megan's," he said. "Seriously. But if you're just trying to be polite and not put me out, don't do that. I need to fix this if I can."

She paused, looking out the truck window. He took great pride in building that log cabin with his own two hands. It wasn't huge or fancy, but it was cozy and it was home.

"Okay," she said. "I'll take you up on your offer. I *am* pretty hungry."

Thank You, God—for giving me a chance to set this right.

Eric grinned. "I even have a tray—you eat in bed."

"Just to confirm," she said, "it will be just me in that bed, correct?"

He wanted to laugh at the silliness of her question, but just in case she was actually concerned he might try to jump in bed with her, he responded with great seriousness.

"Just you," he said. "And when Megan gets home, I'll drive you back over there. If you feel weirded out or something, you can tell me and I'll take you back. No harm, no foul."

"Okay." She laughed nervously and shook her head. "Did Zach ever tell you how when Megan first got into his truck, she made him promise her he wasn't a serial killer?"

Eric laughed. "Must've left that part out."

"Yeah—that was my doing. I could teach a class on how to be wary of men." A shadow crossed her warm brown eyes for a moment, but she shook it off. "How ironic."

* * *

Lindsay stood in the front hall of Eric's home. Boomer sat at her feet, his stub of a tail wagging like crazy, looking up at her. "Hi there, boy," she acknowledged.

There was wood everywhere, and comfy-looking furniture, along with a big-screen TV above the fireplace in the living room.

"Do you watch a lot of television?" she asked. It was strange, because he didn't seem like the type.

"Nah—just movies. Netflix."

"I see."

"Enough talking," he interrupted. "I need to get you into bed."

She raised her eyebrows, even though she knew exactly what he meant, just to make him squirm.

"Uhh…you know. Off your feet."

Lindsay laughed, and Eric shook his head. "Come on, let's go. Doctor's orders."

He took her by the hand and led her into his bedroom, a small room with log walls and a smaller-sized television of its own. The bed was an old iron-framed one, with what looked like a handmade quilt (from his mother, perhaps?) on top of the queen-sized mattress.

"Wait," he said suddenly. "Have a seat while I change the sheets for you." He gestured toward a plain wooden chair in the corner. "That's where I sit if I'm wearing dirty clothes and need to take them off without getting the quilt dirty."

"Lovely," she said brightly. "Does this mean it's covered in dirt?"

"Nope." Since she apparently wasn't moving fast enough, he walked her the few steps to the chair and put his hand on her shoulder, gently setting her down. "Sit. Don't move a muscle."

Bossy, bossy.

"Do I get a treat if I obey?" she asked sarcastically. "Is this how you trained Boomer?"

Eric looked like he wanted to say something back, but instead he turned and walked out, returning quickly with a pile of fresh sheets.

Lindsay watched as he made the bed, tossing the old sheets into a hamper by the master bathroom door.

"Thank you," she said as he finished up. "I appreciate it."

"Let me check the bathroom real quick and give it a once-over." Eric strode past her and emerged a few moments later. "We're good."

"Hang on, I'm going to need you to show me how to use the remote."

Lindsay went into the bathroom, finished up and washed her

hands. No more spotting, thank God.

Seriously, thank You, God. That was so scary. I want my Little One to be okay. Please.

Although it was a strange thing, to share something so personal with Eric, she felt he'd genuinely want to know. "Everything's good," she said, and smiled. "No more spotting, so it seems like that was a one-off from the fall."

"Thank God," he said. "You still need to get into bed, though. It can't hurt to rest for a day and give your baby a break from all the adventure."

She got under the covers. Beneath the quilt was a fluffy down comforter, and a soft, clean sheet. The pillow was fluffy, too. "You sleep in a very comfy bed. I like this."

He was taking such good care of her. She'd have to be careful to guard her heart around him…because Eric was the sort of man she'd only wished Grant could have been.

If she forgot to be cautious, all she had to think about was how devastated and alone her father was, ever since Mom died. Even when love worked out and resulted in a happy marriage and two daughters, someone was always going to leave—one way or another.

And the end result was the cruelest pain imaginable.

* * *

Eric brought the tray into his bedroom where Lindsay lay, resting sweetly in his bed, with her legs elevated by a pillow under her knees. She clicked off the news on the television.

"Peanut butter and jelly on whole wheat bread," Eric announced. "I'm not an advanced chef, but I can make a mean

PB&J, at least."

"That looks perfect." But instead of reaching for a sandwich, she took his hand. "Will you say grace for us?"

Eric closed his fingers around her small, warm palm, and bowed his head. "Lord, thank You for this food; please bless it to our bodies. Thank You for Lindsay and her baby being okay. You sure did give us a good scare. Please keep them both safe, God. And help me to do whatever I can to help make that happen."

"Amen," she murmured.

They both ate in silence for a moment, their mouths too full to speak.

After swallowing and taking a deep sip of water, Lindsay smiled at him. "What do you suppose God wants you to do, to help keep me and my Little One safe?"

"I don't know. But I wish I did."

Eric's heart was beating faster now. Why had he gotten so personal with his prayer in front of her? God already knew what was in his heart. He didn't have to pray that out loud…and yet he had.

Because he wanted her to know.

"You're being so nice to me," she said, smoothing the quilt over her still-flat belly. "I'm having a hard time understanding how you don't already have a girlfriend."

She laughed, as if she were joking, but Eric could tell it was a serious question.

"Come on, I've had girlfriends before." He shrugged. "But love don't last. Never lasted for me, anyways."

"How so?"

"I had this one girlfriend, after high school… She wasn't a

Christian. Didn't have the same life goals. She wanted to move to Hollywood and be a movie star. Didn't want kids, nothing normal like living in Idaho." Eric smiled wistfully. "And stupid me, I loved her—I really thought I did. But love ain't enough to fix a relationship doomed from the start."

Lindsay nodded thoughtfully. "Doomed, because you didn't want the same things in life?"

"Yeah." It had been a while since he'd thought about his former girlfriend. Whether or not the love between them had been real, the broken heart he'd experienced after it ended wasn't something he'd ever repeat on purpose. "We just weren't on the same page."

"What happened with her? Is she an actress now?"

"Nah. She moved to L.A. Last I heard she was living with some wannabe drummer or something."

Lindsay sat back against his pillow, her dark hair framing her face. "Do you miss her?"

Did he?

No.

"She taught me a lesson I needed learning. After her, I'll only date a woman who has the same morals and goals as me. Love and lust ain't the top priority, I don't think. 'Cause that stuff won't last anyway."

She inhaled sharply.

Oh, man.

Did he just blow it? Was she mad he didn't believe in love?

But instead of glaring at him, she shook her head, as if in amazement.

"I feel the same way you do, Eric. I mean, who needs love when it's not going to last and just end up hurting you even worse? I want to be with someone I can trust. Someone who I respect. Who I know wants to protect me and my baby." She sighed. "I'd take that over romance any day."

If anyone wanted to protect her and her baby, it was him. Could she see that? Did she know?

That guy Grant didn't deserve to be anywhere near Lindsay or the baby.

"Maybe," Lindsay said slowly, "after the baby is born, you could be like…a strong male figure in his life. Teach him boy stuff, that kind of thing."

"Be his dad," Eric agreed.

She stared at him in stunned silence, her lips parted.

He hadn't meant to just say that.

It just came out of him, so naturally. He'd been agreeing with her. Of course, he'd be a positive male role model in her child's life.

He wanted to be even more than that.

Eric could be a father-figure to her child, the way his own father had been for Zach, since Zach's father had abandoned them.

"I'm sorry," he said. "I meant—I was agreeing, of course. Everything you were saying, that sounds like stuff a father would do. That's why I said that."

"Okay." She still seemed almost out of breath, maybe unsure of either herself, or of what he would say next.

"I don't have to, if you don't want me to," he said. "It was just a suggestion."

"I want you to. Yes, Eric—I definitely want you to."

Wow. Was this why God had shown him the vision of himself with a woman—Lindsay, surely—holding a baby?

Lord, is this how You are giving me a family?

Eric never expected direct answers to his prayers. He prayed and asked questions of God way too often, he figured, to get a personalized response on each one.

Until the vision. His one and only vision from God. He was sure of it.

But now, deep within himself, Eric could feel the answer.

Yes. This is it.

Eric grinned. *Thank You, God. Thank You, thank You. Please don't let me jack this up.*

"Lindsay," he said softly. "I just want to give you a thought, something to pray on, something to mull over. No need to answer right away, okay?"

She looked up at him from her pillow and nodded. "Okay…"

"You have a baby coming, with no father. And I have an empty house, with no wife, and no chance of having children of my own."

"What are you saying, Eric?" She didn't sound mad… just… curious? Excited, even?

Was that possible? Did she want this too?

Yes, she does.

Eric felt the Holy Spirit whispering within him as clearly as he could feel the softness of the quilt on the bed beneath his fingers.

"Maybe," he said, "instead of just being a father-figure in your baby's life, I could be his *actual* father. You and I could get married, and you could live here with me, and we'd raise the child together. As partners."

"Like… co-parenting?"

"If that means parenting together, then yeah," he said. "You wouldn't have to worry about being broke anymore, 'cause I'd take care of my wife, my family. That's what I always wanted to do anyways, 'fore I even met you."

"You just met me. No one does this."

"I may've just met you, but I've been hearing about you from your sister all year. That girl can't say enough 'bout you."

"She's told me about you too."

Eric grinned. "So we ain't strangers, not really."

Lindsay's eyes welled with unshed tears. "You are an amazing, generous man to offer this to me. To us. But you don't know what you're getting into. I've got tens of thousands of dollars in debt. If we got legally married, you'd be taking that on."

"Haven't had nothing good to spend my money on all these years." Eric shrugged. "Already got a good truck. Got a house, and no mortgage 'cause I built it myself. I could pay off your debt with you, if you'd agree to be my wife."

Her jaw dropped, her mouth opened like a small letter O, and she stared at him with an expression of pure surprise.

"Why?" she asked. "Why me?"

"I like you, Lindsay. I… I care about you, and the baby. I want only good things for you both."

"What else? There has to be something I'm missing here. What's in it for you? Sex?"

Heat rushed to his ears. Hopefully in the dim light of the bedroom she wouldn't notice, but he turned his head and stared at the embroidery on the quilt instead of looking at her intense gaze.

Lord, give me the words. If this is really Your will, help me out.

He took a deep breath, and looked at her. "You're right. There is something in it for me. Last few months I moped around, sure as all get-out I'd never have a family. Never'd find a beautiful woman who liked being with me, who respected me as a man, even though

I can't give her children, and who'd marry me anyways."

He smiled wistfully. "I always wanted to be a dad. My folks are awesome—you'd love 'em. They want to be grandparents, too. You should see how happy they are that my brother's wife's got a baby on the way—"

"Is that it? You want to be like your brother?"

"No." He sighed. Telling her everything would make him sound out of his mind. But the truth was all he had, and she deserved to know why he felt so confident they'd make it, despite having just met her.

Please don't let me mess this up more. Help me.

"I see you," Eric said finally, "and... and you look just like the woman in my vision."

There. He'd said it. Now she knew.

"Vision?" she echoed uncertainly.

"I haven't just heard about you before...I've *seen* you before."

"In a photo," she suggested.

He looked at her and shook his head. He tapped his temple. "In here. I think that's why it already feels like I know you. God showed me you were coming, and the baby, even."

"My sister must've told you I was coming."

Eric shook his head again, very slightly. "Do you believe God can show someone something true?"

"Yes...of course."

"This ain't something that's ever happened to me before. I don't know if it'll ever happen again. But God showed me, clear as day. You and me and the baby. I can't ignore that like it didn't happen. It happened. And now...you're here."

Lindsay didn't look nearly as taken aback as his brother had.

"You really feel this was a vision from God?" she asked. "How sure are you?"

"I was ninety-seven percent sure when it first happened, and I told my brother about it. But then, when I met you…well, I'm a hundred percent sure now. I don't think I'd have the guts to propose what I'm proposing if I wasn't so sure."

He liked how she was taking it all in—she didn't dismiss it right away like his brother had. As if maybe, just maybe, he was valuable enough to God to get a special vision created specifically for him.

To have a gorgeous woman in front of him who believed in him that way…how could he give that up?

"When I saw your baby's heartbeat on that monitor, I just… I want us to be a family."

"This is crazy," Lindsay whispered. "I thought the same thing, at the same time, even. How it would be, if you were my baby's father."

"I think it's what God wants, too. For me to ask you. You don't have to be head-over-heels in love with me. I don't expect that. We both know how that stuff ends up."

She nodded. "Unfortunately. Yeah."

"But we'll each be filling a big gap in each other's life. You need a husband and provider, and I need a family. We can do this together."

"Like a business arrangement?"

"Like a *marriage* arrangement," he said. "Like in the olden days. Those marriages-of-convenience lasted forever, compared to now, where half the people who marry for love end up divorcing."

"That's true," she mused.

"New love, lust, that all fades, Lindsay. But having common

values and filling each other's needs—that lasts."

* * *

Lindsay couldn't believe what she was hearing from Eric. But it was the answer to her prayers.

Was it "settling" if she married someone when they weren't in love, even if they had the same Christian values and the goal of raising a happy, healthy child together?

Not really, not if she didn't want to get so attached to a man that she ended up completely destroyed when the relationship ended—which it would—either by divorce, abandonment, or, best case scenario…after many decades together, right when she was completely and utterly in love and not whole without him…death.

Just like what had happened to her dad when her mom died.

By accepting Eric's proposal, could she be missing out on the perfect man for her?

Unless this was God's plan all along. And Eric was, in fact, the perfect man for her.

What did "perfect" mean, anyway? A hundred years ago, marrying a wealthy, educated man was considered the perfect match. And while Eric wasn't like the hedge-fund managers or lawyers from New York that she'd previously dated, he was still an incredible guy.

"Let me think about this," she said. "Okay?"

Hopefully he wouldn't change his mind in the amount of time it took her to make up hers.

Eric nodded and patted the quilt next to her. "You got it."

He took their empty lunch tray and walked to the door of the bedroom. "Want me to send Boomer in here for company? He's a big teddy bear."

She grinned. "Sure."

A minute later, Boomer bounced in and jumped up on the bed at her feet. True to what Eric had said, having the dog there was indeed comforting and cuddly. It was like having her feet next to a giant oven, if ovens were covered in brown curly fur.

Arranged marriages, marriages of convenience, this wasn't a new idea. Many women still did it in other countries. It had been going on for centuries. Plenty of happy, loving couples had come from marriages like that.

The fact was, she'd already given up her virginity just to have the *chance* at what Eric was offering as a definite. Why not marry him? It wasn't like she had men banging down the door to be with her. Most young men didn't want to take care of another man's child. Eric was different, because this was his chance to have a child at all.

Grant was out of the picture, and her baby needed a dad. More than that, she needed a home for her and her child. A warm, safe, loving home where they'd be taken care of.

While her sister had offered to let her live in the guest cabin, it was really tiny, and might not be the best place for a rambunctious child to grow up. Kids needed more than a hundred square feet to run around, didn't they? There was no room for a crib in there, even. Would she even be able to carry her Little One up the ladder to the loft bed in the first place? Or climb up when she was heavily pregnant?

As much as she felt good having the guest cabin as a backup in case she couldn't get a job and an apartment of her own, she'd have a problem if she did get a job, with a newborn at home. Where would she bring her baby? Would she make enough money for a nanny to care for her child? Maybe. Or maybe she'd be working just to pay the nanny, in which case she may as well stay home and raise her child herself.

Get by on food stamps.

Unless she could get a job where she could bring her baby to work with her, and keep him by her side. That would be ideal. Something part-time, where she could have her child with her so she could breastfeed and hold him, and spend most of her time with him and not slaving away at a job she hated.

Nothing like that existed, as far as she knew. Maybe if she started a freelancing company of her own, of some sort. She could do taxes, she was certified for that. But the fact remained that she wasn't in a position to say no to a free home, food, healthcare— Eric said he'd take care of everything so she could raise her baby.

Their baby.

He would be theirs, to raise together, just like a real couple.

They *would* be a real couple—they'd be married. How weird would that be, to call Eric "my husband"?

Hmm.

What should I do, God?

There were so many upsides to just saying yes.

For one, she was attracted to Eric Hunt. It wasn't like he was hard on the eyes, or elderly or something. He was a bit rough around the edges, but maybe that was a good thing. The men she used to date in Manhattan were a little too smooth for her taste. So smooth they were slimy.

Maybe it was better to have a regular guy. Someone who didn't care what other people thought about him. Who didn't care what people would say when they realized he was raising another man's child.

Would they tell people? Would people ask?

It was a small town.

And she didn't want her baby raised in a lie. He'd grow up someday, and when he found out the truth, he'd feel betrayed. It'd be much better to make it just a natural part of his story from the beginning.

She imagined tucking her child into bed—he looked to be about four years old in her mind, and as adorable as a puppy. Eric would help her tuck him in. They'd say their evening prayers together. And if her boy asked for the story about how he was born, she'd tell him how he was extra lucky, because his father had *chosen* him. "Daddy chose you when you were still in my womb," she'd tell him. "And he chose me. Maybe when you're grown up you'll want to meet your biological father, whose genetics you share. But Eric is your Daddy. Your *real* Dad."

That's what she'd tell him. And it wouldn't come as a shock, because she'd have told him the same story since he was a baby.

But how much harder would that story be to tell, if Eric wasn't in the picture?

She'd be tucking her boy into bed, all by herself. They'd pray together, and this time, her son would ask why he doesn't have a daddy, like the other kids.

"Your biological father is in New York, and maybe you'll meet him someday. And maybe…someday…you'll have a stepfather."

Ugh. That was not nearly as lovely of a story to tell a child.

In fact, the whole scenario really only worked with Eric by her side.

Why shouldn't she marry him? He was handsome, healthy, strong, stable. He had a ranch and his own home and a truck. Eric could take care of them, and be a real father to her child.

Lindsay would be a fool to turn that all down, just because they didn't know each other well. It wasn't like he was a stranger who'd emailed her from out of the blue. She wasn't a mail-order bride, risking everything sight-unseen. Her sister's husband-to-be had grown up with Eric. Eric was the most well-vetted man she'd ever meet.

So why *shouldn't* she marry him?

She took a breath, matching it to Boomer's slow, soft snoring at her feet.

You tell me, Lord. Tell me if this the right thing to do.

The answer came to her so fast, she heard it within herself even before she'd finished asking the question—*YES.*

Whoa.

Okay.

That "yes" feeling was strong. Really strong. No doubts in her mind sort of strong.

"Eric," she called. "Can we talk?"

Eric opened the door to the bedroom. "I didn't mean to freak you out, earlier."

Lindsay laughed. "That's okay. It's a freaky sort of situation."

He laughed. "Yeah."

"Do you really want to get married and have this baby together?" she asked.

Chapter Six

LINDSAY COULDN'T BELIEVE how she'd just asked that question. So casually.

Even though her whole body trembled as she spoke.

As if it weren't the biggest deal in her whole life—and in his, as well.

Please don't have changed your mind.

Eric cocked his head, as if it took him a moment to replay what she'd said to him, so he could be sure.

"Do you?" he asked.

"Well…" Her voice caught in her throat. "You tell me first." She laughed, to soften the intensity of the moment, and he grinned at her.

It only pertained to the rest of their lives. That's all.

"I'd be honored to marry you, Lindsay," he said, all laughter gone from his face. "If you'd have me, I'd take care of you both. You might even come to be real happy as my wife, if you give me a chance."

"How about you?" she asked. Her heart raced in her chest. It was so loud, the blood throbbing in her ears. Could he hear how nervous she was? "Do you think you'd be…happy, with me?"

"We're practically strangers at the moment," he admitted. "But after living together, raising a kid together, I'm sure it would happen eventually. We've got great chemistry to start us off, at least."

He was right. The romantic tension, the heat between them was real. He had to be feeling it just as she did.

They could definitely be happy together.

And as long as she didn't do anything stupid like lose her heart to Eric along the way, there was no reason their marriage couldn't be a successful partnership—and the perfect situation for her baby, especially compared to what she had to offer her child on her own.

"This is the craziest thing I've ever done, agreeing to this," she said. "But it feels right. I can't explain it."

Eric grinned. "Ditto everything you just said."

"Can we do it before the baby is born?"

"I'd go with you to the courthouse next week, if you'd like. Then you could move right in."

Oh my goodness. This was too crazy.

Was it possible he was just doing this as an elaborate way to sleep with her?

No, that was even crazier. A handsome guy like Eric surely had his pick of the ladies. But if he was determined to save himself for marriage, as she was—well, had been—maybe he was getting tired of waiting for his wedding night.

"Have you ever been married before, Eric?"

He shook his head. "Nah. And I'm glad, too. It would've been awful to marry a girl who expected to have kids with me, and then have to give her the bad news. With you—my biggest fear is no longer an issue."

"Your biggest fear?"

"You already know I'm sterile. And the problem's a non-starter, because you're already pregnant. It's…perfect."

It was perfect.

But she had to test him, to see how much this was about sleeping with her, instead of about raising a baby together.

Lindsay cleared her throat. "What if I told you…I don't want to sleep with you?"

His expression faltered. "Ever? Do I disgust you or something?"

"No!" she said quickly. "No, of course not. I mean, I might *want* to sleep with you, but I don't think I should. Even if we were married. At least not until we knew each other much better. Trusted each other. I don't want to get hurt, emotionally, the way I was with Grant."

"I'd never hurt you, Lindsay."

"I know." Did she know? "But…I've had this awful experience, and really recently. The last thing I want to do is repeat it."

"We wouldn't be repeating that mistake," he argued. "For one, I wouldn't get you pregnant, and two, even if I did, I'd be your husband, and I'd never leave you."

"It's this," she said quietly. "I don't want to be 'logicked' into having sex." It may not have made sense to use *logic* as a verb, but hopefully he'd get what she meant. "I don't want to be worn down—to have to be convinced."

"Like I'm doing right now," he said, exhaling heavily. "Sorry."

"I know you'd probably want a wife you could sleep with," she said. "And I'm not saying 'no' forever. Just 'no' for the amount of time it would take us to naturally be…ready to take that step."

"What if that doesn't happen?" he asked. "Not trying to 'logic' you or nothing, but—what if you never want to sleep with me?"

It was a legitimate question.

Especially assuming he was against adultery, and not intending to take a vow of celibacy for the rest of his life.

"It took me five years of knowing Grant to sleep with him, and look how that turned out," she said finally. "I don't know what the right amount of time is, because it's not like I've gotten this right before."

Lindsay paused. What could she say to make him understand just how frightened she was of losing herself again? And worse— of never being whole again if it ended?

"I ain't against love," Eric said. "I just don't trust it to last. That's why I don't have to be in love with you, to want to marry you. But maybe you need to be in love with me to sleep with me."

"Maybe."

That would be worse, somehow. To love him, and not have him love her back.

"People who are 'just friends' sometimes do that whole 'friends with benefits' thing," she said slowly. "…so if we're married, I guess I'll just—"

Don't. Don't do it again. Don't prostitute yourself, even if the price is higher this time.

The phrase "I'll just sleep with you anyway" had almost passed her lips, but she stopped herself.

"I don't know, Eric," she said finally. "I think our marriage would have to go from being a marriage of convenience, to being…real. In every way."

He'd said maybe she needed to love him in order to sleep with him. But her wary heart told her that *he* needed to love her, before she could be that vulnerable to him.

If he loved her, then she could trust herself with him.

Maybe.

She mentally braced herself for his reaction, because she wouldn't blame him if he were mad. Here he was, offering her everything, and she was telling him he'd have to give even more—his heart—before she'd give herself to him. Especially since she'd already given her body to a man who had offered her only a few nights off the street.

Would he call the whole thing off?

"I really like you, Eric," she whispered. "I want to marry you and raise the baby—our baby—together. I can promise you a family, but I can't promise you that one thing. I'm sorry."

Eric was still, quiet. His broad shoulders were straight with tension as he listened to her.

"I understand if you don't want to marry me anymore," she added. "I'll be sad, but I'll understand."

Please don't change your mind.

He took her hand in his, covering her palm with his own strong, calloused one. "I still want to marry you. Not having sex won't be a big change for me, anyway." Eric laughed. "But if you're open to letting me try to court you, even while we're married, then I'm in."

Lindsay smiled and gently squeezed his hand. "I'm in, too."

* * *

The following day back at Megan's house (well, Zach's house, but soon-to-be Megan's, and that's where she was staying, anyhow), Lindsay couldn't keep the smile off her face.

Last night, when Megan came to pick her up from Eric's, she didn't dare tell her about their arrangement, though. Not yet. Her sister was still ticked off that Lindsay had risked her and the baby's safety by going riding.

At least she didn't have to stay on bed rest, now that the spotting was done with. But she'd learned her lesson. No more heroics or adventures, if that's what one would call slowly riding a gentle horse across a flat field. Lindsay intended to keep her feet firmly planted on the ground for the rest of her pregnancy.

Megan entered the kitchen in a fuzzy bathrobe over her flannel pajamas. "Good morning!"

Lindsay grinned at her. "Bathrobe but no socks or slippers? Aren't your feet cold?"

"If you're asking if I'm getting cold feet about the wedding, the answer is definitely not," she said, sliding across the floor to grab a coffee mug.

"I'm not that clever," Lindsay said. "I literally meant your body is dressed for a different temperature than your feet are."

Megan laughed. "Right."

Lindsay brought her own coffee to the table and smiled again. "I have to tell you something."

"You've already shocked me more than ever possible already, so do your worst."

"This is a good thing. I think you'll like it."

"Oh really?"

"Eric is a great guy, would you agree?"

"Absolutely. He's been Zach's best friend since they were kids. I'd trust him with my life because of that alone."

"Would you trust him with your sister's life?"

Megan frowned. "What are you talking about?"

"Has Zach told you anything...personal about Eric?"

Megan took a sip of coffee, which was her way of waiting a

second to think before responding. "He may have. I think I know what you're talking about."

"Because Eric told me himself. About his issue, medically."

"You tell me, and I'll tell you if I know already."

"That won't work. What if I'm just telling you his secret, instead?"

"We'll say it at the same time," Megan suggested. "Starting with the words 'Eric can't…'"

"Have kids," Lindsay finished for her.

Megan nodded. "You didn't give me a chance to finish, but yes. That's what I was told as well. I feel so bad for him."

"I kind of thought maybe you were thinking about Eric when you said that we could find me a husband who'd want me, not despite my condition, but *because* of my condition."

"Yeah, I was, actually. I didn't expect him to tell you so soon. How did that happen?"

Lindsay shrugged. "I was telling him all sorts of things. He came into the doctor's office with me for the ultrasound. It was really personal, very intimate, in a way. It made us become fast friends, I guess."

"So is that what you wanted to tell me? That you know about Eric?"

"No. It's more than that." Lindsay grinned, but what if Megan wasn't as excited about her plan as she was? Even though she'd suggested it herself, the timing was way too soon, surely.

Or was it?

"Eric suggested that we get married. That way I could move in with him, and have the baby born into a two-parent household and Eric would take care of us. I'd be on his health insurance, so I'd be able to get all my prenatal exams, and the delivery would be covered."

"You're not considering this just for health insurance, are you?"

"No! No, of course not. I really like Eric. He's kind and generous, and he's got a good head on his shoulders. Also a good-looking head, also good-looking shoulders."

Megan giggled. "Right."

"And he's always wanted to be a dad. For him it's an opportunity to be a father, to have a family. He's excited about that! Way better than Grant's reaction when I told him I was pregnant."

"You can't marry someone just because he's better than Grant. Literally a stick in the mud would be better than Grant."

"I know. But think about it—it solves all of my problems. Everything I've been worrying about, praying about. Housing, solved. Healthcare, solved. Having a father for my child, solved. And having a partner to help me and care for me, especially when I'm in that stage where I'll need all the help I can get. It's perfect."

"But you don't love him, Lindsay." Megan raised her eyebrows. "That's tough, because loving a man is a huge part of getting married, don't you think?"

Lindsay shrugged. "It's a marriage of convenience. Those happened all the time in the not-so-distant past, right? And even nowadays, there are countries with arranged marriages. That's practically the same thing, but those couples aren't even choosing their partner themselves."

"I guess…"

"So why not here, and now?" Lindsay continued. "He needs a family, I need a husband and provider, and my child needs a father. Win-win-win, all around."

"What happens when the newness and excitement about being able to live in his house and afford everything you need for your child wears off? Will you look at him, and wonder… *'what if my true love is out there somewhere?'*"

Would she?

No.

There was no need to. Eric was a great guy. It didn't matter if they weren't in love. That was actually ideal, as far as Lindsay was concerned. But they'd have the best to offer their son, because they'd both love *him*. That was for sure.

"I think…any man who loves my son and takes care of him, that's a man I'll be happy with. Even if it's not a romantic love, I'll love him as family, just for that."

"So you're just going to sleep with a man you don't love?" Megan asked. "I mean…again?"

Heat filled Lindsay's face. "No. We talked about that. Separate bedrooms for us, at least until we decide, mutually, otherwise."

"And he's fine with just giving you everything and not even getting the benefit of sharing your bed?"

"I wouldn't call it 'fine.' He understands, and he won't push me. I told him I was open to the possibility of sharing a bed in the future, and so… we're going to get married."

"When?"

"Not sure. You don't really want to ruin your special day by doing a double wedding, do you?" Lindsay asked.

"I don't think it would ruin it, but if you're not in love, I'm not sure if that's something I want in my wedding. It almost sounds like you're doing a business arrangement."

"A *marriage* arrangement," Lindsay said, echoing Eric's words.

"That sounds like it should be handled at the courthouse, perhaps." Megan sighed. "But I don't want to kick you out of the wedding, if you were excited to do a double wedding."

"Nope. I couldn't care less about the wedding." Lindsay laughed. "I mean, I couldn't care less about my *own* wedding. I care deeply about yours. I want it to be perfect for you. In fact, since Eric and I can move in with each other after we make everything official, we'll have more time to plan your wedding with Zach."

"You're really serious about this, aren't you," Megan murmured. "This feels too fast."

"I know. It feels fast to me too. But I have to go back to the doctor in a couple of weeks, and I may as well be on Eric's health plan when I go. I think as long as we both go into it with realistic expectations, we should be fine."

"Don't you expect to be married to a man who loves you and cherishes you? Isn't that an expectation that's reasonable, Linds?"

"I used to think so," Lindsay said. "But not anymore. Now I just want a man who wants to take care of me. Of us." She placed her hand on her womb. "I have to start thinking about someone other than just myself. This is what's best for my baby, and it's not a bad deal for me, either. It's a great deal."

"I'll support you in whatever you want to do," Megan said. "And when you get the marriage license, I'll be your witness if you need one."

"Thank you," Lindsay said. "I appreciate it…more than you know."

Megan pushed her chair back. "But if you ever want a divorce because you're just not feeling it, I'm going to remind you that you've made your bed, and knew that going in."

"That sounds fair." *Please, God, don't let that ever happen.*

"So when's the big day?"

This was happening. For real.

"First thing next week." Lindsay tried to smile, but faltered.

"You don't have to do this," Megan said. "You can stay with us. We'll help you get a job, and find a daycare. You don't need to get married for the baby's sake. Not if you don't want to."

"I'm terrified, Meg," she admitted. "But I *do* have to. And I want to, as well. Even if I'm scared to death."

"Don't do it," Megan said suddenly. "Not if your heart's not in it."

"This is a logical decision." Lindsay picked up her empty breakfast plate. "A decision I made by using my brain and my gut, not my heart—unless you count my love for my baby. That's the heart in this."

"Just wait," Megan pleaded. "Wait until you've thought more about it. Why so fast? Why not wait a couple more weeks?"

"I'm not going to fall in love in a couple weeks, but my situation would be better if I were already married, like…two months ago. If I'm going to rush in anyway, why not rush in right now?" Lindsay laughed, but it wasn't from humor.

It was more of a don't-cry-just-laugh, laugh.

"Fools rush in," her sister reminded her.

Lindsay sighed and looked down at her still-flat belly. "We sure do."

"I want you to talk to someone about this, first. I bet she'll ease your mind about going it alone."

"Why *should* I go it alone, if I don't have to, Meg?"

"You'll see her tomorrow at church anyway, okay? Please—

don't jump into the deep end so fast."

What her sister didn't seem to get was that to Lindsay, getting married wasn't the deep end. *Not* being married was swimming in the deep end…and if she didn't do it, she might drown.

Chapter Seven

SUNDAY MORNING, THE clean spring air was brisk, belying the sunlight that filtered through the trees. Lindsay swiped her hands down on the dress Megan had lent her. It was cute, but not exactly Lindsay's style. Then again, it fit. And beggars couldn't be choosers.

It was a casual dress, which was good, considering there were quite a few people in jeans and sneakers attending church that morning as well.

"I just really love the church here." The breeze made Megan's cheeks pink from the chill in the spring air.

They walked from the gravel parking lot over a footpath worn into the grassy lawn toward the church.

"Everyone's really warm and welcoming," Megan said. "And you'll finally get to hear Zach sing! That was one of the things that made me fall in love with him."

"I can't wait." Lindsay wrapped her arms around herself for warmth.

Wearing her sister's cardigan in lieu of an old rain jacket she'd been offered was a slightly more fashionable choice, but less functional in the chilly weather. The wind zipped right through the knitting.

"You've been talking about Zach's guitar skills since you met him. I'm worried you've overhyped him."

"Impossible." Megan laughed, and took her sister's hand to pull her toward the entrance of the old timber-framed church.

They walked through the great big wooden doors, and a friendly-looking middle-aged woman greeted them with a smile.

"Good morning!" she called. "Welcome to church. Megan Moore, and is that your sister? Your twin sister? How could you not tell me there are two of you?"

Lindsay blushed. "I'll take that as a compliment, since I've got five years on her. Lindsay Moore."

"Ginger-from-the-general-store. But you can call me Ginger." She winked. "I can't believe I haven't seen you—I usually get to meet everyone first." Ginger shook Lindsay's hand, pumping it up and down with enthusiasm and genuine warmth.

"It's so nice to meet you, Ginger."

But there were people behind them trying to get through, so Lindsay followed Megan to the pews.

Apparently Zach had gotten there earlier to set up or something for the worship music, but Eric Hunt was there, looking handsomer than ever, with his brown Stetson on his knee instead of his head.

He'd combed his dark locks back for the occasion, but that was his only nod toward formality. His formfitting sky-blue T-shirt, which showcased his biceps and shoulders a little too well, would've been just as at home in a gym as it was in this low-key, understated church.

It was packed.

Was it possible that all 650-something residents of Bear Creek Saddle were in the church that morning?

No. Probably not.

Guess it wasn't that big of a church, and so it *felt* really packed.

Eric stood when they got to that row.

"Good morning, ladies." Eric smiled and nodded at her. He scooted down on the pew to make some room between himself and Jay. "I've been saving you a seat."

There were those butterflies again.

She could see his blue eyes from all the way down at the other end of the pew. Maybe because they matched his T-shirt. Had he done that on purpose? Did he know the blue of the shirt made his eyes stand out even more?

Megan prodded her. "Well? Are you guys going to like, run into each other's arms and twirl or something?"

Lindsay turned and quieted her sister with a stern glance. "Don't say a word."

Lindsay nodded at Eric with a smile, and proceeded to carefully walk past the row of legs and knees and feet. She figured it was less obnoxious to sidestep while facing them, than away from them, although that was also a little awkward.

Climbing over Chris and Jay would've been more of a challenge, but they both stood.

Chris nodded at her, acknowledging her existence in a non-combative way, which was a plus.

Jay touched her elbow lightly to guide her. "Eric told me you're okay, after all," Jay said quietly in her ear.

"I am," she responded. Thank God. "Thanks for your help with Smoky."

Finally she sat…right next to Eric Hunt—her future husband and adoptive-father-to-be of her child. The perfect spot.

Saying "her husband" in her head didn't make it feel any more real.

Was Megan right...were they being completely insane? And if so, did it matter—if it was for the greater good of her child?

"That's a pretty dress," Eric said.

She couldn't exactly take that compliment, considering she hadn't chosen it, and it wasn't hers. "Thanks. You should've seen some of the dresses I had back in New York. I didn't get too many opportunities to wear them, other than the occasional work event or cocktail party. I'm a big fan of the LBD."

"Ell-bee-dee? What's that?"

Right. There was zero reason for him to know that. "Little black dress."

"Ah. Well, I'm a big fan of the WFC."

As if he could see the confusion in her eyes, Eric laughed. "Whatever feels comfortable."

Lindsay laughed. "I'm learning to appreciate that style. My feet have been feeling great since I've started wearing sneakers everywhere. Megan doesn't have much in the way of heels to borrow...though it's not like they're exactly appropriate footwear for the ranch." She looked down at her plainly adorned feet. "I used to wear heels every day. I loved my Louboutins. They had this sassy flash of red when you kicked up your heel—"

She looked over at Eric, and while he was looking at her, she could tell he wasn't even pretending to care about designer shoes she didn't even own anymore.

"Are you going to miss having all that stuff?" he asked pointedly.

The subtext was clear: if she stayed with him on the ranch to raise her baby, she wasn't going to find herself back in expensive high heels anytime soon.

"I don't know," she said softly. "I don't think so."

None of that stuff, as much as she'd enjoyed it in New York, was worth missing out on a chance to give her child a father who'd love him and take care of him.

Shoes were nice, but not nearly as important as her having a partner in life going forward.

"It's not important," she added. "I won't bring it up again."

But now it seemed like she'd made Eric uncomfortable. He looked away, running his large fingers along the brim of his hat where it sat on his knee.

Guess he was back to silence.

Great.

On the other side of her, Megan nudged her with her elbow.

"Remind me after," she said softly in Lindsay's ear. "I want you to meet Zach's mom, Mrs. Walker. She raised Zach as a single mom. Seeing as how Zach turned out great, and she's just fine, I think it would be really good for you to talk with her."

Lindsay glared at her sister. "Please do not bring up my condition in church. And I definitely don't want to tell your fiancé's mom about it!"

Megan shook her head. "Then just meet her, and then you can call her later and talk to her privately about it. She'd probably ease a lot of your worries. Linds—you promised you would."

No, Lindsay hadn't exactly "promised" to speak to anyone about it. But…maybe it wouldn't hurt. Just to get another point of view.

Right then, the churchgoers fell quiet, as Zach got on the

platform in the front, his guitar in hand.

"Good morning, friends," he said. "Will you stand with me, and let's sing a song of praise to the Lord together."

Lindsay stood, and looked over at her sister. Megan was beaming up at Zach, pure adoration in her eyes.

Lindsay wanted to feel that way about a man. And to have a man who was worthy of that adoration as well.

Unlike Grant.

Would she adore Eric one day that way, or would marrying him mean settling for a loveless life in exchange for safety and security for her and her child?

Would that be so bad? At least she wouldn't get hurt emotionally.

Zach strummed his guitar and sang the opening verses of *How Great is Our God*. He had a microphone on a stand, and his voice led the congregation.

"He's really good." Lindsay elbowed Megan and repeated it. "Why didn't you tell me he was this good?"

Megan laughed and began singing along at the chorus. On the other side of her, Eric was singing along quietly. He could definitely carry a tune, although he didn't have the golden tongue Zach did.

But the deep baritone of his voice made her want to sing too, especially since they were singing a song she'd heard on the radio and knew the words to.

She sang along, not daring to sing quite as loudly as Megan. But the more she sang, the more she forgot that she was in a new church, surrounded by new people, watching her brother-in-law-to-be singing, or that she was standing next to a man who made her feel nervous and excited at the same time.

A man who'd seen her and her baby in a vision from above, and who trusted in it enough to propose.

God was giving her a way out of the mess she'd made of her life. Beauty from the ashes.

And so she sang louder, and praised the Lord.

* * *

Later that afternoon, Lindsay bit the bullet and called Megan's soon-to-be mother-in-law, Mrs. Walker. She seemed really nice when she met her after church, and she certainly had raised an incredible young man in Zach.

So maybe Mrs. Walker *would* have some good advice to share with her about being a single mom in the small town of Bear Creek Saddle.

Just in case either Lindsay or Eric got cold feet before they went through with it. She shut the door to Megan's bedroom and, with her phone, sat next to Zach's big goofy black Lab on the bed.

Was Inky even allowed on the bed?

After the initial pleasantries, Lindsay couldn't hold off getting to the point. "Mrs. Walker, I'm not sure if Megan told you or not, but I've actually come to Idaho in a bit of a situation. I know when you and Zach's father got married, and then he left when Zach was so young—"

This wasn't working.

"I'm so sorry, Mrs. Walker," Lindsay added. "Please don't be mad that Megan told me that. Zach told her. How you raised him so well, I mean as a single mom. And the thing is I am...well..."

"It's no secret 'round here," Mrs. Walker said with a chuckle in her voice. "You really can't keep a secret too long in this town. Especially once Ginger finds out, but don't tell her I said so. That's just between you and me."

Right.

"Good to know." Lindsay sighed. "I won't be able to keep *my* secret too much longer, but I'm kind of hoping to hold on to it for a little while…"

"Are you pregnant, Lindsay?" There was no judgment in Mrs. Walker's voice.

Just concern.

"I am. And the father is out of the picture. I never intended to raise a child on my own. To be honest, I really don't think I can do it. But I'm having the baby, so…" Lindsay ran her palm down Inky's back, and he nuzzled his snout against her arm. "Do you have any advice for me?"

"It's hard, honey," Mrs. Walker said. "I'm not gonna lie. When Zachary was first born, I 'bout near went crazy. Having a baby when you're on your own ain't easy. It gets a little better once they sleep through the night—around three months in, if you're lucky—but ultimately, *you're it*. You're the end-all be-all in that house. There's no one to turn to when you need to just take a break. You can't take a break from being a mom—especially when there's no dad."

A pit formed in Lindsay's stomach. "I had a feeling about that. How did you manage?"

"Lots of prayer, lots of prayer. Definitely helps to have some friends around. The church has a food room if you run into hard luck. We made good use of it when Zachary was little. And you know… I'd be happy to babysit for you once in a while, if you need me to."

Her chest clenched with emotion. "That's really nice of you, Mrs. Walker. Really kind."

But Lindsay couldn't depend on everyone else to help her. Like Mrs. Walker had said—she'd be the one ultimately responsible for her baby.

"I'm not sure that I'm going to be good at this," Lindsay admitted softly. "I mean—I was good at my job. I was really good at it. But I can't treat a child like they're a client, or a financial sheet. I can't… I'm not really sure what I'm going to do."

Inky licked her hand, as if to remind her to pet him. She rubbed behind his ears.

Lindsay felt comfortable talking with Mrs. Walker. She was a good listener, and had hard-won advice to offer.

"What do you mean, honey? You already said you're keeping it."

"Yeah…but I've considered that maybe it would be best if I gave my baby up for adoption, someone who would be ready for a baby. Someone who'd be amazing at being a mom, and who had a husband already. I really do want my baby to grow up in a two-parent household." Lindsay winced. "I didn't mean that as an insult, Mrs. Walker."

"None taken. To be honest, honey, I wish Zachary had grown up in a two-parent household as well. There's a lot of things a daddy helps with and provides for a child that I did *not* feel qualified to provide. We were lucky that *my* father was in the picture, so Zachary had his grandpa, and some of the men at church were wonderful influences on him."

"Really?"

"Eric Hunt's dad, for example—he'd take those boys camping, taught Zach how to play ball, all those things I would've wanted Zach's dad to do with him."

"So, like a father-figure?" That had been what she was thinking when she'd first asked Eric to be part of her baby's life, before he suggested being an official father. Just having a father-figure to be sort of a surrogate dad to her child would help, a lot.

But it wouldn't help too much at three a.m. when she was alone with the baby.

Being married to Eric—now *that* would help. He'd be the surrogate dad *and* he'd be there for her, too.

"Just remember, honey, you're not doing this alone. By the time you have this baby, everyone in church is going to notice that you're pregnant and had a baby—you can't exactly hide that—" Mrs. Walker laughed cheerily, though the thought made Lindsay shiver.

She didn't want everyone knowing.

Everyone *judging*.

"So everyone will give you a helping hand when you need it," Mrs. Walker said.

She sounded so confident. So sure.

Lindsay wished she had that same confidence.

"What do I do when I'm exhausted and it's three a.m. and the baby's screaming and I ran out of diapers and my milk isn't coming in or the baby won't latch, and I end up leaving the stove on or something and cause a fire?"

"Oh, my. You've really thought that one through, huh?"

Mrs. Walker didn't laugh, perhaps because Lindsay had just told her a version of her greatest fear—that she was not enough, that she'd make terrible mistakes that would ruin everything for her child—and Mrs. Walker knew it wasn't a joke.

All of those things could happen—they could all happen at once.

And Lindsay would be completely and utterly overwhelmed.

At least if she were married, Eric could run out to buy diapers for her while she stayed with the baby, or take over a feeding so she could sleep, or use a fire extinguisher or something.

Something.

"Well," Mrs. Walker said, "use a microwave instead of the stove, so you don't burn anything down. And other than that… I'm sure *all* of those things will happen. That's just part of parenthood. You left out the part where you're changing the diaper, and in the moment he's not covered up, your baby pees all over you!"

Now Mrs. Walker was chuckling again.

Lindsay smiled, momentarily forgetting that Mrs. Walker wasn't in the room with her, and wouldn't be able to see that she appreciated her sense of humor. She really did.

She just wasn't in a laughing mood. "I ran out of diapers, remember?"

"Oh honey. That's when you pray. Because even if you're not enough, God is."

Lindsay definitely wasn't enough.

Whatever her sister had hoped she'd get from this conversation, it had only served to bring all of Lindsay's fears about raising her baby alone, onto the surface.

Also, now she needed to buy a microwave.

Eric's proposition was looking better by the second.

God, give me a sign that marrying Eric is what You want me to do.

She'd felt that "yes" inside of her, so strongly, when Eric first proposed. But now her certainty was fading fast in the face of self-doubt. What if marrying Eric wasn't what she was supposed to do, after all?

It almost didn't seem fair that God had given Eric a sign—the vision of them, together as a family—but not her. Seriously. Two thousand years ago, God had sent an angel to tell *both* Mary and Joseph, separately, about Mary's special pregnancy.

Please tell us both, Lord. I want to know for sure, too.

If only God could give her a crystal-clear sign. Something to tell her, "*Yes, this is what I have planned for you.*"

Because if it wasn't, Lindsay didn't know how she'd be able to handle being a single mom. The thought of giving up her child to adoption, while logical, hurt her heart.

This child growing in her womb was already everything to her.

And she'd do *anything* to give him the life he deserved.

Chapter Eight

"He who finds a wife finds what is good, and receives favor from the Lord." Proverbs 18:22 (NIV)

ERIC WASN'T ALONE on the front porch outside of Megan and Zach's log cabin, but he sure wished he was. Nothing like a big, unwanted intervention to ruin a beautiful morning.

After sitting together at church, he and Lindsay had spoken for over an hour on the phone before bed.

She was still in.

So was he.

He'd been so sure she'd change her mind about marrying him, but if anything, Lindsay was more resolved now than before.

Today was supposed to be the big day—they just needed to make it legal, really.

She'd already told her sister, and while Megan felt it was too fast, Lindsay assured him her sister would support their decision.

His own talk with the guys hadn't gone over nearly as well.

Not one of his friends approved.

Now Zach, Jay and Chris had followed Eric back to Zach's

place, where Megan and Lindsay were staying, so they could all try to talk Eric out of it.

"Will you stop breathing down my neck, already?" Eric glanced over his shoulder at Zach, who was chomping at the bit to get in the door. "You can't just use your key."

"It's my house!" Zach pushed his arm past Eric to get to the door, but Eric side-stepped directly into his path.

"The girls might be sleeping," Jay said. "It's only seven o'clock, and they didn't have to be up at five for milking."

"You'll scare 'em half to death if all four of us just barge right on in," Chris added.

Zach put his hands up in surrender, his house key dangling from the keychain on his finger. "Fine. Knock again."

Inky was barking up a storm inside. If the sisters weren't awake already, they were now.

"They're not expecting us all," Eric said, gesturing at his friends. "This is going to feel like an ambush to Lindsay. It's not fair."

"You shouldn't be marrying her," Chris said for the millionth time. "You guys barely know each other."

"I want Lindsay to be my wife, and to raise her baby as our own. She said yes. Why is this so difficult for you guys?"

The door opened, and Lindsay stood in the doorway, freshly showered, with no makeup on and her hair still damp, her expression one of complete surprise.

She looked beautiful.

"Hi…everyone." Lindsay backed away from the door, as if unsure what to do. She turned her head back toward the kitchen and called to her sister. "Your fiancé's here! And…mine."

Wow! He was her fiancé. The word seemed so strange coming

from her, but it was true. Eric caught her eye, and she smiled, clearly sensing how weird the whole situation was.

She looked back at them, and opened the screen door, motioning them all inside. "Jay and Chris are here too," she added, for her sister's benefit. "So maybe put clothes on."

Eric laughed, but the firm look from Zach made him stop.

Why did they have to be such buzzkills? This was supposed to be exciting. They should want him to be happy, not desperate to stop him from doing what God had called him to do.

"We just made a pot of coffee," Lindsay offered. "Are we…all going to the courthouse together?"

"No," Chris said sharply. He pushed his dark hair out of his eyes and crossed his arms.

"Please, have a seat," Lindsay suggested to the group.

Zach took his place at the head of the dining table, and everyone seemed to know not to sit in Megan's seat, to his right.

"Come on." Eric offered Lindsay a half-smile and took her hand, leading her to the table.

They sat next to each other, with Jay across from Eric, and Chris at the other head of the table.

Lindsay leaned over and whispered in his ear, her breath soft and warm on his cheek, and still minty from toothpaste. "What's going on?"

Megan entered from the bedroom, where apparently she'd gotten dressed, if she really hadn't been dressed before. That might have just been a joke…he was still getting used to Lindsay's sense of humor.

"I already tried to talk her out of it," Megan said, looking straight at Zach.

Zach glanced around the table. "I love all of you guys. We're a family here. So let's consider this a family meeting."

Eric shook his head. "It ain't right for you to butt your nose in where it don't belong. No offense. I love you, man. But this is between me, Lindsay, and God."

"I don't care if you think it should be that way," Zach argued. "It's not. Because when things go south, we're going to be the ones to pick up the pieces."

When. Not "if." Nice way to show support, huh?

"Megan," Lindsay said, "are you really okay with this being a so-called family discussion? It's our own decision."

Megan shrugged. "I see what Zach is saying. I mean, if you change your mind, you'll end up living with us or in the practice cabin out back."

"I'm not going to change my mind," Lindsay said. "I don't see what about our situation is so confusing to you guys."

Eric took her hand under the table. It wasn't fair for Lindsay to have this sprung on her. She probably already felt left out and like an outsider. Now, no one in her new so-called "family" at Bear Creek Saddle Ranch wanted her to marry into it.

"This isn't cool, guys," Eric said. "I've had enough of this. What do you think you can say to change our minds?"

Chris eyed Lindsay coolly. "She slept with another man and wants you to raise *his* child."

Ouch.

Eric took a deep breath, and sighed. "Okay, I thought about it. Not gonna change my mind."

"The biological father isn't in the picture," Lindsay added. "And with Eric being there for our child from the beginning, from even before birth, it's no different than if we'd already been married and I'd had to use a sperm donor to get pregnant. We'd be in this position no matter what, having a child together."

"No offense, Lindsay," Jay added, "as much as I've heard about you from Megan, I never took you for a small-town country girl. Will you even be happy here?"

Lindsay's face froze.

Oh man…oh man—did Jay just put a crack in Lindsay's resolve? Wasn't he supposed to be the nice one? If anyone was going to do it, Eric would've bet on Chris, who was blunter than blunt.

"I suppose I never intended to be a small-town girl," Lindsay admitted slowly. "But it's beautiful here. And it would be a lovely, safe place to raise our baby. It's just…different from what I'm used to."

"He's not particularly fancy," Zach pointed out, gesturing to Eric.

"She has eyes, Zach." Still, Eric straightened in his chair.

There wasn't going to be much in the way of a makeover. The fanciest Eric ever got was when he put on his non-muddy boots and non-muddy cowboy hat. That was about it.

"I like him the way he is," Lindsay said. "And he never knew me when I was wearing my designer clothes, or had my nice apartment on the Upper West Side. Eric only knows me as broke and wearing hand-me-downs, and he wants me anyway. That's saying something."

Megan broke in. "Let's look at this the other way around. Linds—you're marrying Eric because you want someone who will be a good father and provider, and you enjoy his companionship, correct?"

"Correct." Lindsay looked at Eric, her eyes wide. "I hope that's okay by you."

"Of course," Eric said, grinning. "That's what I want to be for you."

"And Eric," Megan continued, "you want to marry Lindsay because she's pretty, nice, and smart, and is willing to be your wife and raise her child with you as the father, since you can't have your own, correct?"

No one blinked. Everyone at this small table knew about his condition by now, so it wasn't a surprise.

"Correct," Eric said. "And I enjoy her company, as well."

"Great." Megan stood from the table and paced a bit. "Now I want—just for a thought exercise—to flip it on you. There is a possibility, at some point in the future, God forbid, that something could happen to change why you are getting married. What if she miscarried—"

"God forbid," Lindsay exclaimed.

"Or what if, at some point down the road, something happened where you didn't have a child anymore? I mean…even just when that child grows up and goes off to college. But what if, God forbid, you lost your child too soon. Would you still be okay being with each other, if not for that baby's sake?"

The thoughts Megan had just put in his mind made Eric sick to his stomach. He didn't want to think about his beautiful baby being anything other than healthy, happy, and at his side.

"And Lindsay," Megan said, pointing toward her sister. "What if the ranch went bankrupt, and there was no money left at all? What if Eric could no longer provide for you and the baby the way you were expecting him to? Would you still want to be married to him?"

Lindsay stood, facing her sister. "Yes. Because I have faith in him. Even if he lost everything tomorrow, I know he would do everything in his power to take care of us. God forbid, if he were disabled or something, I could get a job and take care of him. We'd make it work."

"That's right," Eric said, pushing back his chair. "And if something were to happen to this child, we'd need each other to lean on. Maybe we'd try for another at some point. People use sperm donors and such for medical issues all the time these days. We could have more than one kid, even, if she wanted to."

"That's right!" Lindsay turned to Eric and wrapped her arms around his neck.

The room around them ceased to distract him. His friends' voices became like a tinny radio playing at the bottom of a well, for all he could hear them.

He whispered in Lindsay's ear. "I still want to marry you, today, if you do."

She nodded her head toward the bedroom door, and put her finger to her lips, slipping past him.

Lindsay walked back to him a few moments later, looking more polished, her purse over her shoulder. She smiled at him, flashing her beautifully white teeth. "All set."

With that, and without even a glance behind her at the crowded kitchen table, she took his hand, and they walked out of the house.

He opened his truck door for her. "You ready for this? Courthouse?"

"Before they try to stop us again." She grinned. "I'm liking you more and more every day, Mr. Eric Hunt."

* * *

Lindsay couldn't believe she was actually doing this. Marrying a man she'd only known for one short, intense week.

Am I insane? Should she stop this train now, so she could get off with her dignity before it crashed?

A small voice within her whispered resolutely: *Keep going.*

All right. She'd keep going.

Eric looked up the number to the courthouse and called. "What do we have to do to get married today?"

He nodded, repeating everything the person on the other end said out loud so she could hear.

"We have to go to the county recorder's office first to get the license," he repeated. "Coeur d'Alene? Okay. That's not too far."

Lindsay clenched her hands in her lap. This was getting real. Very real.

"Social security cards. Okay. Driver's license, state-issued ID or birth certificate, okay. Rings."

Her eyes widened. *Rings!* What would they do for wedding rings?

"Get the license first," he was repeating, "then have the judge do the ceremony. Okay."

He turned to her briefly, going against his own rule of never taking his eyes off the road, but then he was back to staring out the window carefully. "Linds—we need an appointment with the judge."

He'd called her by her sister's nickname for her. It worked—and it sounded just right coming from him. "Can you make one now?" she asked.

Eric chuckled. "The lady heard you ask in the background. Yes—the judge has time today, if we're willing to wait."

Lindsay's heart raced with excitement, and maybe just a touch of anxiety. "That's great!"

"The Kootenai County Magistrate Judge is in the courthouse on the same street as the county recorder." He spoke into the phone again as he drove. "That's right, we've never been married before."

The woman's voice on the other end of the line kept talking rapidly, and Eric answered and asked questions as fast as she could keep up.

"We're not related, no." He winked at Lindsay, and she giggled.

"Hey, do we need witnesses?" she asked.

"Not in Idaho," the woman's voice came through the phone, but Eric answered for Lindsay's benefit.

"Nope. We're good."

The ride to the county recorder went by faster than it should have. As the scenery flew by her window, the soaring mountain peaks covered in evergreen trees and topped with snow, the fields of cows and sheep grazing, even small homes with small acreage and a horse or two in the backyard, she took it all in.

This would be her home now. Not Manhattan.

Was she really ready to make such a big change?

She had to. For her Little One.

Sure, tons of babies were born in New York City every day. They had great lives, many of them, at least. She'd seen stay-at-home moms and nannies take little toddlers to the playground, rolling over the cracked sidewalks in their strollers, passing the traffic and the fumes and the throngs of people. The kids seemed happy enough. Yes, there was a bit of a rat problem near the garbage cans, but the city was doing its best.

But in New York City, she couldn't just let her kid go outside to play, and have faith he wouldn't get kidnapped or harmed. Here in Bear Creek Saddle, Idaho, she could raise her baby with an old-fashioned way of parenting. Teach him to be independent and to enjoy the outdoors. To not fear every stranger—because in a small town, there were no strangers.

Even herself—she wasn't a stranger when she'd arrived, because she was Megan's sister. The small mountain town wasn't the sort of place anyone arrived in accidentally. There were no tourist attractions to draw new people.

Bear Creek Saddle was the best well-kept secret in north Idaho. Not only was she not a stranger when she'd shown up, she even got a free ride from the airport. That didn't happen in most places.

"This is the right thing," she said, breaking the silence in the truck as they pulled up to the county recorder. "Right?"

"Right." Eric turned to her and smiled. "I've always wanted to get married to a girl like you. I feel like I'm getting more than I deserve here."

Lindsay laughed, his words bringing exuberant butterflies to her stomach. "I feel the same way! You're offering me so much, and I just want to be worthy of that. I'm going to try to be the best wife and mom I can be."

"And I'll try to be the best husband and father I can be." He nodded. "If I ever get it wrong, then this is how we fix it. Communication."

"And prayer," she added. "Can we pray before we go in to get the license?

Eric turned the truck's ignition off and unbuckled his seatbelt.

He was so handsome, so kind. She'd never meet anyone better, so it really didn't feel like settling, even if she was technically settling for a marriage of convenience.

It was a smart match, and it felt right in her gut.

Her soon-to-be-husband—

(oh wow, that sounded so good)

—took her hands in his and bowed his head. "Father, thank You for putting Lindsay into my life. Thank You for everything that led us to here, right now, because we don't always know Your plans, and don't understand why things go the way they do in our lives."

True. So true.

"But with my condition, and her condition, and the bond that we feel, the friendship we've formed in such a short time, thank You. Thank You for the vision You gave me before she came to the ranch, so I would know what to do."

Lindsay smiled. She believed now, as much as Eric appeared to, that his vision really came from God. It definitely could have been…she'd heard of much more unbelievable miracles that had happened by God's grace.

"Please be with us today, Lord, and bless this marriage. Let us always do Your will and not our own, so we don't mess up this amazing chance at a normal, happy family that you've given us."

"Yes, Lord," she added. *Yes to all of it.*

"We love You and pray in Jesus' name…amen." Eric kept his hands on hers and lifted his head, gazing into her eyes. "Man, I'm a lucky guy."

"Same," she said. "And amen and amen." That man knew how to pray. From the heart and from a humble place. It was wonderful to be with him in the moment.

Eric looked over at the entrance to the county recorder's office.

"Oh, hang on," he said with a groan. "Let me put my gun away."

He reached around to his right flank and slowly pulled out what looked to her like a cop's gun, keeping the muzzle pointed down and away from her and himself.

What. On. Earth.

"Oh my goodness," she gasped. "Megan told me you guys all have guns—I thought she was just trying to scare me!"

Eric reached over her and put the gun into his glove box, right in front of her, and used a small key on his keychain to lock it.

She froze, pulling her body as far back against her seat as she could. What if that thing went off accidentally? At least the gun wasn't ever pointed at her, but still.

Eric must've seen her expression, because he raised his eyebrows. "Only thing that scares me, is not being allowed to bring protection into these places."

"Why would you need a gun on you all the time, anyway?"

He shook his head. "Same reason you always wear a seatbelt. You don't intend to need it—you'll always drive safe as you can, but it's good to keep it strapped on, just in case someone rams into you."

"You don't need it around me," she argued. "Guns aren't allowed in Manhattan. I'm not used to it and I don't want to get shot."

"Then don't purposefully shoot yourself," he said, a bit sharply. "That's where most of the gun deaths come from, especially the ones that happen in the home. Gun won't go off unless you pull the trigger, and it won't shoot you unless the muzzle is facing you."

"I don't like it," she said again.

Was this going to be a deal-breaker?

Maybe.

But for her, or for him?

Eric paused. Maybe he was thinking the same thing.

"This is Idaho," he said simply. "Even if you don't want me carrying a gun, everywhere you go, *someone* will be carrying one. Guaranteed."

Really?

She glanced out the window. There were a lot more people down here in Coeur d'Alene than up in Bear Creek Saddle.

"Notice how polite everyone is?" Eric asked. "That might be why."

This was a lifetime of her only seeing guns on cops and in the movies, versus someone who grew up with them and considered wearing one to be as normal as bringing his wallet with him.

"Never had to use it other than for target practice," he added, "an' I pray to God I never do. But you telling me to not carry, is like me telling you to not put on a seatbelt. This is part of who I am. I protect people. Think of me as your personal armed bodyguard."

"That's one way to look at it," she said slowly. "I guess all the important people, the politicians and celebrities wearing million-dollar diamonds, get armed guards."

"And now you have one, too." Eric grinned.

"But…it's so safe here. I don't need that level of protection."

Eric gestured out the window. "Look at all the people walking around. It's not that we don't have criminals out here. It's just, most criminals wouldn't risk messing with any one of these folks."

"Why not?" she asked. "I think I've seen only one cop car since we got into town. How is carrying a gun under your shirt where no one can see it going to stop a carjacker, or mugger or rapist or something?"

It still didn't make sense to her. Smart people knew not to mess with a cop because they could see the gun on their hip. If everyone was hiding them, how would it help?

"'Cause the bad guys know half these good folks are armed—*but they don't know which ones.* Could be that little ol' lady. Could be that man in a business suit, eating his lunch. You don't even need a license to conceal-carry a gun in Idaho anymore. People just do it, and criminals know and don't want to risk getting shot at."

Okay. That was a good point. As strange as the concept was, the way he put it seemed to make sense.

Could she learn to live in a house with a gun?

Lindsay frowned. "I don't want our kid near that thing."

He looked at her with a surprised, happy expression. "You said 'our kid.' I love that. Thank you."

Lindsay smiled. "Yes. He'll be ours, not just mine. That's why I want to do this in the first place. Don't forget the rest of that statement, though."

"I'll get a safe and keep it locked up when it's not on me. Top priority."

"Fine," she said finally. "If Megan got over it, I guess I will too. Just don't expect me to ever feel comfortable around them."

He clapped his hands together, like the bang of a gavel. Done.

"This is how we do it, Linds. Communication. We're off to a good start, I think."

"You're right." They weren't getting into fights and screaming at each other or calling each other names, as she'd seen other couples do. Eric always seemed to keep his head on straight and tried to work things out. "That's a good sign."

She looked up at him, and the look on his face…for a moment it looked like he was going to kiss her, maybe even just a peck on the cheek? But then he stopped himself.

"Let's get this license thing out of the way," he said, "so we can get in line at the courthouse."

Out of the way, right.

"We're good, right?" he asked.

"We're good."

Everything was just barreling along.

Fast.

Lindsay's chest tightened, her insides quivered.

Lord, give me one more sign that this is Your will and not simply my own desperate wish to be married for this pregnancy.

Just one more sign.

* * *

Eric glanced over at the piece of paper in Lindsay's hand as they exited the county recorder's office. It was a marriage license which would allow them to get married, but it didn't mean they were married yet. They still had to get the judge down the street—which was appropriately named "Government Way"—to sign it.

His bride-to-be looked amazing, her cheeks flushed with color, her dark brown hair caressing her face.

The ring.

Eric still needed to get her a ring—but how? When? They had to sign in for the judge to see them. Maybe he could make a quick run for rings while she waited there, after they both signed in.

Talk about waiting till the last minute.

Could he pick out the perfect ring for her in five minutes flat?

It's in Your hands, at this point, Lord. Just show me what to do.

They got back in his truck.

* * *

Lindsay's thoughts were all over the place as Eric brought the truck to a stop in a parking spot in the small, paved lot in front of the courthouse.

"You aren't ready to be intimate, I know," Eric said, suddenly. "But I was thinking…"

Please don't try to convince me to have sex.

Where was her sign from God that this was the right thing to do?

"What were you thinking?" Her trepidation filtered into the question.

"We're gonna go inside and kiss in front of the judge—'you may now kiss the bride.'"

Oh, wow. She hadn't even thought about that part of the ceremony. She hadn't thought about the ceremony at all, really…she was so focused on what would happen after it, when they were living together as man and wife.

"So I figure maybe we should do that for the first time when it's just you and me." Eric glanced at her, as if to check in on how she was receiving his suggestion. "Alone."

Lindsay laughed nervously. As a healthy human woman with working eyes, she was attracted to Eric. The man dripped testosterone and cowboy-yumminess.

Yes—she *wanted* to kiss him.

But she couldn't afford to let physical lust interfere with their ability to form a real relationship. One based on everything a marriage should be based on, including complete trust.

And as much as she didn't want to get emotionally entangled with him…after talking to Megan about it, the idea of being physically intimate without him loving her first, bothered her.

If he didn't love her, she couldn't trust him not to leave. But if she loved him first, she'd be the one ending up heartbroken.

Then again, it wasn't like they had to be in love just to kiss.

She licked her lips.

Wiped her hands on the skirt she'd borrowed from Megan.

"Right now?"

"Yeah, right now." He paused. "I don't want to make you do something you don't want to do, Linds. If you're not up for it, we don't even have to kiss during the ceremony."

Not kissing at all? That didn't seem right for a marriage ceremony.

"Okay, I guess." Lindsay took a calming breath. "Just so we don't bang noses or something when we get in there."

Eric took his hat off and set it on his knee. He reached over to her, and he was suddenly close, very close.

"You haven't even unbuckled yourself yet," he said softly.

With a slow, steady movement, he wrapped his arm around her shoulder, and dropped it behind her, his hand brushing against her hip and the top of her thigh as he unclicked her seatbelt.

"Thank you," she whispered.

Eric paused, and in that pause, she took everything in. His face. The ever-present stubble on his olive skin. His blue eyes, gorgeous against his skin and dark hair.

His lips, full and smooth.

He took her face in his hand, cupping her cheek. His hard, calloused hand was unexpectedly gentle…and softly, slowly, Eric kissed her lips.

Yes, this.

This was perfection.

Eric's mouth on hers was everything she'd ever imagined it would be. The kiss could have gone on forever, but it ended much too soon.

It was Eric who pulled away, leaving her breathless, wanting more.

"How'd that work for you?" He grinned. "'Cause it worked good for me."

Her legs were jelly, her stomach fluttery with nerves. Ha—he knew the effect he'd had on her.

"That was fine." So nonchalant, to match his own calm and cool demeanor. Even if she was anything but calm and cool on the inside, after that kiss. "How's my lipstick?"

"Might be a bit smudged." He grinned again. "Sorry 'bout that."

She reapplied and rubbed her lips together. It was *definitely* worth messing up her makeup, but he seemed a bit too sure of himself for her to tell him that.

Seemed as if her lips would be the only thing about her that was formal for the occasion. There would be no wedding dress, no bouquet. He'd changed out of the muddy boots he'd been milking the cows in, which was a nice gesture, at least.

But this was all just to make it official, getting married, so they could be a proper couple…so what did having a big wedding day matter?

"I never thought I'd get married like this," she admitted. "I imagined a white gown. And guests."

"That marriage license is good for a year." Eric took her hand in his. "We don't have to do this—I want you to be happy."

"I'll start showing soon." The thought of going to church with a big belly and no wedding ring was almost reason enough to jump in with both feet. But ultimately, Eric was a good man with good Christian values, and he wanted to protect and take care of her and her baby. She couldn't afford to change her mind because of some last-minute jitters. "I just want to do it. Let's do it."

As if he could see the fear in her eyes, Eric gave her a soft, encouraging smile. "You don't have to be afraid, Lindsay. I'm going to do everything in my power to be a good husband and father. I won't let you down."

His words had a calming effect. It was clear he wanted this to work as much as she did.

"I promise you this," Eric added. "When you finally fall in love with me, we can renew our vows and have it be a proper wedding."

When they fell in love. Not "if." She wished she had the confidence Eric had. It had to be the vision from God that gave Eric that confidence.

"That would be perfect…thank you, for saying that."

She put her hand on the door to get out, and Eric came around to help her get down. She needed all the helping hands she could get right now, and especially after her—their—baby was born.

Thank God for Eric, and for the vision that led to his proposal.

One more sign, Lord.

I need one too.

Please.

Chapter Nine

INSIDE THE COURTROOM, they waited in a hallway lined with folding chairs, paperwork in hand. Lindsay's phone was going crazy with texts, as was Eric's.

"Let's turn them off," he suggested. "I don't think we need to listen to all of their arguments again."

"Good idea…once was definitely enough." Or in the case of her sister, a hundred times. "Megan's waffling back and forth between saying I should go for it, to saying it's crazy." Lindsay turned her phone off—the second time she'd done so since arriving in Idaho. "She's certainly making *me* crazy, but that's all she's accomplishing."

"We still have a bit of a wait." Eric glanced up at the big clock on the wall. "I need to run out and get us the rings. You stay here an' hold our spot. I'll be back, quick as I can."

Lindsay's expression must have shown her concern, even though she didn't say a word, because he put his hand on hers.

"Don't worry. I looked up a place on my phone—there's a silver jewelry store a couple miles from here. I won't be able to get you gold or diamonds there…just something simple to cover our bases for now."

"That's totally fine," she said. "You don't have to get me

anything expensive."

Eric smiled and squeezed her hand. "I'll try to find something nice. And if you hate it, we can throw it in the garbage bin on the way out and go buy you one you love. Sound good?"

Lindsay laughed, and covered her mouth since it sounded so loud in the quiet hall. "Just get back here as fast as you can."

Eric left, leaving her sitting alone between two empty chairs. The elderly lady to her right was knitting something out of gray and yellow yarn.

Was that a sign? Knitting a life together?

No. It's just yarn.

Lindsay sighed.

The minutes ticked by on the big clock, each moment bringing her closer to becoming Eric's wife.

A short, middle-aged woman with dark blonde hair and a skirt-suit opened the door to the waiting area. "Eric Hunt and Lindsay Moore? It's your turn with the judge."

Already?

Lindsay looked back toward the entrance, adrenaline flooding her veins. He wasn't back yet.

"I'm sorry, my fiancé stepped out for a moment—"

"Uh-oh," the woman said, and clucked her tongue. "Quick, go get him!"

Lindsay ran down the hall and out the front door.

What was she doing? He hadn't just stepped outside, he'd gone ring shopping. She fumbled with her phone, powering it back on.

It was taking forever to reboot. No wonder she never turned her phone off in the first place.

Even if she could call him right then and there, and he

immediately left the jewelry store, he wouldn't be back in time.

Wait. Eric didn't even have his phone turned on.

They were going to lose their spot.

Her stomach dropped.

What if *this* was the sign?

Just not the sign she wanted.

A sign that maybe…they weren't supposed to get married?

"I'm back!" Eric hollered from across the parking lot. He'd spotted her before she'd seen him pull up.

"Quick!" Near-frantic, she waved him inside. "They're waiting on us."

"Just in time, then." He exhaled heavily.

They didn't have vows written, they didn't have flowers. They didn't have—

"We have rings now, right?"

"We do," Eric assured her. "I didn't know your ring size, so I guessed."

Oh, no. Why hadn't she thought to tell him before he ran out? "Don't worry about it, it's fine."

Please, God, let the ring be too big rather than too small, so it doesn't get stuck.

Unless the ring getting stuck was supposed to be her sign?

Lord, help a girl out!

Eric took hold of Lindsay's hand and they rushed forward toward the woman at the chamber doors.

"We're here," he said. "Sorry 'bout that."

"Late to your own marriage ceremony." The woman clucked her tongue again, as if to scold him.

"Real sorry," Eric said, taking his hat off and holding it in front of him. "We're ready."

The woman smiled—she was probably caught off-guard by his good looks and puppy-dog eyes. It was enough to warm up any woman who might have been considering a harsher response.

"So sorry." Lindsay smiled the sweetest smile she knew how to put on.

"You'd be surprised…" the woman said, shuffling her feet forward as they followed behind her into the small courtroom. "I seen it all before, workin' here."

The judge was an elderly man in his seventies, with wisps of silver hair encircling his bald head like a crown.

"So. We're doing a wedding ceremony today, are we? That's good, that's good. My favorite thing to do here, to be honest. Always makes my day. Been married over fifty years, myself."

"Congratulations, Your Honor." Lindsay looked for his name on the placard in front of him. It said JAMES FITZGERALD in all caps, gold on black.

"Lindsay, is it?" he asked, glancing down at their marriage license with a chuckle. "I'm supposed to be congratulating *you*, not the other way around."

"Thank you," she said, accidentally in unison with Eric.

"No witnesses, though?" Judge Fitzgerald asked, peering behind them at the empty room. "Are you eloping?"

"I thought we didn't need witnesses," Lindsay said. "I don't know if—"

"Just us today, sir," Eric said quickly. "I mean, Your Honor."

"Very well, very well. Well, this is exciting. We'll have Lucy take a photo of you two afterward if you want. Shall we begin?"

Lindsay glanced at Eric. He had a huge smile on his face.

Lord, not one more sign for me?

No?

The judge cleared his throat, looking at each of them in turn. "We are gathered here to join you, Lindsay Moore, and you, Eric Hunt, in the union of marriage."

This was happening. Right now, sign from God or not.

"It's a contract," he continued. "A legal contract, but it's also a spiritual one. This contract is not to be entered into lightly—but thoughtfully and seriously...and with a deep realization of its obligations and responsibilities."

Lindsay's stomach fluttered again. Nerves. Or...was it possible she was feeling the baby fluttering around, already? She glanced over at Eric and caught his eye.

He smiled reassuringly, and nodded.

"Please remember," the judge was saying, "that love, loyalty, and understanding are the foundations of a happy and enduring home. You have to be kind to each other."

Kind. She could do that. Eric deserved that, and so much more.

"Here we go," the judge said. "Ready?"

Here goes nothing.

"Do you, Eric Hunt, take this woman, Lindsay Moore, to be your lawfully wedded wife, to have and to hold, in sickness and in health, in good times and bad, for richer or poorer, keeping yourself unto her for as long as you both shall live?"

"I do." Eric swallowed hard.

This must be just as crazy for him as it was for her. But at least he'd had that vision to hold on to. Perhaps this was a test. What if God wanted her to hold on to Eric's vision? To trust in it, even though she hadn't gotten a sign like that herself?

"Do you, Lindsay Moore, take this man, Eric Hunt, to be your lawfully wedded husband—to have and to hold, in sickness and in health, in good times and bad, for richer or poorer, keeping yourself unto him for as long as you both shall live?"

"I do," she said.

Oh, wow.

"Do you have rings to exchange?"

Eric nodded and pulled a thin, folded paper bag out of his back pocket. "Got them right here, hang on." He turned the bag over, and two thin, silver bands spilled into his waiting palm. "Here," he said to her, "you can hold on to mine."

She reached over and gingerly picked up the bigger ring, and of course her jittery nerves had her hand shaking like a leaf in the wind. The other ring fell to the floor with a clatter.

"I'm so sorry!" she gasped.

"It's okay," Eric said, and they both dropped to their knees at the same time to retrieve it.

Eric was looking where the sound of the ring falling had emanated from, but in the periphery of her vision, Lindsay had seen it roll under the straight-backed blue chairs behind them.

Dear God, is THIS the sign? Are you trying to tell me something with this?!

And then, a glint of light off something in the corner. "I see it!" she exclaimed. "I'll get it."

Lindsay stepped over the chair and picked up the ring, which now had some dust on it from the floor.

She held it to her face and blew on it to get the stuff off.

Oh.

My.

Goodness.

This was her sign.

This was her sign that could only be from God, because who else would be able to align everything so perfectly?

"Are you okay?" Eric asked, worry edging into his voice. "Is your ring all right?"

"More than all right," she breathed. "It's perfect, Eric."

Tears gathered in her eyes, and she blinked rapidly, tilting her chin back to keep them from falling down her cheeks.

"Gave you a scare, did it?" the judge asked, looking concerned.

"No," she said, shaking her head. "No. It's just—my father bought my mother a ring in Israel on their honeymoon that had Hebrew engraved on the inside. It's this, what's written inside this ring, but the ring you got me is the English version."

The judge raised his bushy white eyebrows in surprise. "What's it say in there? May I ask?"

Eric answered for her. "It's from the Song of Solomon—*I am my beloved's, and my beloved is mine.*'"

"Exactly." Lindsay wiped her eyes carefully. "That's it." She laughed, and looked heavenward. "Thank You, God, for that. That's a good one."

"Amen," Eric said, grinning. "Wow, now I'm really glad that ring spoke to me. I was worried you'd think it was cheesy, since—"

She knew what he was going to say. Since they weren't exactly "beloveds" just yet. Lindsay shook her head.

No need to tell the judge that. They had their reasons to get married, and it was between them and God.

Thank You.

"All righty," the judge said. "Now that's sorted, shall we continue? I don't think we have time to start over."

"Please," Eric said, "continue. Sorry 'bout that."

"You're first, Eric. Repeat after me: 'I, Eric Hunt…'"

Eric held the ring between his thumb and index finger carefully, poised above her raised left hand. "I, Eric Hunt…"

"Do take thee, Lindsay Moore, to be my wife," the judge continued.

"Do take thee, Lindsay Moore, to be my wife…"

Was Eric's hand trembling, now, as well? Or was she just trembling all over, making the whole world move?

Eric continued repeating the judge, bit by bit.

"To have and to hold…in sickness and in health…for richer or for poorer…till death do us part."

"Put the ring on her, Eric," the judge said, "and say…"

"With this ring I, thee wed." Eric slipped the ring, engraved with the same verse as the ring her father had given her mother in Israel, onto her left ring finger.

It fit perfectly. Somehow, he'd gotten the exact right ring size.

Thank You. Thank You for showing me Your hand in this, after all.

Lindsay then repeated the same script back, and put the larger silver ring onto Eric's hand. "With this ring, I thee wed."

They stared at each other, their hands touching, her heart beating so loudly within her eardrums that surely he could hear.

"By the authority vested in me by the State of Idaho," Judge Fitzgerald said, "I now pronounce you husband and wife. Eric, you may kiss the bride."

Husband. Bride.

It was real. They were married now.

Eric cupped her face, just as he had done in the car, and she rested her cheek against his strong hand. He leaned in and kissed her gently, and when she smiled, he kissed her again.

"Well then." The judge sat back in his chair with a smile, folding his hands across his ample belly. "It was my honor to officiate your wedding, Mr. and Mrs. Hunt. I wish you all the best, and a long, healthy and happy marriage."

"Thanks so much, Your Honor," Eric said. "Means a lot."

"Do you have any advice for us?" Lindsay asked.

"The couple that prays together, stays together," the judge said. "And as long as you remember how much you love each other, you'll be able to weather any storm."

She glanced at Eric, and he met her eyes. To the judge, they probably looked like they were thinking about how strong their love was, gazing at each other with romantic affection.

But this marriage wasn't based on romantic love, and both she and her new husband knew it. Would they still be able to weather the storm of raising a child together?

Chapter Ten

"Therefore what God has joined together, let no one separate." *Mark 10:9 (NIV)*

ERIC COULDN'T BELIEVE it. They were married now, for real. He had a wife. A pregnant wife!

As they drove up the drive to the front of his cabin, Eric's pulse raced. This was a huge deal. A big responsibility now. God had given him a family of his own.

As much as his recent diagnosis of infertility had rocked his identity as a man, this newfound responsibility bestowed upon him felt like the cure.

Because now, he wasn't just a man, he had two new titles: husband and father.

Please help me not mess this up.

Lindsay was reaching for the door handle already, as usual, but Eric jumped out and went around to offer her a hand down from the truck. Maybe they'd need to look into getting a smaller vehicle, one she'd feel comfortable getting into and out of when she was later in the pregnancy, and one that would comfortably fit a car seat for their child.

Their child.

Thank You, God. Thank You for this chance.

They walked in silence to his door—*their* door—and after he unlocked it, with Boomer barking like crazy inside, he looked down at her small frame and grinned.

"I want to carry my bride over the threshold."

Lindsay shuffled her feet, and nodded hesitantly.

"Is this weird?" she asked. "I mean, you don't have to. It's not like we're really—"

Eric picked her up off her feet, bringing her face to his level, the movement cutting off her words before she could finish that awful thought.

That they weren't married for real.

"We are," he said. There was no uncertainty for him about that. "We made a promise in front of a judge and God, and a promise to each other. It's real. You're my wife."

It was as if she weighed nothing at all in his arms. But having her so close to him, the lavender scent of her shampoo, the warmth of her body in his arms, made him lose his thoughts.

Lindsay wrapped her arms around his neck, but he couldn't be sure if it was a tender gesture of affection, or to help her feel more secure in his arms.

Eric carried her over the threshold.

"Welcome home, Mrs. Hunt."

A small smile crept upon her face, which was a huge improvement to the uncertainty he saw just moments before.

"Thank you." Still held in his arms, Lindsay looked at him, her grip around his neck firm. "You're…my husband."

It was an incredible statement. Yes, he was her husband.

He nodded solemnly.

"I don't particularly want to set you down," he said. "Having you in my arms feels pretty good."

Was there any chance at all that she'd be willing to let him carry her into the bedroom?

"I think…" Lindsay said softly, "I think you should probably put me down."

It was if she could hear his thoughts—and wanted to stop them before he got started.

He set her down in the front hallway. Even though it pained him to let her go.

"I'm already falling for you," he admitted. "How 'bout you? Do you think it was getting married that did it?"

Lindsay's smooth cheeks pinked. "Maybe that's a man thing. Having official paperwork that says we're married makes you even more bonded to me, maybe? Or was it standing up before the judge and God, like you said?"

"Perhaps." Was it different for her?

"Women tend to bond to men they sleep with," she said, as if she wasn't talking about herself, but a distant relative. "I read that once. Not all women, of course, but in general, when a woman and a man have a one-night stand, the woman ends up hurt because she'll start bonding, and he won't."

"This ain't no one-night stand," he reminded her. "I'm not going anywhere. You won't have to worry about that ever again."

At those words, she smiled, and walked over to the kitchen sink. She washed her hands and dried them on a dishtowel he kept on the counter, but she put it away by folding it over the handle on the oven, instead of just throwing it back on the counter like he would've done.

"I appreciate that," she said. "But I think what I'm saying is…if we sleep together, I'm going to have a hormonal bonding to you that isn't real, the same way you're bonding to me simply because you made a commitment in front of others."

"What are you saying? That this ain't real?"

"I don't know." Lindsay pursed her lips, taking a moment before speaking again. "I want to bond with you the right way, to create a healthy foundation for our marriage."

"Okay," he said. "I get it. It's all fake, and no marital relations."

She rolled her eyes.

"Don't make that face." Eric didn't like where this was going. "It's rude."

Lindsay didn't respond. She walked back over to the kitchen table and sat, her elbows up on the tabletop, staring at the wedding ring he'd given her.

"Communication, right?" she said, still staring at her hand. "I apologize. I probably made a face because I felt as if *you* were rude by summarizing something I'd just said that was important—like, really important—you boiled all that down to 'it's all fake, so no sex.'"

Huh. Wasn't that what she was getting at, though?

Should he even bother trying to get his wife to sleep with him? Or would that just tick her off, or make her feel uncomfortable?

"Do me a favor," Eric said. "Tell me if you have something against sex in general, even if it's with your husband."

"You'd rather I have something against sex, than have it be I want to grow our relationship first?" she asked, raising one eyebrow.

"I don't think so, no. Just had to check. I know your experience with Grant wasn't so good."

"It was not ideal, no," she said. Her expression grew distant, her lips a straight, thin line. "I don't ever want to feel like...like I owe a man my body. So please, even though I'm your wife now, don't use that as a bargaining chip or something."

"All right."

This was going to be tough. It sounded like he shouldn't ever expect Lindsay to want to sleep with him.

And after the baby was born—from what he'd surmised—most couples took some time off anyway, because of physical issues for the mom, and being too sleep-deprived to be intimate.

It was beginning to feel like he'd just signed up to be celibate for the rest of his life.

God, soften her heart toward me, and remove my temptation whenever I look at her. Make me see her as You do, instead.

That would be great.

"I'll wait till you're ready," he said finally. "And if you're never ready...well, I knew this was going to be a marriage of convenience. I made my bed, now I got to sleep in it, I guess."

Alone, apparently.

Lindsay rested her forehead in her hand. "Don't be dramatic. If I never feel secure and loved enough to want to sleep with you, that's not on me."

"Then let me try. Let me do something romantic for you."

She popped her head up, her hair disheveled from her hands. Looking around his small log home, she shrugged. "I don't even know what I would consider romantic. I never had a chance to find that out about myself."

He didn't know what was romantic, either. Probably not waking up early to milk Daisy, or falling off a horse.

"Can I try the normal stuff, like taking you out to dinner, flowers, dancing, writing you poems and stuff?"

Would that even work, as closely guarded as she was?

Could he even pull off trying to do that stuff? It had never really come up before. Yeah, in high school he'd made a girl a mix-tape, and she'd been pretty excited about it, but she didn't fall in love with him over of it.

What could he do to fast-forward to the part of the marriage where they were in love?

"Do you write poetry?" Lindsay asked, a look of interest flashing through her eyes. "I never would have guessed that about you."

Oh man.

"Sorry, no...I don't write poetry or nothing like that. I just know sometimes guys do that in the movies and girls like it."

She laughed. "Oh, well. I think it's less that girls like poetry, and more that we like the idea of a man thinking about us, and creating something just for us, and pouring his heart into it. That's what would interest me, anyway."

"I'll have to get to work on that, then." Could she tell he was internally grimacing?

"So..." She looked around again, her gaze landing on him once more. "Now what?"

"We should probably eat something. I'm starving." He strode to the stovetop and turned it on, since the pan from that morning was still sitting there. "Want eggs?"

"That would be great, thank you," she said. "I should probably make them, right? Didn't you say that it would help you if I could take care of the house and cook, so you could get everything figured out with work?"

"I figured I'd take my wedding day off."

She laughed. "Right. But, I can make eggs, at least. How many do you want?" Lindsay stood and opened the fridge, rummaging around to find the eggs. "You—I mean, *we*—only have three eggs in here."

"I forgot to collect them this morning, with the guys giving me a tough time over the marriage thing."

"Collect them…?"

"Yeah, the chickens are out back. You can just go and take some from where they lay 'em. I get eight eggs a day from my ladies."

Lindsay didn't look as sure of herself now. "Um…maybe I should make something else for lunch. I don't know how to gather eggs, or clean them or whatever it is you have to do."

"No need to clean them," he said. "It's really no big deal, you just have to go out back—"

With a quick, decisive movement, Lindsay shut the stove off. "We have a problem."

He frowned. "Was the pan burning or something?"

"No." She sighed. "I have a confession to make."

Eric froze. "I suppose we're gonna be learning a lot of new things about each other, now. Lay it on me."

"I can't cook."

Eric looked at her, speechless. She couldn't cook at all? How had she survived all these years?

"I didn't marry you so I could have a personal chef," he said.

"But I was hoping you'd be able to take the cooking on to help out."

"I'm pretty good at making macaroni and cheese from a box in the microwave, eggs, cereal with milk, and heating up frozen meals, but again, only in the microwave. I pretty much live on Lean Cuisines."

Huh.

"Did you just never...have an oven in New York?" Eric frowned.

Lindsay laughed dryly. "Don't be silly. Of course there are ovens in New York. I'm just a little skittish around hot things."

Hot things?

Eric pulled a chair out from the table and straddled it backwards so he could see her in the kitchen. His house—*their* house—was so small, she wasn't more than a few feet away.

"It's stupid," she said. "I burnt my arm on a hot pan of gingerbread cookies that was fresh out of the oven. It was a long time ago...I was five. For some reason, my mom didn't realize she had to tell me not to touch them. And I haven't been comfortable putting things into or taking things out of an oven since."

"Since you were five," he repeated.

There was no way that could be true. But why would she make it up? Did she just hate cooking?

"You can use oven mitts, you know," he said. "You don't have to touch anything hot."

"I realize that," she said, waving off his suggestion. "It's not logical, obviously. I'm not dumb; I know that."

"I didn't say you were du—"

"—the reality is," she interrupted, "I never learned to cook because of it. Dumb as it may be. I'm barely okay with making things in a pan, and even that is iffy. I learned how to cook eggs out of necessity for protein."

Oh boy.

"I'm great at making cold sandwiches from cheese and deli meat," she said, "and I can use a toaster for frozen waffles. But…if making eggs here on the ranch requires me to interact with actual live chickens, I have a feeling that's one dish that's out."

"You don't look malnourished," he said finally. "You sure that's all you know how to do?"

Lindsay stood in the kitchen and just stared at him.

She had to be pulling his leg, right?

Eric laughed. "I get it. Good one."

Lindsay exhaled heavily, her cheeks puffing out before releasing.

"You're setting low expectations so I'll be surprised when you go all gourmet on me," he said. "That's cute. Guess I'm still learning your sense of humor."

"No, Eric."

She wasn't laughing with him.

From the look on her face, it was clear—she was upset. For real.

"I don't need gourmet food," he said quickly.

"I should have told you this before I agreed to take on the role of housewife and stay-at-home mom," she said softly. "I'm sorry."

"Don't worry 'bout it." Eric shrugged, as if her omission of something that would affect their daily lives three times a day wasn't a big deal.

"I'm willing to learn," she said. "And to get over my issues with using an oven."

"Then I'll be your guinea pig," he said. "I'm not picky. I'll eat burnt food."

That seemed to help. Lindsay's shoulders relaxed a bit. He hadn't even realized she'd been tensing them until they dropped an inch at his words.

"I'm sure I can figure this all out," she said, with more conviction this time. "If I can work in finance, surely I can figure out how to follow a recipe and turn a few dials on a stove, right?"

"Right. And if you can convince people to invest their money with you, you'll be able to convince our chickens to let you have some eggs, too."

Lindsay smiled, but her eyes looked too bright. As if she was hiding unshed tears. "I'll become a proper Idaho rancher's wife and mother."

Eric stood and pulled her against his chest. She wrapped her arms around him, and pressed her face into his shirt.

"I don't know how to be a wife, Eric," she whispered. "I've spent my entire adult life working on my career and my social circle. Now I've lost all of it. My friends, my job, my money. All of my possessions. It was all for nothing."

"If none of that had happened, I'd never've met you." He smiled to soften his words. "God has a plan. This happened for a reason. It wasn't for nothing."

"Your friends and family are going to hate me," she said. "They're going to think I'm taking advantage of you. That you got the short end of the stick."

"Don't say that." He ran his hand over her silky hair. "It ain't true."

She looked up at him, her eyes wide. "How are we going to even explain to your parents that we eloped, and they've never even met me?"

"I'll talk to them," Eric said. "They're getting what they said they wanted…my brother, too. It's just gonna be a bit sooner than they all expected, that's all."

"I wonder what Megan's going to say," Lindsay said. "And now I'm scared to tell her—isn't that silly?"

"She reacted pretty well to the fact that you're pregnant and lost your job, right? Getting married's a good thing. Megan wasn't as against it as the guys were."

She nodded. "Okay."

Lindsay took her phone out of her purse and held it tentatively, as if it might bite her.

"I have twenty-three text messages and two voicemails." She laughed, but it was clear she was nervous.

She pressed a few keys and put the phone on the counter in front of her, on speakerphone. It rang.

"Lindsay!" Megan exclaimed when she picked up the phone.

"You're on speaker, Meg. I'm here with Eric."

"Hi, Eric," Megan said, as if nothing was wrong.

Not exactly the tone he'd expected from her…what was going on?

"Hey," Eric said.

"I'm sorry I missed your calls," Lindsay added. "I turned the phone off. We have something to tell you."

"You got married at the courthouse," Megan said. "I already know. So does Zach, because I told him."

Lindsay glanced at Eric in confusion, and he frowned, raising his arms. He had no clue how the word had gotten out so fast.

Lindsay stared at the phone. "Where did you hear that?"

"Are you kidding?" Megan asked. "You really think you can keep a secret like eloping in Coeur d'Alene from spreading like wildfire? Ginger—from church—her daughter was emptying the wastebaskets there, and she heard the ladies up front talking about it, and she told her mom, who of course, called me to congratulate me on your marriage."

"I'm so sorry you found out that way," Lindsay said. "We didn't mean for that to happen. That's why I was calling you now."

"I would've come with you, been there with you, just like you and Eric will be there for me and Zach at our wedding." Megan sounded...hurt.

"None of you guys liked the idea from the get-go," Eric interrupted. "I got texts from everyone saying to sleep on it, to wait."

"I would've *been there*," Megan repeated. "You didn't even give me a chance."

"I'm sorry," Lindsay said. She looked genuinely crushed by her sister's words. "We're planning on doing a renewal of vows with everyone there, when...when the time is right."

Megan sighed audibly, her breath coming through the speaker. "Did you just do this so you could live together?"

"That's only a small part of it," Lindsay said. "We want to be a family. Living together before my—our—baby is born will give us the chance to get everything worked out ahead of time."

"I never should have suggested a double-wedding," Megan said. "This is my fault, for even putting the idea into your head."

"What double-wedding?" Eric asked.

Lindsay shook her head. "See, Megan? I didn't even mention it to him. He thought to propose all on his own."

"Let's have dinner tonight at my place," Megan suggested. "You two and me and Zach. This isn't the best conversation to have over the phone."

"Is Zach mad?" Lindsay asked.

"He's…I think he's surprised, to be honest. Neither of us thought when you were walking out our door this morning that you were going to run straight to the judge."

"We'll be there tonight," Eric said. "Just remember…what's done is done."

"Are you going to invite Chris and Jay?" Lindsay asked. "Because…maybe don't. I don't think I can take all of you ganging up on me like that again."

"I'm sorry," Megan said. "It'll be just us. But Eric should still go talk to them. They'll get used to the idea eventually, Linds."

Man. That was the last thing he wanted to do.

Eric nodded and tapped Lindsay on the shoulder silently, so she'd see him. He put his hat on, pulled it down low over his head, and tipped it in her direction.

She could keep talking to her sister, and maybe they could work it out before dinner. In the meantime, he was going to find his best friends, and get them to understand.

One thing was for sure. If anyone tried to break them up now that they were married, it didn't matter that they had a history together since they were kids. It didn't matter that they owned the ranch together.

Lindsay was his wife now, and they were having a child together. This was his family now, and he would protect them, and their relationship, by any means necessary.

Even if that meant losing his friends, and losing the ranch.

* * *

This was it. Lindsay was officially a married woman. She had a husband—and a handsome one at that. More importantly—*most* importantly—she had a father for her baby...*their* baby.

So she was going to move in today. Of course, it's not like she had much to move, per se. She didn't have even much in the way of clothing, other than what she'd been borrowing from Megan. She'd sold almost everything else. Maybe, when she got brave enough, she'd asked Grant to ship her anything she'd left at his apartment.

No. She couldn't do that. Because if she contacted him, he'd want to know what was going on.

What was she going to say? *I took the money you gave me for an abortion—oh and ha ha ha, I'm keeping the baby?*

He'd be furious. Not that any of that mattered. A child's life mattered much more than that. But surely Grant would be upset he had no say in the matter.

She didn't want anything from him. She didn't want child support. She would happily sign it all away, just to keep him from trying to get any custodial claim in the future on their baby.

Would that even be right to do?

Didn't matter now. Now that she was married, she didn't need Grant to help take care of their baby, because Eric had vowed to do so in his place.

Thank You, God, for Eric. Thank You so much for putting him in my life. In our *lives.*

How was she going to be a good wife for Eric, so he didn't regret his decision? Surely marrying her for the sake of the baby would eventually make him realize that he could have just waited to find someone he was in love with, and married her, and used a sperm donor or something to have the baby. Maybe his brother would've even offered up his DNA, so that the baby would still have been Eric's bloodline.

Stop thinking like that. None of that mattered now.

Eric had chosen her, because he felt God had called him to do so.

Thank You, God.

And if anything, God had affirmed for her she was making the right decision by agreeing to this marriage arrangement. Lindsay looked at her silver wedding ring. She wiggled it a bit, carefully sliding it off her finger so she could see the engraving on the inside. The same engraving, the same verse that was on the ring her father had given her mother.

That could not have been just a coincidence.

That was God.

No matter what happened with her own heart in this relationship, she was doing it all for a higher purpose—for her baby.

And God knew that she would do anything for that child. She would jump in front of a moving car for him. She would starve to give him the last crust of bread. She would throw herself in front of a bullet for this baby.

But she didn't have to do any of those things, at least not right now. All she had to do was take care of herself and give the baby a good healthy place to gestate inside of her. Surely she could handle that, at least.

And in the meantime, she'd be able to get to know Eric better. And he'd be able to get to know her.

Yes, they were doing it all backwards. But sometimes that's how life worked, right?

Lindsay had seen a library down off of Main Street. It looked much smaller than any of the libraries she'd patronized in New York, but if they had some books on how to cook simple meals for beginners—maybe even something in the children's section would be appropriate for her skill set at this point—that would be a good start.

And there was always YouTube. YouTube could be her teacher.

She'd make it work. She'd mastered new skills before and she could do it again. If she wanted to keep her marriage, she had to do her part.

At some point, she was going to have to learn how to trust her new husband, to feel safe and secure in their relationship, or she'd never be able to share a bed with him. And that was a big deal for Eric.

Lindsay *had* to make this marriage work—for her baby's sake.

Chapter Eleven

ERIC FLIPPED THE headlights on the truck as the sky grew darker. A whitetail deer darted across the road, disappearing into the forest, followed by a fawn.

"Don't run over Bambi," Lindsay said, pointing.

She seemed to be getting more accustomed to all the wildlife in Bear Creek Saddle, but he loved the look of wonderment and surprise on her face whenever she saw something on four legs. It was so cute.

Hopefully his folks would agree. Having them accept her as their daughter-in-law was so important to Eric.

He'd never been so nervous about going over to his parents' house—not since the time he and the guys had been brought home by the sheriff, after getting caught sneaking onto Ol' Man Hilderson's property during a sleepover.

This dinner at his parents' house would have much more serious long-term effects than when the sheriff had brought him home. His folks were already upset and hurt he'd gone off and eloped without even telling them—without them even having met Lindsay.

They thought it had taken him so long to make time for a family dinner because he and his new bride were "busy being newlyweds," as his mom had said.

Eric purposefully didn't suggest otherwise.

His parents could *not* find out he'd been spending the last three weeks sleeping in the guest room that would eventually become the nursery.

At first, they questioned Eric's motives up and down, and he told them the truth—most of it. He'd told them how he'd had a vision of Lindsay before he met her. That he felt called by God to propose. That he just knew she was *The One*, and how he wanted to spend the rest of his life with her.

All of that was true.

He left out the fact she was pregnant with another man's child, or that it was an arrangement of sorts rather than a traditional fall-in-love-then-get-married sort of deal.

He didn't want to tell them their plan was to get married and worry about the love stuff later, if it ever came at all. It wouldn't matter—because their goal was to be a happy, healthy, stable family for the Little One growing inside of Lindsay's womb.

His parents would never understand that. They were madly in love with each other, and always had been, it seemed. They were one of the lucky couples, the ones who *didn't* turn to each other after years together and realize they'd fallen out of love and had nothing in common, and no reason to remain married.

That was Eric's biggest fear.

The last thing he wanted was to get a divorce. But by going into his marriage with their expectations lined up with reality, he and Lindsay probably had a better chance of making it than most couples these days, who divorced at the drop of a hat.

Maybe his dad would understand why Lindsay didn't want to be a single mom—maybe he'd understand how much Eric wanted to be a father to that baby, in the way that Mr. Hunt had been like a second dad for Zach growing up.

Maybe.

Tonight was not the night to find out. They just needed to meet Lindsay, that was all. They could just meet her, and see how kind and caring she was. Surely when they saw how well the two of them got along together, how beautiful and gracious she was—they'd understand why he just had to marry her.

They had to see.

Right?

Because if his parents knew right off the bat when they met her that she wasn't in love with him, or that she'd married him mostly for the child's sake and not because of any particular affection on her part for him, they'd never support the marriage.

Eric had a feeling Lindsay would never feel like their marriage was "real," as she put it, if no one else around them acted like it was.

And if Lindsay never got comfortable within their marriage, what was to stop her from leaving him, and taking their child with her?

Not to mention…he'd straight up miss her. Having Lindsay in his home—*their* home—made his days so good. Eating dinner with her (so far, no eggs unless he gathered them himself like he used to do, but she was working her way up to it) was way better than eating alone like he used to do after a hard day's work.

If she ever changed her mind about staying with him, he didn't know how he'd be able to unlearn what it was like to share his life and home with someone he cared deeply about.

That wasn't going to happen. It simply couldn't—he wouldn't let it.

Eric glanced over at Lindsay when they stopped at the stop sign. She looked amazing. She wore the same dress that she'd worn to church one time, the pretty one with the flowers. She had a touch of lipstick on, maybe some mascara—Eric couldn't really tell about those things.

He just knew she looked fantastic.

"You're quiet," he noted.

"What if they don't like me?" Lindsay kept her hands tightly together in her lap. If she squeezed them any tighter, she was liable to crack her knuckles.

Eric checked the rearview mirror. No one was behind them, so he just sat at the stop sign. He made it a point to not drive and look at his passenger.

Making that mistake and getting into a car accident once was enough for him. And now felt like an important time to look at her.

"Linds—just be yourself. You're good at talking to people, right? You're a people person. You have—what did you call that? Customer relations skills?" He grinned.

"I guess I could kind of think of it that way," she said slowly. Her fingers relaxed a little in her lap. "I just know that they can't be happy they're meeting me after we're already married, and they don't have a say in the issue."

"About that." How was he going to tell her this? She wasn't the type of girl who'd ever want to lie, just like he didn't want to.

It wasn't really lying if they didn't tell everything. Some things were personal.

"I want them to get to know you," Eric said, "and not have any weird ideas about why we got married. They don't know that you're pregnant, or that we weren't in a romantic relationship before we got married."

"How do they think we got married a week after meeting? Were we in some sort of secret relationship while I was in New York?" She frowned, clearly not liking the idea.

"No, no…some people, they meet and it's like love at first sight. That happens. I say 'love at first sight' ain't real, though. That's probably *lust* at first sight."

And if that was the case, he definitely had that.

"But I haven't said none of that to my folks. They can just think what they want."

"Okay." The sun was setting outside, and a ray of pink-orange light highlighted her face as she bit on her lip. "Do they know about your condition?"

"I haven't told them yet. Told my brother, but he knows it's not his story to tell. They'll know when the time's right. I don't like to stress out my mom—she's been through enough."

Even though she'd been in remission for a long while now, keeping unnecessary stress from touching his mom was an unbreakable habit now for him and Ryan.

Lindsay shook her head. "So we just tell them we fell in love and had to immediately elope and not invite them to our wedding, for no good reason? And we don't tell them I'm pregnant, and that we got married so we could co-parent the baby? Isn't that like… wouldn't that be lying to your parents?"

"We're just not giving them very personal details about our very personal relationship," he corrected her. "I know it's kind of splitting hairs—and they're going to find out everything in time. They deserve a chance to get to know you first, without all that baggage. You know what I mean?"

"That makes sense... I guess a lot of those details are kind of personal. Like they don't need to know we're sleeping in separate bedrooms."

Eric didn't even want to know that.

"Yeah. It'll just worry them." A car pulled up behind them and tapped the horn. Eric raised his hand to let the driver know he heard him.

Eyes back on the road.

Hands at ten and two.

He drove, his stomach clenching with unease. Would his parents notice something was different about this marriage? What if they got the wrong impression of Lindsay? He really wanted them to like her as much as he did.

She was going to be the mother of their grandchild, and they didn't even know it.

* * *

Lindsay put on a big smile before Mrs. Hunt even opened the front door to their home. It was a modest one-level ranch-style home, on a decent amount of land—five acres? Ten acres?

She didn't really know how to judge, other than that it wasn't a quarter-acre suburban lot and it wasn't a sprawling ranch with thousands of acres. But it looked like a really lovely home to grow up in. Just very different from her own upbringing, living in a second-floor walk-up apartment in the middle of New York City.

Eric's childhood home was the kind of house she'd seen in

Hallmark movies about small-town, hard-working middle-class families who lived somewhere in the middle of the country.

"Welcome!" Mrs. Hunt's face lit up when she saw Lindsay and opened the door, gesturing them inside. "I can't believe we are *finally* getting to meet you."

The word "finally" stuck out. Clearly his parents weren't pleased they were first meeting her after the marriage. What parent would be? She couldn't blame them.

Eric bent down and gave his mom a kiss on the cheek, and hung his hat on a hook by the door. He didn't even look to see where the hook was—he must've had muscle-memory from doing it so many times.

Eric's dad had been sitting in a recliner in the living room, which Lindsay could see from the front hall. He stood when they entered and walked toward them. Just as she went in to give him a peck on the cheek, he stuck his hand out to shake her hand.

It was an awkward little dance.

Mr. Hunt chuckled. "I'll take the hug, sure." He turned to Eric. "She's beautiful, son. You picked a good one."

Lindsay didn't know what to do with her hands. Or her face. Keep smiling, probably. If she could've gone back in time and had this dinner prior to running to the judge, she'd do it in a heartbeat—just to avoid the uncomfortable situation they had on their hands this evening.

What if they thought she was a gold-digger who'd stolen their son?

Even worse: was it possible that she was?

No. At least, she hated the thought of that being the case.

This marriage wasn't for her. It was for the baby. That had to make it right...right?

But if it was solely for the baby, she would've given him up for adoption instead of entering into a lifelong relationship with their son.

So if his parents ascertained some selfish thinking on her part, they wouldn't exactly be wrong. And now she'd potentially ruined the Hunts' youngest son's chance of marrying for true love.

He was stuck with her, and so were they.

Not exactly the best grounds to have a friendly, no-pressure meet-and-greet dinner.

"Ryan really wanted to be here tonight," Eric's mom said, "but he had to work late and Tiffany wanted to rest, being pregnant and all." She clasped her hands together. "Isn't that such exciting news?"

"I'm real happy for them." Eric smiled and did sort of a fist-bump thing in front of himself, as if to punctuate the sentiment.

Was that a flash of jealousy in his eyes, though?

But then it was gone. Maybe it hadn't been there at all.

It wasn't crazy to think maybe Eric mourned not being able to impregnate a wife he loved, who loved him back. Ryan had everything going in that regard, and right now it seemed like Lindsay had given Eric the short end of the stick.

Because it wasn't as if Eric seemed afraid of love, like her. He'd told her he just didn't think it was a good basis for a marriage compared to more fundamental values and goals. And now she wanted him to fall in love with her so she could trust him with her security and her child, but without her having to fall in love with him back. Trusting him with her heart would be a step too far.

Eric discreetly brushed his hand against hers, and gave her a silent look that seemed to say, "Don't do that."

Don't do what? She lifted her hand to make a "what?" gesture when his parents turned so they could follow them into the dining room.

Ohhh.

Without even realizing it, she'd had her hand resting on her lower abdomen, over her womb—something she'd been doing ever since she found out there was a baby growing inside there—and only noticed after she moved it to communicate silently with Eric.

That was something only a person with a stomachache or a pregnancy would do, and they couldn't afford his parents finding out the basis of their marriage. Nothing could give the secret away.

Not tonight.

Not yet.

Eric put his arm around her shoulder and squeezed her against him. This was good. Maybe he could just keep his arm on her, and she could be conjoined-twins with him all night. At least then she'd know what to do with her legs: follow him.

"You guys are probably starving," Mrs. Hunt said. "Everything's all ready. Go ahead and sit."

Mr. Hunt sat at the head of the table, and his wife sat on the other side at the end. Fortunately, Eric and Lindsay sat next to each other. If he had to communicate silently with her again, he wouldn't have to kick her from across the table.

She just had to focus on not ruffling any feathers, and get through this dinner without making his parents hate her.

This was her one chance to make a good first impression. If she blew this, his family would think of her as some sort of gold-digger (ranch-digger?) who was taking advantage of their son.

It would be impossible to regain their trust after that.

Mr. Hunt said grace, and he prayed just like Eric did—comfortably, humbly, and simply. Eric's hand on hers calmed her jittery nerves. She didn't want him to take his hand away when they said "Amen."

There was a big plate of lasagna and a bowl of steamed zucchini and squash on the side. Would Lindsay ever be able to prepare a meal like that? Or any meal that wasn't prepared and frozen?

"Oh, let me get the bread." Mrs. Hunt got up from the table and ran over to the kitchen, where she pulled a long French bread loaf out of the oven.

"Wow, did you make that?" Lindsay looked at the piping hot garlic bread in amazement.

"Nope," Mrs. Hunt said with a laugh. "They sell it at the deli area of the supermarket, and you just have to pop it in the oven to warm it up. It goes great with lasagna. I hope you like Italian food."

"Absolutely," she said truthfully. "I love it." She took a bite. Delicious. "I could use some recipes, actually…I want to learn how to make Eric's favorites."

Her mother-in-law raised her eyebrows, which made her look just like Eric when he did the same thing. "Maybe I should keep them a secret to keep you guys coming here every week for dinner."

"Mom." Eric gave his mother a look.

"What?" Mrs. Hunt widened her eyes innocently. "I can't have her hiding you away from me."

Whatever happened to a man leaving his mother and cleaving to his wife? Having at least some recipes might help with the cleaving aspect…assuming that included a man and wife having dinner together.

As much as Lindsay wanted to say something to that effect, she couldn't afford to do anything to mess up this dinner. Whether or not Eric's mother liked her, she was going to be their baby's grandma, and part of their life. It wasn't worth it to mess it all up just to get a point across.

"Okay, okay," his mom said, responding to Eric's own raised brow. "I'll just give away all the family secrets."

"As you should, Darlene," his father said pointedly. "Lindsay *is* family now, remember?"

"We'll happily be here anytime you want," Lindsay said quickly. They needed some damage-control. "You're a much better cook than I could ever hope to be, and I'm sure Eric won't want to miss out on seeing his mom."

Mrs. Hunt beamed. "She's smart," she said to Eric.

Lindsay exhaled. *Thank You.*

"She's definitely smart." Eric gave Lindsay a smile and, on his lap where his mom couldn't see, gave her a thumbs-up sign.

Butter up mom. Got it.

Suddenly a wave of nausea overtook her. Why wasn't morning sickness happening in the morning? It was nighttime, for goodness' sake. The tasty lasagna she'd been eating turned in her stomach.

"Excuse me," she said. She didn't want to open her mouth too much, because she had food in it still and she didn't want to spit it out. "Bathroom?"

"Two doors down," her father-in-law said, pointing.

Eric looked concerned.

Lindsay ran to the bathroom as another wave of nausea overtook her.

Why now?

Running from the table to be sick might clue them all in that she was pregnant. Since they didn't know Eric was sterile yet, they'd probably think she'd had a one-night stand with him and then a shotgun wedding after she came up pregnant.

But the timing didn't work for Lindsay's pregnancy to be from an affair with Eric, and Mrs. Hunt surely would figure that out. If she'd gotten pregnant from Eric, it would've taken at minimum two whole weeks before they would've found out, even if they got married immediately when they did.

But they'd gotten married after only one week of having met.

Whether Mrs. Hunt suspected Lindsay's pregnancy or not, it was no wonder his mom was suspect about their marriage.

Lindsay washed her hands and face and looked up into the mirror above the bathroom sink. Her face was getting a bit rounder. Already? Was that possible?

She took some toothpaste from the tube on the counter, and swished it around her mouth with some water.

Makeshift mouthwash. It would do. If only she had her purse with her, so she could brush her hair and reapply her lipstick.

She came back to the table. Surely she'd been gone too long.

Lord, I'm probably bugging You with all of these requests, but please let me eat this meal Eric's mom made and just keep it down, for the sake of peace in this family.

She took a tentative bite.

Nope. Not ready yet.

"So," Mr. Hunt said, spearing a zucchini on his fork. "I hear you grew up in New York and lived in New York City. What was that like? I bet Idaho's pretty different—a big culture shock."

"Are you liking it here? You guys aren't going to move to New

York, are you?" Mrs. Hunt asked.

"No, no," Eric said quickly. "Were staying right here in Bear Creek Saddle. You don't have to worry about that, Mom."

"It's so beautiful here," Lindsay added.

That was true. It was really beautiful. But it definitely was a culture shock, too. She didn't want to give them any reason to think she had anything negative at all to say, though. About *anything*.

Lindsay smiled. "I love the mountains."

"But no skyscrapers here," Mrs. Hunt pointed out.

"Yes, but with Megan living out here, I really wanted to be with family. Family is so important."

Eric was nodding. Good. She'd said the right thing.

"And then you met Eric!" Mrs. Hunt exclaimed. "How did you meet—tell me everything. This has to be the fastest engagement and marriage in the whole world."

Lindsay glanced at Eric. Clearly his mom didn't think their marriage was a good idea. It was coming out in her words, even if she was trying to not say it outright.

"Mom, people get married all the time even faster than we did. Sometimes…you just know you belong together."

"Yes," Lindsay jumped in. She could say that all night and never be lying. "I saw Eric was the right person to marry. And once you know… well, then you know!"

She smiled big, and looked over at Eric. She hadn't said anything untrue. And… well, she *did* know. She knew that she needed someone to help her raise her child, and someone to provide for them. It didn't hurt that Eric was young and handsome and co-owned the same ranch where her sister lived.

But those were all big-picture reasons. His mom seemed to be searching for the details, the spark of romance.

Could she tell it was missing?

Maybe they needed to act more in love, to be convincing.

Lindsay hooked her arm through Eric's at the table, and leaned against his shoulder. He smiled—probably because he knew exactly what and why she was giving them a little public display of affection—but his smile looked like affection for her, as well.

Perfect.

While she'd only done it to help his parents feel better about their relationship, the feel of his warm, muscular body pressed against hers made her feel better, too. More connected, not just physically, but emotionally.

Eric made her feel…safe.

"It seems like it happened so very fast," his mom said again. "Where exactly did you meet, again? Something extraordinary must've happened for Eric to marry you without even introducing you to us first."

Oy.

"Well, I'm blackmailing him," Lindsay joked, looking up at Eric. He winked at her. "He didn't have a choice."

Eric and his dad laughed. But his mom stared at her with an open mouth.

"She's joking, Mom."

Mrs. Hunt looked over at Eric suspiciously. "I'd know her sense of humor better if only we'd all gotten a chance to get to know each other *before* you two made a life-changing decision without even thinking about conferring with us. You didn't even talk to Pastor Jim, Eric! Why?"

"Because I didn't want anyone trying to change my mind." Eric set his fork down a little too hard, and it clanged. "I prayed about it and made a choice that felt right, Mom. You'll just have to trust me."

His mother shook her head. "This, from someone who has no concept of what marriage is because you have no experience with it. You're supposed to talk to other married people, first. Like me and your father."

Lindsay recognized the pain behind her sharp words. This wasn't just anger…Eric's mom sounded hurt.

What would Lindsay do if a client said this to her, about making some sort of move on their behalf they weren't on board with?

The customer is always right, and it doesn't cost anything to apologize.

It was her motto at work when it came to talking to anyone who had an issue. And Mrs. Hunt had very legitimate issues about their marriage—even *without* knowing it was built on a foundation other than love at first sight.

Lindsay took a deep breath. "You're one-hundred percent right, Mrs. Hunt, and I am so sorry. We should've met with you before getting married, and we both should have sought out your counsel, and gotten your blessing."

"That's right. You should have." But her mother-in-law's face softened.

Eric stayed silent, as if he didn't want to mess anything up, but his eyes stayed on them intently, following every word and expression.

"You raised an amazing man," Lindsay said. "I hope we can move forward and get to know each other better from here, even though we kind of jumped the shark by getting married first."

Eric nodded and his mother very slightly shrugged her

shoulders in grudging acquiescence.

"Did you two meet on the internet or something, like Bill and Allie?" his mom asked. "Is that what this is about? You can tell me."

"I came to visit my sister Megan, and your son was kind enough to pick me up at the Spokane airport," Lindsay said. "And when we met for the first time, our eyes just locked from across the baggage terminal, and we hit it off right away."

"Absolutely." Eric grinned broadly, and took a big bite of lasagna.

That was a good idea. If her mouth was full, she couldn't speak. And maybe they'd stop asking so many questions.

Her nausea was gone now, thank God.

Who knew the skills she'd amassed during her time at the bank would be so useful on the home front?

Eric had known. He was the one who'd suggested she utilize her people skills to begin with. He must have realized it would make her more comfortable to connect to an area she had some level of expertise in—and it had.

Maybe he knew more about her than she'd even thought.

But his mother was right to be concerned about them getting married so quickly, especially since they barely knew each other.

Even Lindsay was worried about that.

Chapter Twelve

ERIC WANTED TO shove the stack of paperwork right off of his desk. It was too much to handle, even though he'd only been printing out a portion of the data he'd been combing through on his computer. How was he supposed to deal with business stuff, when the sheer amount of receipts and scores of spreadsheets threatened to overtake his life?

It was times like this—and he'd had more than enough of them since they'd taken over the ranch from Bill—when the wood-framed window in the old farmhouse bedroom he called his office was more of a distraction than anything.

The low afternoon sunlight called to him. There were so many chores on the ranch that needed to be tended to before sunset. And, to be honest, he'd rather be out there, riding around on Smoky, then cooped up in the farmhouse with the other guys.

No one was having a good go of it.

Eric rolled his chair back, and stood and stretched.

Enough of this.

They needed his new wife's help, and with tax season coming up fast, his friends were probably finally desperate enough to accept it…even if they were still having trouble accepting the fact that he'd gone off and gotten married behind their backs.

The one guy he couldn't be sure of convincing was Chris. Chris had always been wary of outsiders. Now that Lindsay was his wife, even if only in name, Chris would have to concede—she was no longer an outsider at Bear Creek Saddle Ranch.

Wouldn't he?

Eric strode down the narrow corridor and pushed open the half-closed door to Chris's office.

Chris's head was facedown on the desk, as if he'd just thunked it on there in frustration.

"You look the way I feel," Eric noted.

Chris popped his head up and scowled. "You're supposed to knock."

"Your door wasn't closed."

"Well," Chris said, "I was just doing some thinking."

"Me too."

"You go first," Chris offered.

Eric leaned against the doorframe. He would've gone over to sit on the corner of Chris's desk, but it was as covered in paper as his own was. Eric shook his head.

"All right," Chris said. He leaned back in his chair. "I was thinking 'bout how when Lindsay first got here, she wanted to help us with all this stuff."

Wow. Maybe he wouldn't be as hard to convince as he'd thought.

"She'd be good at it, too," Eric said, being careful to not seem overeager.

The fact was, Lindsay clearly missed having her job. She was putting her all into trying to learn how to be a homemaker, but things kept happening to discourage her.

Last night, when she'd pulled the chicken out of the slow-cooker for dinnertime, Eric went to carve it and found the plastic bag of giblets the grocery store had shoved in there, still inside. She hadn't even known to look for the bag, much less not to cook it for eight hours inside their dinner.

It was so unexpected, he'd laughed until tears streamed down his cheeks, but she was not amused. To Lindsay, it was one more bit of proof that she'd only be respected for her skills with numbers—and the household budget wasn't enough of a challenge for her.

If Eric could secure this for her, maybe she'd be happy. He hadn't married her to get a cook and a maid. Yes, he wanted her to be there for their child, but there were plenty of ways she could do both. Many women did. Especially since she'd be working right there on the ranch, and there was no reason she couldn't make her own hours.

"We need her help," Eric said. "Maybe if we just ask her to take a look at our situation, and she can tell us if we're on the right track, and what she could do to help us get it all straightened out."

"Fine." Chris sighed heavily in surrender.

Fine?

After weeks of being adamantly against the idea of anyone else seeing the inner-workings of the business side of their ranch, Chris was finally willing to admit defeat?

"Okay." Eric wanted to whoop for joy and punch his fist in the air, Rocky-style, but something told him Chris wouldn't appreciate the theatrics.

Zach appeared behind the doorframe with Jay. They must've heard them talking. Eric stepped out of the doorway to let them in, and they all stood in Chris's small office.

"Couldn't help overhearing," Zach said. "We're on board with that. We need the assistance, and she's family."

Eric nodded.

The tension in the air was thick with unsaid words.

"What am I missing here?" Eric asked. "Your wedding's next week, man." He playfully hit Zach's shoulder. "Shouldn't you be walking around on cloud nine?"

"Eric," Zach said somberly. "We might be in the red by a lot of money, depending on how this shakes out come tax time. Tens of thousands of dollars, even. I've spoken to Megan about it, and she still wants to get married, even though whatever we might owe in taxes would become her debt then, too."

"Of course she does," Eric said. "She loves you."

The men glanced at each other uncomfortably, avoiding Eric's eyes.

Oh.

Ohhhh.

Eric had promised Lindsay he'd take care of her debt, take care of her, and their child. What if all he'd done by marrying her was put her into even more debt?

"What if I can't take care of her and the baby?" Eric asked softly. "She doesn't love me the way Megan loves you. Not yet."

Jay cleared his throat. He looked like he was about to say something, but a glare from Zach shut him down.

Jay just raised his eyebrows and shook his head.

"I know," Eric snapped. "You told me so, right? You all told me so."

That was the one big problem with a marriage of

convenience—it was no longer convenient if one half of the couple wasn't fulfilling their end of the deal. And right now, that was Eric.

"If you bring Lindsay in," Jay said, "she's going to learn about all of this. And that might not be the best way to start your marriage."

"I'm not keeping it from her on purpose," Eric said. "I didn't think of it as some big secret."

Chris and Zach looked at each other. What was Eric missing?

"I just figured we'd get a handle on where all our money was going to, straighten it out, do our taxes, and get back to making a profit," Eric said. "Businesses have good years and bad years all the time, right?"

"Right," said Jay. "But what if the ranch is no longer profitable, and it's just digging us into a bigger hole each month? We won't be able to make payments if this keeps up. We may be forced to liquidate our assets to pay the bank back."

Eric froze. "Are you saying…we might have to sell the ranch?"

"It's just one of many possibilities," Chris interrupted. "No one knows. We haven't been doing a perfect job with our paperwork 'cause we've been busy being ranchers. Ain't our fault we never done this sort of thing before."

"It *is* our fault," Zach said. "We knew we were getting behind with all this stuff. We should've hired someone to help from the get-go."

"Lindsay could help with that, too," Eric said. "She could get this sorted, and continue to help us throughout the year so we don't get so backed up again."

"We agree on that," Zach said. "She's in, if she wants in. And we'll make sure she can have a baby-friendly schedule when it's time, that sorta thing."

The other guys nodded in agreement.

"She'll be real happy 'bout this," Eric said.

But would she still be happy when she found out Eric might not be the stable provider he'd told her he was?

* * *

Lindsay collapsed onto the couch, exhausted. Part of her exhaustion was from the pregnancy, for sure. But most of it was the vacuuming. Why did her sister love cleaning so much, again?

A key turned in the lock on the front door. Boomer, living up to his name, barked a greeting in his booming doggy–voice as Eric walked in.

"Hey, Eric!" She sat up straighter. A light sheen of perspiration covered her lip, which she dried with the back of her hand, then she ran her fingers through her hair to tame it. "You're home early."

His handsome face betrayed his excitement, but about what?

"I hope you haven't gotten too attached to vacuuming," he joked.

She grinned, rolling her eyes as she patted the vacuum beside her, where she'd left it when she sat down, not bothering to return it to its proper space.

"Ol' Sucky and I are trying to bond," she said, "but it's a work in process."

"The guys and I could really use your help in the office. You'd said you were interested in working there, and we could pay you and everything—we'd have to if we weren't hiring you, but someone else, of course."

Lindsay couldn't believe her ears. "Your friends are okay with this?"

"They're more than okay with it," Eric said. "We're desperate. Actually… I have to tell you something."

Uh-oh. That didn't sound good. What was going on?

Lindsay channeled her inner-Eric and chose to respond with his favorite response—silent-waiting for more information.

Eric sighed, and sat down on the couch next to her. With his denim-clad legs spread, his knee touched hers. She made no move to pull away.

It was nice, having him close to her.

"We've kind of made a mess of the business side of things, looks like," Eric said. "At first it was going great—but the more successful we got, the less time there was to spend in the office, because there was so much work to do on the ranch, you know?"

Lindsay nodded slowly. What kind of mess were they in?

* * *

Lindsay furrowed her brow as she sat in Eric's office in the farmhouse, scanning the papers on Eric's desk. So far what she saw wasn't terrible, numbers-wise—but it was extremely disorganized. No wonder they were behind.

"So you're telling me that all of you guys documented everything in a similar way?"

Chris shook his head. "We kinda all did our own way."

"How did you get your taxes done last year?" she asked. "What's your accountant say?"

The guys, standing above her, looked at each other over her head.

"Did you even call your accountant?" Lindsay set the papers down and leaned back heavily in the chair.

"We don't have an accountant," Zach said finally. "He wanted to charge way too much money."

"Yeah—and he wanted us to get a bookkeeper, which we definitely couldn't afford," Jay added.

Lindsay sighed and shook her head. "I can tell you right now, if you had paid for a bookkeeper in the first place, you probably wouldn't be so upside-down in your finances. And the cost of your accountant should be made up by how much you save on taxes. Right now, you're going to have to go over everything with a fine-tooth comb and put it into an organized fashion. And you definitely need an accountant."

"Are you gonna be able to help us, Lindsay?" Eric asked.

His eyes look so hopeful. She didn't want to disappoint him. She could definitely do the bookkeeping. But—especially when multiple assets and partners were involved—an accountant was a necessity, not a luxury.

She relayed this to them as best she could. The severity of their situation finally seemed to be dawning on them.

"You guys are great at what you do," Lindsay said. "You're ranchers. That's what you're great at. The stuff you're not great at—the stuff you don't even *want* to do—that's something you should delegate. Think of how much more money you could've made, if you were focusing all of your energy on getting the ranch to be the most productive it can be, instead of squirreling away in the farmhouse."

"She's got a point," grumbled Chris.

"Let me hire an accountant," Lindsay said, "and I'll work with her to get everything under control. What I can do right now is start going through everything, compiling what you're going to need, and put it all into a nice neat notebook and zip file and get it ready for the accountant, so she won't have to put as many man-hours into it—which will cost you less. That'll also give me a huge jump-start on figuring out where money is coming in and leaking out."

Zach sighed with apparent relief. "Okay," he said. "That seems like that's what we gotta do, so we'll do it."

"Great." Lindsay held her hands over the keyboard, ready to roll.

Once Eric gave her the room to do what she needed to get done, she could definitely tidy up this mess. She may not be great at tidying up messes when it came to housekeeping, like her sister, but she could get people's financial houses in order. That's what she was good at.

"If I need to find expenses for each of you—for the ranch— where do I find them? Can you guys give me whatever you have on that? And also I'm going to need a bunch of other stuff."

Lindsay enumerated all of the documents and receipts she'd need from them. There were a lot.

No one was taking notes.

"Okay—maybe everyone can check their email in five minutes for the list from me, and send me back each of the files I need. And *then* I'm going to be able to get to work."

"I already feel so much better about this," Eric said to his friends.

"Me too," Jay said. "Finally feels like we're on the right track."

Zach and Chris nodded in agreement, and when Eric looked at her, it was with an expression of genuine admiration and gratitude.

This was awesome. This was what she thrived on doing.

She didn't need her fancy career in Manhattan. Maybe, if she had the ability to take care of one account really well—the ranch—that would be enough.

Especially considering how complex it was.

"Do you guys have any financial investments that the ranch invests in to bring in more income?"

"No." Zach furrowed his brow, as if her question had exposed their lack of expertise. "Our investment is the land, if that counts. We don't know about investments otherwise."

Lindsay's brain started cranking, the gears turning. There were so many aspects she could help them with.

Cattle futures, perhaps. They could help offset any losses. A stock portfolio. Real estate. They had numerous homes on the ranch that could probably be considered as collateral. Implementing a proper book-keeping system. Maybe figuring out a line of credit to make required improvements. There was so much to be done. She rubbed her hands together gleefully, ready to dive in.

"Eric." She looked up at his handsome face. He was so tall...she loved it. "Does this mean I get your office?"

Eric laughed. "For my wife? Anything."

In her jubilance, jumping up on her tip-toes to give him a kiss on the cheek felt like the most natural thing in the world to do.

Eric's eyes widened, and he grinned, touching his jaw where she'd kissed him. "Wow. Wasn't expecting that. Wish I had more offices to give away."

"Okay, guys," she said. "Everyone get ready for an email in five." Zach, Jay and Chris took her cue and left her to it, closing the door behind them.

Now it was just her and Eric, alone in his office.

"Thank you for giving me this chance," she said. "This right here, this is what I'm good at. Not homesteading."

"Not yet." Eric winked at her.

"We'll see." It might never happen. "You know…I haven't felt in my element since I got here. I stick out like a sore thumb."

"No, you don't."

"That's sweet of you," she said, "but I know I do. I still can't figure out how to cook a chicken, I'm banned from riding Smoky, and I'm sure it hasn't escaped your notice that I haven't collected eggs on my own yet."

He chuckled. "I may have noticed that. But you're my wife. Even Chris and my mom are on board with that now. You belong here, Lindsay. I promise you do."

Did she? Or would she forever be a city girl in the countryside, a foreigner in a foreign land?

Lindsay stood from the desk, and gestured around the office. "Being here, being able to help you guys, finally being able to do something I actually know how to do really well—*this* is my element. And I'm just…really grateful you're giving me a chance to prove myself to you this way."

Eric took a step toward her, wrapping his arms around her waist, and looked deep into her eyes. He was acting more and more like a real husband, instead of a pretend one, every day. She was almost starting to believe him…that it was real.

As dangerous as that was, Lindsay couldn't help but to find herself craving his affection.

"You don't need to prove yourself to me," he said. "I already believe in you."

The warmth and strength of his arms around her made her melt. She could stay like this with him forever.

"Thank you for taking a chance on me," Eric whispered. "On *us*."

* * *

In the following weeks, Eric watched as Lindsay worked her tail off. It was freeing for him, actually—he much preferred being on the field, and he knew the guys did as well. Every now and then they would get a text, asking where she could find such and such information, and they would let her know. She had control of all of the inner workings of the business, and she seemed happier for it—and so did the guys…even Chris, amazingly.

He'd just finished dropping dinner off for her at the farmhouse since she wanted to work late. As long as he didn't have to be both wrangling the livestock and also in the office, he was more than happy to cook for them. Especially since Lindsay really wasn't getting any better at cooking—and she'd be the first to admit it.

She'd hired an accountant from Coeur d'Alene, and the two of them were figuring things out. Thank God. It was a huge stressor lifting off his shoulders.

It was getting warmer out every day, and soon he'd be able to just wear a T-shirt outside. Haying season would begin, with all that entailed. If there ever was a perfect time for Lindsay to be working with them, it was now. They needed all hands on deck, especially since her sister was still pretty busy making custom birdhouses and crafts to sell on Etsy.

Only problem with the stress of the business aspects easing up a bit, was that now his thoughts found their way to worry upon more sensitive issues. Like the baby.

Would he be a good dad?

He'd been so consumed with his own desire to raise a family and leave a legacy for this world, that he hadn't even stopped to wonder if he *should*. Was it possible he wasn't able to have his own offspring because God didn't want him to be a father, for some reason?

Or maybe, the reason was simply so he'd have a reason to marry Lindsay. It was impossible to figure out, and ultimately, maybe it didn't matter much—as long as he did the best he could with what God had given him: another man's child to raise.

Could he be as good as his own dad? And would his child love him, even if he knew that Eric wasn't his biological dad?

And what if Grant wanted to come back into Lindsay's life, and be in a relationship with her? Equally frightening…what if, after the baby was born, Grant wanted to come back into the *baby's* life?

Those were Eric's greatest fears. Because what could he possibly offer Lindsay to keep her with him, if her child's own father wanted to provide for and be with them?

It was messy. Nothing was tied up in a little bow.

At least with an anonymous sperm donor, he and Lindsay wouldn't have had to worry about a biological father wanting to come in and take custody.

What could they do if he asked for custody, even split custody? With Grant in New York and the ranch in Idaho, was Lindsay going to have to take their baby on a plane to New York half the time?

Could the judge make them do that?

Once again, that discontent with his situation bubbled under the surface. If only he was able to father a child himself, the natural way. None of this would even be an issue.

Why me, God? Of all the people in the world to afflict with infertility, why me? Weren't there some child abusers He could go after, instead?

Eric sighed. It wasn't fair, but that was life. Life wasn't fair.

At least God could make beauty from the ashes. He always did.

Yeah, it was a tough break that some stupid, long forgotten injury from childhood was preventing him from having his own biological children now, as an adult. But had that not been the case, what were the chances he'd now be married to the most beautiful girl in the world, with a baby on the way?

His diagnosis had resulted in the best possible outcome for any guy, much less a guy in his particular situation.

And while he'd been worried before that Lindsay wasn't happy in her new role as wife and mother-to-be, now that she had a job she felt confident in again, she seemed to be thriving.

But she still wasn't in love with him. Even worse, he was falling for her. Totally one-sided.

The pain of seeing her say goodnight to him and then politely close her bedroom door was messing with his emotions. The push-pull of wanting her and not being able to have her was taking its toll on their marriage, arrangement or not.

Because it was starting to feel so real to him. Until she rejected him once more, and then he was reminded...nope. Not really real.

She still wouldn't sleep with him, and the guarded look on her face whenever he walked into the room made him not want to push his luck by bringing up the subject.

He'd told her he'd be okay with being celibate forever. But that may have been wishful thinking.

What if she never fell in love with him?

Maybe if he loved her as well as he could, he wouldn't even be worrying about that...he'd prize her happiness above all else, including his own desire to sleep with her.

"That's a conundrum," he muttered under his breath.

Eric kicked the pebble in front of him as he moseyed down the footpath back toward home. He'd left the truck at the farmhouse for Lindsay.

Maybe it was time to start thinking about getting Lindsay her own car—something that would fit a kid in a car seat in the back seat. He could fit Boomer in the back seat of the pickup truck, and it would do in a pinch, but Lindsay would probably really like having a car she wouldn't have to climb up into to put the baby in and out, right?

Oh, and then there was her debt.

Their debt.

He'd taken on her debt knowingly, with the promise to pay it off. But it wouldn't be smart to use his savings to pay off her debt now, when they might need it soon to save the ranch and the very roof over their heads. So now…she might be taking on whatever hole they'd dug themselves into by not keeping proper track of their income and expenses—and she might end up in *even more* debt.

And if there was a hefty sum for the ranch to pay off come tax time, it was going to come out of all of their own salaries and profits. It might be a lean Christmas.

There had to be something he could do to get the money.

Would she love him if he had enough money to instantly pay off her debt from getting scammed, and give their baby everything he could possibly need or want?

More importantly…would she love him if he didn't?

Chapter Thirteen

LINDSAY HAD TRANSFORMED the kitchen table in Eric's—in *their*—home into wedding-planning central. Not for herself, not yet. For Megan, of course. Right now, Lindsay really needed to figure out some balance with her new work in the office, tentatively developing relationship with Eric inside of marriage, and the one thing she should've been focusing on that she'd practically forgotten about—Megan's wedding.

The wedding was next week. She'd only done a few things to prepare—talking to Megan that first night about what she envisioned, and she'd called around and gotten some quotes for catering.

It looked like they'd have to go all the way to Coeur d'Alene or Spokane to get a bunch of competition to compare prices with. One of the downfalls of living all the way up in Bear Creek Saddle.

But did she really miss Manhattan? Sure, you could get twenty different types of pizza from twenty different pizza shops, and have it all delivered. There were a gazillion restaurants all within walking distance from your front door. Shopping was out of this world. Whereas in Bear Creek Saddle, shopping was limited to Walmart and Cabela's for hunting gear.

To the town's credit, the mom-and-pop stores were really fun to shop, like Ginger's General Store. She wasn't going to find a Gucci bag there, but she could find huckleberry jam, and worms for the garden in a fridge in the back, and "that's almost as good," as Eric would say.

Lindsay chuckled to herself. She wrote down some names and numbers on a notepad, and called them all, never mentioning a wedding, just trying to get the cost to cater a chicken or fish dinner to fifty or so people.

Unless Bill and Allie at Freddie's Diner could handle the gig? They were guests too, obviously, but it wouldn't hurt to ask them.

She sighed, rubbing the bridge of her nose. Time was running out. And she really didn't want to tell Megan, a week before the wedding, that she'd given up and had to give Megan all the tasks to take care of.

That wouldn't be right.

Party-planning was something Lindsay had always enjoyed. Excelled at, even. They didn't need a venue—the ranch itself provided a beautiful backdrop. They could rent a tent, rent some chairs to line up for the rest of the wedding ceremony. Maybe a flower trellis to get married under. Lindsay started jotting down ideas, incorporating Megan's ideas from before. They could use the chairs that they had for the ceremony and bring them in under the huge tent along with some rented tables. She spent hours making phone calls, getting everything sorted.

The cake was the final thing.

"*Do you want to go taste testing with me for the wedding cake?*" Lindsay texted her sister, despite the late hour.

"*Sounds like so much fun!*" Megan texted back. "*I'd love to, but Zach's gotten it into his head to build a gazebo out back, so we can get married in it.*"

What do you think?"

Lindsay quickly texted a GIF of a little girl wriggling with excitement.

She put a line through her to-do list where it said "flower trellis," and in its place, wrote "flowers/bouquet/petals."

"*The gazebo sounds perfect,*" Lindsay texted back. "*Just position it in a place where the sun's not going to be in people's eyes or something. When he builds it, just try to figure out where the seating is gonna be, so there's room for chairs.*"

"*Got it. So I promised to help him build the gazebo tomorrow. Can you do the taste testing with Eric? He likes cake.*"

"*Question: style over substance, or substance over style?*"

"*Just make it yummy and put a cute topper on it, and I'll be happy.*"

Lindsay stood from the table and stretched. Cake tasting. That actually sounded like a lot of fun. As much as it was a bummer she couldn't go do that with her sister, it might be a fun "date" to have with Eric.

She went to the fridge to refill her water glass. Eric had stuck a note on the front with a magnet. Lindsay pulled it off and read his chicken-scratch handwriting:

> *Roses are red*
> *Violets are blue*
> *Can't write no fancy poem*
> *Just blessed I married you*

How sweet was that? Lindsay shook her head and giggled quietly. Well, her husband might not be the next poet laureate, but he'd certainly succeeded in making her smile.

Where was he, anyway?

Lindsay slowly walked through the small cabin. He wasn't in the kitchen, which she already knew, since she could see it from the table, near the living room. He wasn't in the bedroom taking a nap, and the bathroom door was open so… Maybe he stepped outside?

"Eric?" she called. "You in here?"

His voice came back from the guest room, where he'd been sleeping at night.

Every night.

"Come on in," he called.

The door was closed, so she knocked just to be sure, and pushed it open. The last few times this happened, she found him sitting on the edge of the bed with Boomer napping beside him, looking deep in thought (Eric looking deep in thought…not the dog).

Maybe Eric was thinking about them. Maybe he was praying.

Maybe he'd even been regretting getting married.

But this time when she opened the door, Eric had a tape measure in hand and was taking measurements of the room, jotting down notes on the back of a flyer offering an off-season clearance sale on snowplow attachments for trucks.

His fitted shirt sleeve stretched over his bicep as he pulled the measuring tape in, where it recoiled with a click. Eric looked up at her and grinned. "I was thinking we could put the crib over here."

Yes! She thought the word instead of saying it, but the huge smile on her face must've told him all he needed to know.

"We could put a changing table over here, the crib there, maybe a dresser over here… I have to anchor all this stuff to the walls, too. What kind of paint do you want, do you think?"

Lindsay took her invisible wedding-planning hat off, and put on her imaginary interior-design hat. "I was thinking a Noah's Ark theme—all the different animals two-by-two? They make wall decals and have sheets and curtains and stuff for that."

"That's a great idea," Eric said, nodding as he looked around the room to envision it. "And an animal theme would fit either a boy or girl. It's neutral."

"I'm having a boy." This was not the first time she'd told him that...he just didn't believe her—because how would she know?

Eric set down the tape measure, pencil and flyer and walked over to her in the middle of the room, taking both of her hands in his.

"Lindsay, I know you're excited to have a boy. But when we find out tomorrow, if for some reason it's a girl...I don't want you to be disappointed or something."

Megan shook her head. No way. "I won't be disappointed. I'd love to have a girl, maybe someday. But I just feel like this is a boy, so... we'll find out for sure with ultrasound, I guess."

"Just don't want you to be setting yourself up for disappointment, that's all."

Lindsay raised an eyebrow. "Do you know something I don't know, somehow?"

Eric paused. "Don't know nothing about the baby you don't know. Maybe I'm projecting a bit."

"Why? Did you want a girl over a boy?"

Eric shook his head. "I just want a healthy, happy kid. I don't care if it's a purple penguin. But...if we have a purple penguin, and I'm a grizzly bear, do you think a penguin would ever accept a bear as its father?"

What was going on?

"You lost me." She sat on the edge of the guest bed, and patted the spot next to her in front of a sleeping Boomer, who snored quietly and rhythmically. "Girls love their daddies just as much as boys do."

"That ain't what I meant." He sat next to her. "What if once our baby is born, he won't bond with me? What if he knows I'm not his real dad?"

Lindsay put her hand on his broad shoulder, feeling the heat of his muscular back through the thin cotton material. "Our baby will only ever know you as his father. From the moment he opens his eyes, he'll see you, and you're going to be the one who's there for him with me. We're going to co-parent, right?"

Eric nodded.

"So our baby's going to have Daddy helping changes diapers, Daddy helping give baths, Daddy helping put him to sleep, Daddy reading him a book, Daddy to roughhouse with, and you're going to be one of the very most important people in his life other than me. That's what babies are like."

Eric sat silently, seeming to absorb her words. "I suppose you're right."

Lindsay smiled tentatively. She had no idea that he had even harbored these concerns. "Our baby's going to love you. And bond with you. I'm sure of it. Are you worried you're not going to be able to love him as your true son? Is it possible that's where this is coming from?"

Her heart raced and her stomach flipped uncomfortably inside of her as she waited for him to speak. Was it a bad sign that he was taking a moment to think about it before answering?

God, give him peace, and Thy will be done. And give me some words, Lord, please.

"I adopted Boomer when he was just a pup," Eric said finally. He lay down on the bed, resting his dark hair against Boomer's back. "He's a great cuddler."

"Can I try?" Lindsay lay down on the other side of Boomer, the dog's warm body lying between them.

This must be why they had the phrase "a three-dog-night" for when it was really, really cold. Dogs were like little ovens, giving off heat at a much higher temperature than the human body. With three dogs, she could have one on each side, and one at her feet to keep her feet warm. Yes. That totally made sense.

As he spoke, Eric stared up, where thick log beams ran across the rafted ceiling, and leisurely rubbed Boomer's belly. "Boomer's a dog, not a human, and I still love him like family. That was my first thought to myself, when my brother suggested maybe I should adopt. So I figure a human baby...I'm bound to love him."

"I'll do my best not to have a purple penguin then." Lindsay giggled, rolling over onto her side to look at Eric's face.

At that point, Boomer had had it with the cuddling. The big dog groaned and got up, stretching as he slowly slinked off the bed and out of the nursery.

Eric rolled over and laughed. "You scared Boomer away," he chided playfully. "Who's going to cuddle me now?"

With no mountain of dog fur between them, suddenly, it was very apparent—she was lying on top of a twin-size bed with her husband.

Her husband whom she'd never slept with.

"Thank you for the poem."

"Anytime." He smiled.

Eric didn't make a move to pull her into him. He stayed on his side, looking at her eyes.

What would happen if they consummated their marriage now?

What would happen if they slept with each other before they were in love—before she knew if he loved her, especially—even though they were already married?

What if, after sleeping with her, he no longer wanted anything to do with her, the way Grant had done? Grant had been her friend for years. He was enough of a close friend to her she'd felt she could count on him to let her stay at his apartment—and she'd been right.

But sleeping together changed everything.

There were consequences to having sex, and she was living proof of that…as was the child growing inside of her.

"Grant hasn't even called me, or texted me," Lindsay whispered. "It's like he doesn't even care to find out how I'm doing, or if I even had the… procedure… done at all. You'd think he'd want to know if he had a kid out there in the world."

The soft look faded from Eric's eyes. "Why do you even care if Grant calls you or not?" he asked. "You're married to me now."

"That's not what I meant. I was thinking about us, and then I was just thinking about him, and—"

"That man wanted you to *kill your baby*, Lindsay. Our baby. Have you even thought about that, or have you just been secretly pining away this whole time?"

She'd ignore the "pining away" comment in the interest of not adding fuel to the fire. But is that what he really thought of her, just because she'd been honest enough to let him know what was on her mind?

"Of course I think about what he did. Every day. But he's still someone who was in my life for a long time, Eric. Someone I shared something very intimate with, and I guess I'm still…really shocked and hurt he walked away from it all. Grant doesn't even know where I am or what I'm doing. He has my phone number. It hasn't changed. Does he really not care if I've kept the baby and I'm going to give birth?"

"You've been thinking 'bout this for a while now."

"I've been thinking about a lot of things."

"Me too," Eric whispered. "I'm worried that, in your mind, Grant will always be your baby's father. And I will always be the guy on the outside, looking in."

He looked so distant from her now.

As if he wanted to look at anything other than her.

Lindsay didn't like seeing him pull away. It hurt. If she touched him now, would he jerk away from her in anger? Would he rebuff her advances?

She lay there on her side, staring at him as he stared at the wall. Maybe she should make a move, cuddle herself next to him, and just remind him that she was there for him, with him.

His wife.

But if he were to rebuke her advances, she might feel even further from him than ever.

The bridge they'd built between them would snap if the chasm grew any wider.

Could she handle that?

The easiest thing to do would be to walk away and close the door, leaving him to brood silently on his own.

Now that she'd felt the sting of rejection herself, the hurt hiding beneath Eric's distant behavior was clear—and there was nothing she could do about it.

Maybe… maybe this was how he felt all the time. About her. *Oh no.*

The realization hit her like a bag of cement.

She'd had one tiny taste of potential rejection, but for Eric…this whole time, he probably feared any move he made, any overture of affection, would be misconstrued as trying to coerce her.

And she'd been so fearful herself, she'd let him hold on to that. No wonder their relationship was disintegrating in front of her eyes. And their baby wasn't even born yet.

Lindsay took the plunge. Someone had to. She scooted closer to him on the bed, and rested her hand lightly on the back of his neck.

Eric turned and looked at her, his surprise at finding her so close evident on his handsome face.

"I'm glad I'm here with you," Lindsay said softly. "We have a unique situation. A unique marriage. But I wouldn't have married you if I didn't think that at some point it would go from a very odd situation to completely ordinary. Just another couple, together, happy, raising their family."

Without saying a word, Eric wrapped his arm around her back, pulling her close to him, and kissed her. His lips were firm and strong against hers, and she melted in his embrace.

Now they had what they didn't have in the courthouse weeks ago. They had privacy. They had time. They were married, and kissing each other on a bed in their own home.

But what if this ruined the true romantic friendship blooming between them? Would they ever be able to get it back?

Having sex with a man she didn't love had completely destroyed her life in Manhattan. She'd started to actually *like* Idaho, and if everything got messed up here with their marriage of convenience, she'd lose not only a husband, but also be out of a house and a job, and have no support to raise her baby.

Now that Eric had her in his arms, his gentle caresses and impassioned kiss had her wanting to throw caution to the wind and surrender to his touch.

Was she even ready? Her first time had definitely not been the amazing experience she'd been led to believe sex would be. Actually…it had hurt her, both physically and emotionally.

Did she even *want* to do it again?

Her cell phone buzzed insistently. Unknown New York number. Was it Grant? Perhaps all this arguing about him made his ears burn from all the way across the country.

She almost answered it. But if it was Grant calling now—of all inopportune times—it wasn't worth making Eric feel jealous over him. Grant didn't even know Eric existed.

It was time to change that.

She handed the phone to Eric. "You answer it for me."

The corner of his lips lifted in a cautious smile. He knew what she was trying to accomplish by giving him the call.

"Lindsay Hunt's phone. This is her husband, Eric."

His smile dropped as he listened for a moment. "Yup…She didn't know." Pause. "I'll take care of it."

He put the phone down, but didn't speak right away.

Was that Grant on the call? If not, who? Why were they calling her? Was it possibly just a telemarketer? Didn't sound like one. What did Eric say he'd take care of? And what didn't she know? Her instinct was to pepper him with questions.

But if she'd learned one thing from Eric, it was that sometimes not saying anything at all was the best way to get someone to speak freely. So she waited silently—it was probably ten seconds, but it felt like ages.

"That was a lawyer," he said finally. "Real...*not nice*." Eric was probably cleaning up the word he actually wanted to use. "Acting like you took people's money on purpose."

Her throat constricted. They'd never stop coming after her, until she could make financial amends. "I didn't know, Eric, I swear I didn't."

"I hate how they act like you're an accomplice or something. You were scammed, too."

She looked down at her phone on the bedspread. "But what I didn't know doesn't matter when it comes to justice. People still got hurt."

Eric took a deep breath and nodded. "I'll sell my truck, Linds. Still got real good mileage. That'll cover your debt."

"You can't!" Lindsay put her hand to her head. He loved his black pickup truck, and he used it for work. Why was he doing this for her, when *she wasn't even being a good wife?*

"I'd rather pay your debt an' get these guys off your back, and make it right for the people who lost money, than have a paid-off truck anyway."

"I don't deserve you," she whispered.

He gave her a sweet, tender kiss on her forehead. "Here's what I'm thinking—Jesus sacrificed His life to pay our debt. I think the least I can do is sacrifice my truck to pay yours."

* * *

Lindsay was happy to have Eric's hand to hold as they made

their way into the doctor's office.

Dr. Peterson looked down at the papers in front of him. "I see you changed your name." He sounded pleasantly surprised. "Mrs. Hunt—congratulations to you both."

Eric shook the doctor's hand with enthusiasm. "Thanks, Doc. I'm a lucky man."

Lindsay glanced at Eric and smiled. She felt like a very lucky woman. The last time they were sitting in this office, and she was frightened and worried about her baby, all she wanted was to not feel alone—for Eric to be the father of her child and her husband, so that the entire appointment could just be more... *normal.*

And now she had that. Her prayers had been answered.

So why did it feel like the whole thing was a big lie?

It shouldn't feel that way, though... Marriages of convenience used to be the only kind of marriage that existed, practically. And no one thought those couples' marriages were less than legit.

Which made her marriage just as valid as anyone else's.

Eric squeezed her hand as the doctor started the ultrasound, narrating as he went.

He pointed to the screen.

Wow! It was amazing how much her baby had grown in only four weeks. He definitely looked like a proper baby.

He...

Lindsay pointed to the screen. "Doctor, is that what I think it is?"

"Do you want to know?" he asked, with a twinkle in his eye.

"Yes," Lindsay and Eric said in unison. They looked at each other and laughed.

"You've got a good eye," Dr. Peterson said. "Looks like you've got yourself a baby boy. This is earlier than we thought it would be to be able to tell the baby's sex, but sometimes it's just really obvious if he's facing the right way, which he is. We're lucky to get a sneak peek."

Eric looked from the ultrasound screen back to Lindsay with his jaw dropped. "How did you know?" he asked. "She's been calling the baby a boy from the beginning," he told the doctor.

"I don't know how I knew," she said, shrugging. "I just knew. Feels like a boy."

"Well, she does have a fifty-fifty chance of getting it right or wrong either way," the doctor said, nudging Eric. "But whenever a woman says something about her own body, it's best to believe her."

"Good advice," Eric said.

Even though she'd been calling her baby a "he" all this time, it was awesome to be vindicated. She could just picture him, with chubby little cheeks. Would he have her dark brown hair, or Grant's lighter brown hair?

For Eric's sake, she prayed he had dark hair, to match his own.

God, how the baby looks is up to You. But if it's possible to make him look more like my husband than Grant to spare Eric's feelings, that would be amazing.

She was being selfish. It didn't matter what the baby looked like, did it? Eric knew what he was getting into...it wasn't like he wasn't aware the baby wouldn't carry his genetic DNA.

Okay, God, forget that. Just make him healthy, that's all I ask.

After she'd gotten dressed and they were about to leave, Dr. Peterson touched Eric's forearm as they were about to walk out the door.

"Lindsay, do you mind if I borrow your husband for a moment? He can meet you in the waiting room."

* * *

Back at the house after the doctor and a follow-up trip to the bakery about Megan and Zach's wedding cake, Eric carefully made two sandwiches while Lindsay was resting—if you could call going through paperwork on her laptop while lying on her back "relaxing," which for some reason, she did.

Maybe because her feet were up?

"Turkey and cheese," he said. "The baby needs to be made out of more than just cake."

"Only his cheeks will be made out of wedding cake." She laughed. "I'll use the turkey and cheese to fill out his legs."

"Sounds good. You get on that."

Eric couldn't get over the fact they were really having a son. How had she always been so sure? Either way, he was thrilled. It would be great to have a boy to play with his brother's boy. Idaho was a great place to run around and explore as a kid.

"Hey." Eric swallowed a bite of the sandwich. "Did you have any names in mind?"

"I…I've basically been calling him 'Little One' in my mind. I don't have a name yet. Do you?"

Eric shook his head slowly. "But I was thinking, maybe I could name him. I'd like to name him."

"What if I don't like the name?"

Eric frowned. Why would he choose a bad name she wouldn't like?

"It's something I could contribute, at least, if I got to name him," he admitted.

Lindsay set her sandwich down half-eaten. She put her hand on his arm. "Eric, of course you've contributed to this child. You're literally contributing everything *except* for some chromosomes. Who cares where the DNA came from? You're the one who's with me for these appointments. You'll be there when he is born. You're going to be the man our little boy looks at and says 'Daddy, Daddy!'" A smile came across her face as she said the words. "You don't need to feel disconnected from our child."

She was right. Of course she was right.

But… why was there still that tiny part of him questioning it?

"Eric…" Lindsay whispered, "think about it… You find out you can't have children naturally, and even though God has literally answered your prayer with a vision of our family together right when you thought you'd never have one, and now *here I am, your pregnant wife*—it's almost like Satan's still poking little needles into you every now and then. Trying to tell you how your child is somehow not yours, even though you…you *have to know by now*— no matter how he came to be—he's yours."

Eric looked at her. That was exactly what it felt like. How had she grown to know him so well, to know what was in his heart and mind?

"It's dumb of me to have thoughts like that. I know. Don't know why I even let 'em take up space in my head."

"Eric…you don't need to listen to that voice. That voice trying to pull us apart after we married with God as our witness…after God's given us exactly what we each had been praying for…that voice turning you from our baby *is not of God*."

Whoa.

She was right.

It could be the enemy taunting him about whether or not he'd feel connected to this baby, simply because he wasn't biologically Eric's blood.

Did it stand to reason the biological drive to breed, and pass on one's own genetics, was so deeply ingrained he wouldn't be able to work past it?

If that was going to be the case... Eric clenched his jaw. *No.* It couldn't be.

He wouldn't let it.

Love for a child was a choice. And he chose to love that baby, to die for that baby if he had to.

That baby was his son.

Chapter Fourteen

"A cord of three strands is not quickly broken."
Ecclesiastes 4:12 (NIV)

THE DAY HAD finally arrived for Megan and Zach's wedding, and the early summer weather was perfect for an outdoor wedding. It was a big day for Lindsay, as well, simply because this was her sister, and her best friend. Eric was almost as excited about it as Lindsay was, since he was Zach's best man.

It was funny to consider how, even if Lindsay hadn't shown up early to Idaho (and pregnant), she and Eric would still have found themselves walking down the aisle together, her as Megan's maid of honor, and Eric as the best man.

They would have been placed into each other's lives either way.

But the way it had turned out, Lindsay was now the "matron of honor" instead of a "maid of honor." That was a good thing, considering there was no hiding her baby-bump anymore, no matter what she wore.

Lindsay arranged the back of Megan's wedding dress so the fabric swirled like in a wedding magazine.

"You look beautiful." Lindsay stepped back with an approving nod. "*Ravishing.*"

"Ravishing?" Megan giggled. "You totally stole that word. Dad used to say Mom looked 'ravishing,' remember?"

Lindsay laughed. Yes. She'd definitely borrowed that word from their father.

Megan stared at herself in the full-length mirror hanging off of the back of Zach's bedroom door, where they were getting dressed.

"I just wish mom could be here." Megan looked up at the ceiling and fluttered her eyelashes. "I better stop talking like this, I don't want to cry."

Lindsay smiled wistfully, even as her heart twisted. Though it had been two years since their mother had passed, it was hard not to get emotional on an important day like today.

So why hadn't she gotten sad about Mom not being able to be at her own marriage ceremony?

Because it hadn't felt…real. Not like this.

"Zach is going to be stunned when he sees you," Lindsay said, trying to change the subject—to lighten the mood so Megan wouldn't cry.

But Megan was having none of it. "At least Mom has a good reason for not being here." She turned away from the mirror and looked sideways at Lauren. "Dad has no such excuse."

Their father hadn't been the same since their mother died. It was one of the reasons Lindsay feared giving herself fully to Eric—because *all* relationships had to end, one way or another.

Till death do you part.

As much as it hurt to see their dad move from New York to London—away from the walk-up apartment they grew up in, away from their friends, and from every location that reminded him of his wife of over thirty years—he'd jumped at the chance to take a job thousands of miles away. But Lindsay and Megan were both grown women living on their own when their mother passed. And he had to do what was best for him.

"I don't know why I thought he was going to come this time." Lindsay shook her head.

Was Dad being cowardly, by not facing his fear of pain from the loss?

Or was *Lindsay* being cowardly, by not even allowing herself to risk what she'd seen her father go through?

Megan sighed. "He said it was work but…" She waved her hands, her normally bare fingertips now gleaming with a French manicure. "I think that seeing me in a wedding dress would remind him of when he and Mom got married."

"That could be it," Lindsay agreed. "But we are not going to let this ruin your big day."

Megan squared her shoulders and lifted her chin a notch.

Lindsay looked over her shoulder in the mirror and grinned. "That's more like it, Meg."

Megan smiled back at her sister. "I can't believe Zach and I are finally getting married."

Lindsay laughed. "Finally? It really hasn't been that long of an engagement."

"Well, less time than you and Eric had, at least."

Lindsay raised an eyebrow at her sister, but smiled and shook her head.

There was a knock on the bedroom door. "Megan, honey? It's just me."

Sounded like Zach's mom.

"Come on in," Megan called.

"Oh my goodness." Mrs. Walker closed the door behind her and put her hand to her heart. "My daughter-in-law is gorgeous."

Megan leaned in and air-kissed her on the cheek, to avoid getting lipstick on her. "You know my sister, Lindsay Hunt, right?"

"Of course. We spent some time gabbing on the phone!" Zach's mother gave Lindsay a knowing smile. "Eric's secret bride. Welcome to the family."

She liked that—Eric's secret bride. It made eloping and not inviting any of their friends or family sound romantic.

But there was definitely something to be said for a big wedding ceremony like Megan and Zach were having today. Something that wasn't a secret at all.

Was it the secrecy making her feel as if she wasn't truly married yet?

"Thank you." Lindsay shook her hand with two of her own.

Mrs. Walker took Megan's hand, her eyes tearing up. "I know you're probably sad your mama in heaven can't be here today. But she's watching over you, know that."

"Thank you," Megan and Lindsay said in unison.

It was a comforting thought.

"And while I can never replace your mother—and I'd never try—as Zach's mom…well, I'm yours now, too. That's how I feel, and I hope you feel the same way. Anytime you ever want to talk, or if you need anything, I'm here for you."

Megan embraced the woman, and Lindsay took a step back, feeling…what? A little left out, maybe.

But that was silly. This was Megan's mother-in-law on her

wedding day. They were supposed to have moments like this.

Megan's day had nothing to do with Lindsay's own experience of getting married. Because Megan was getting married for real, for true love.

Lindsay had gotten married for her child's sake. And right now, her priorities were God first, baby second. Her baby was everything, and she was going to give him everything she could—including a loving father.

Her internal pep talk worked. Lindsay smiled as the two women hugged.

Her phone buzzed with a text from Eric.

"I hate to interrupt," Lindsay said softly. "Everyone's here."

"*It's go-time for the bride!*" Eric texted. "*Bring her out so we can get these two lovebirds hitched.*"

Lindsay showed her phone to Megan, who giggled nervously.

"I can't believe this is happening." Megan took a deep breath, and held out her trembling hands.

Lindsay handed her the bouquet of deep shades of purple flowers and baby's breath, wrapped in white satin to match her dress. "When you're holding the bouquet, no one will notice your hands are shaking."

Megan nodded resolutely and held the bouquet. "I can do this."

Would the day ever arrive when Lindsay could say the same thing?

* * *

Eric stood toward the back of the lawn where they'd set up dozens of chairs for their guests. The gazebo Zach and Megan had built—mostly Zach, from what he knew—looked awesome. It fit so perfectly on the two acres Zach had landscaped as his backyard, it was hard to believe it ever hadn't been there.

The gazebo was strong and sturdy, and stained to match the log cabin. It would be there for generations to come.

Maybe their baby would grow up to get married under that gazebo, someday.

Lindsay had done a great job setting up the area for a wedding. It looked just like the wedding pics she'd been poring over on Pinterest. The chairs she'd rented had fancy purple covers on them, because Megan had chosen a lavender color scheme or something like that.

All sorts of purple flowers were at the base of the gazebo, and a few tall tables with matching tablecloths and pitchers of iced tea, lemonade, and glasses were spread out for when guests got thirsty sitting outside—though it wasn't overly hot yet, in early June. Lindsay had even set up a little sign, should they need it, pointing guests toward the bathroom inside the house.

Smart lady, his wife.

Still felt so strange to call her that. But that's what she was.

A little ways toward the side, a huge tent was set up with tiny white lights strung on the inside. He couldn't see the lights now, with the sun shining down, but after sunset it should really be something.

Even though Bill and Allie were catering from Freddy's Diner, Eric had insisted Bill make sure they hire other people to do all the work, so they could just enjoy being guests. Bill was like a father to Eric, Zach and the guys—even though he was only in his mid-forties. They'd been working on the ranch for him since they were kids together. It was only when Bill found Allie that he ended up leaving the ranch and selling it to them.

But they hadn't told Bill what was going on with the finances. Eric didn't want Bill to think he'd made a huge mistake selling the ranch to them.

But maybe Bill could give them some insight into how to do it right....

No. It wasn't fair to burden Bill with their troubles.

It was their own fault for getting into a mess in the first place. They should have known they couldn't just go from being ranch hands to owning a complex business and not make any changes to their behavior and what they did.

It was obvious enough now...and Eric wanted to kick himself for it. If he told Bill, maybe Bill would do the kicking for him.

He scanned the crowd. Lots of people from church; Bill sat right in the front with Allie. Everyone was dressed to the nines— lots of dress cowboy hats, nice boots without a speck of mud on them, pretty dresses and carefully curled hair.

The pastor stood on the gazebo with Zach.

He was a lucky man, Zach. He knew his wife loved him, and he loved her back. Zach also knew his wife was going to sleep with him, so that was a bonus.

Must be nice.

Eric sighed. It wasn't right to be jealous.

Lindsay hadn't been able to find a live band or harpist, which for some reason she wanted. But they had one of the girls from church in charge of pressing play on the music, and the sound system with speakers set up on each side was good enough that it sounded great anyway. Megan had already made playlists with enough music to play all night long. Knowing Zach, he'd probably bring his guitar out at some point to serenade her, too. He was good like that.

A chord sounded as the music turned on.

Eric turned toward the door to the house, and Lindsay came out in her long dress, the color of lilacs, and waved at him.

Lindsay smiled and nodded toward the woman from church who'd offered her four-year-old granddaughter as a flower girl—a sweet golden-haired child named Pammy.

"Go on, sweetheart," Lindsay told the little girl. "Just like we practiced."

Pammy walked down the aisle, dropping purple rose petals on the way from her little white basket. Lots of "awwws" in the crowd. She was so adorable. Everyone's phones came out as they clicked away to capture the moment.

Lindsay came over to him and took his arm.

"You look amazing," Eric whispered. "You're going to upstage the bride." He winked at her. Not because he didn't think it was true, but because Lindsay wouldn't *want* it to be true. She was a good sister, and really wanted today to be Megan's day.

Lindsay smiled, her face relaxing a bit. "You look really good, too."

Eric had needed to buy a new suit for the occasion. Hopefully he'd get to use it again when he and Lindsay renewed their vows at some point.

When she loved him.

There was no hiding her baby bump, though she'd tried with the billowy lilac dress material and a strategically placed sash. The rest of her was thin enough that her rounded belly would've looked out of place if she hadn't been pregnant…so surely people were noticing.

No one had mentioned it yet, though.

That was probably just good manners—not mentioning a pregnancy until the woman announces it. And he knew Lindsay didn't feel comfortable enough making announcements like that to everyone in church or at a party like this.

For some reason, she acted like she still didn't fit in here in Bear Creek Saddle.

Did she not want to fit in? Did it not fit her identity as a Manhattan exec?

Maybe that wasn't even her identity anymore. Did she feel she'd failed somehow, to go from being a well-off Manhattan banking executive to being a wife and mom on a ranch in north Idaho?

Maybe he'd ruined her life… maybe she'd let him ruin her life, for their baby's sake.

Lindsay gently squeezed his arm, and they walked forward together, smiling at everyone they saw. They took their places next to the gazebo.

The first chords of "Here Comes the Bride" began to play, and everyone stood and turned. Zach's mother would be giving Megan away, since her dad had bailed, and Zach's father was out of the picture.

Zach had turned out okay. Great, even. Maybe if Eric had never married Lindsay, and she'd had the kid on her own, her kid would turn out great too.

Eric was sure of it, in fact.

But…if he hadn't been there to marry her, Lindsay may've given up her child for adoption to a married couple. Maybe it was because she'd lost her mom, and felt that having her dad alive was like a backup of some sort.

But if a father moves across the ocean and never visits, it's not much of a backup.

Not like a father and mother were interchangeable, anyway. They each contributed something different yet equally important when it came to child-rearing. He knew that from watching his own parents, and those of his friends.

Megan appeared in her wedding dress, holding on to Mrs. Walker's arm.

Eric turned and looked at his best friend. Zach was grinning from ear to ear—pure joy on his face.

When Megan reached the gazebo, the pastor addressed the guests.

"Please be seated."

Everyone sat—they were accustomed to following Pastor Jim's instructions at church, and this didn't seem much different, except with it being outside, of course.

"We are gathered here today, the family and friends of Zachary Walker and Megan Moore, to witness their joining in holy matrimony. Praise God."

A few people in the crowd said "Amen!"

"I've gotten the opportunity to know both Megan and Zach better over the past couple months," Pastor Jim said. "When Zach told me how he prayed for God to give him a wife, and then, *boom!* he meets Megan, I could see clear as day—God wants us to *know* this union is His doing."

The pastor looked at the bride and groom before continuing. "I hope you both continue to be part of our church family. Life will get busy now that you're taking on the responsibilities of being a spouse. God willing, you'll even be parents at some point. Busy,

busy! And time will *fly by*. Just don't let life be too busy to nurture your relationship with each other, and most importantly...with God."

Lindsay would definitely agree with everything the pastor said, as Eric did. God first, above anything and everything. That was one of those values and life goals they'd agreed on as a basis for their marriage.

Surely with the same values and life goals for all the big things, the little things could work themselves out?

But love, and trust, weren't really little things...

"In marriage," Pastor Jim was saying, "as in life—you've got good days and bad. What's special about marriage, however, is now you have a partner to work with you and to help see you through it. One strand alone can be easily broken. Two strands—Zach and Megan together—is stronger that one on its own. But a cord made of *three* strands—that's Zach and Megan with God added to the relationship—cannot be easily broken."

Another "Amen!" from someone in the crowd.

The pastor smiled at the couple. "Are you ready?"

They both nodded, with those smiles of theirs lighting up the gazebo.

Zach took a small folded sheet of paper from his inner coat pocket. The pastor was using a small handheld mic, and he handed it to Zach, so everyone could hear. Being outside, the sounds of the ranch and the slight breeze in the air would've made it hard to hear in the back without it.

Zach cleared his throat. He looked a bit nervous. But then he looked out at the crowd, and then he looked at his bride, and took a breath.

"Megan—on the first day we met, I saw you in a gas station when you first came to Bear Creek Saddle, and I learned that you are beautiful. On the second day we met, you punched me in the nose, and I learned that you are strong."

Laughs from the audience. Everyone had heard that story by now. There'd been a bit of a misunderstanding about Zach's intentions when he'd tried to save Megan from a bear who'd wandered too close to her camp.

Zach grinned. "And from then on, each day that I saw you, I learned something new. I'm still learning new things about you, and I'm falling even deeper into love with you every day. I can't wait to spend the rest of my life with you."

He folded the paper and put it away.

Megan smiled, and gently wiped under one of her eyes. She'd probably gotten a little weepy at his words and was worried about her mascara running, the way Lindsay did sometimes.

She also had her vows written down. Lindsay had practiced them with her the night before.

"Zach, I'm so blessed you didn't write me off completely after I punched you in the face."

Everyone laughed—including Eric—and Megan looked up from her written vows, grinning out at their guests. "I had no idea he was going to mention that in his vows, too!"

Megan laughed and went back to her notes, written in tiny lettering on an index card.

"You are exactly the man I want to be with forever. I respect your skills as a rancher and craftsman, and your ability to take charge of any situation and lead. And, as you know, I absolutely adore when you play the guitar for me."

People in the audience clapped, since Zach often played worship music at church on Sundays, so everyone was familiar with his talents there.

"I love you so much, I don't even have the right words to express it. Thank you for everything. I love you."

Those were really sweet vows. Eric looked over at Lindsay, who was wiping her eyes just as her sister had done.

The pastor took the microphone back from Megan. "That was lovely," he said. "Zach, please place the ring on Megan's left-hand ring finger and repeat after me. 'With this ring, I thee wed, in love and truth…'"

Zach repeated the same words that Eric had said to Lindsay in the courthouse.

Then it was Megan's turn, and she did the same, her delicate hands trembling as she slipped the ring on Zach's finger.

There was definitely something to be said for saying vows in front of their entire community. Standing in front of everyone and proclaiming that you were married under God was a much stronger statement than doing it quietly, privately, where no one would even have to know if they didn't want them to.

Maybe they really should have just waited to get married, until they both felt it was truly right. Even if the wedding included a toddler.

But then they wouldn't have been able to live together for the first year or so of the baby's life, and that was important to Lindsay.

It was important to Eric, too. So much bonding and relationship-building happens between a baby and his parents in that first, crucial year.

"I have an important question, now, for each of you," Pastor

Jim said. "Ready?"

Eric caught Lindsay's gaze across the gazebo.

"Zach, do you take Megan as your lawfully wedded wife, to have and to hold, in sickness and health, for richer or poorer, to love and cherish, as long as you both shall live?"

Zach looked at Megan. "I do."

"And do you, Megan, take Zachary as your lawfully wedded husband, to have and to hold, for richer and poor, in sickness and health, to love and respect…as long as you both shall live?"

"I do," Megan said.

"I now pronounce you man and wife." Pastor Jim smiled widely. "Zach, you may kiss the bride."

Zach pulled Megan in close to him, and as he planted a big kiss on her lips, everyone stood and cheered.

It was a beautiful moment. One they'd all surely remember forever. Cameras clicked—photos for the wedding album.

But Eric and Lindsay would have no wedding album.

Why was it so important to Eric to tell the world that Lindsay was his wife, the way Zach was doing today?

Chapter Fifteen

AT THE RECEPTION in the big white tent afterwards, as everyone danced around the happy bride and groom, Lindsay couldn't take her eyes off her own husband. Eric looked so handsome.

During the ceremony, Lindsay had been completely focused on making sure everything went off without a hitch, and that Megan was taken care of.

But now that everyone was under the big tent, grabbing food buffet-style and finding their reserved seats at the big round tables, it was finally time to eat and enjoy herself, too. They were all sitting together with Chris, Jay, Eric's parents, along with Zach's mom, and Eric's brother Ryan and his pregnant wife, Tiffany.

Her new brother and sister-in-law.

Megan and Zach sat with them as well, so this was definitely the "cool" table to be at. The only thing missing was their own father. And their mother…

But a wedding was no time for mourning—the atmosphere was jubilant. Half of the area under the tent was reserved for dancing, though the thought of dancing with all those people watching made her stomach flip with unease.

Lindsay only knew how to dance alone to songs she liked. Even then, she probably looked ridiculous. But at least no one was around to witness it.

Before they went to get their food, Eric wrapped his arm around Lindsay's waist and brought her over to their table.

"You did a great job with planning this, Linds." He gestured around the tent. "Look at it all."

"Thanks. I'm almost amazed we pulled it off." She glanced over to the buffet. "We better go get a plate before it's all gone— I'm half-starved. Want me to get you a plate of food, too?"

He shook his head. "You've been on your feet all day. I'll get you a plate."

He was right—she had been on her feet all day. She didn't dare look down at her ankles, because they'd probably be swollen at this point in the early evening. That never happened before she got pregnant, but it did now.

She'd take him up on his offer.

"Thank you, sweetie." She gave him a delicate kiss on his cheek.

It felt so natural to do, showing him affection, even calling him "sweetie." But was she laying it on a little thick, just to show his parents that their son hadn't made a mistake, or was she behaving the way she would tonight anyway, if they'd been alone?

It was difficult even for Lindsay to tell.

The rest of the reception went by in a blur. Lindsay got a chance to talk to Eric's sister-in-law, who was due that winter, just like Lindsay. It was good to be able to relate on that level. Ryan looked just like his little brother Eric, although Eric was even better-looking (if that was possible), in her own opinion.

Maybe she was a bit biased.

Megan and Zach looked so happy together. Everyone at the

party swung by their table to wish the new couple well, and it was also a great opportunity for Lindsay to meet any of the people she hadn't officially met before.

There were a lot of them.

Every single one of them seemed as if they lived in a world that was out of her reach.

A close-knit, comfortable, loving world. Everyone loved their husbands and knew they were loved back. No one was scared to death of having a baby; no one held the private shame of nearly aborting their child or considering giving him up for adoption.

No one else lived in a reality where they had married someone for convenience because they needed to be taken care of.

No... Lindsay was alone in that world. And as much as she wanted to fit in with everyone in Bear Creek Saddle, she wasn't very good at it.

She couldn't even take care of her own household. She couldn't ride a horse. She had no clue how to garden, or bake a cake without using a box mix, or homeschool her children—which it seemed half of the people there did. She didn't know how to do *anything* the way people did it in Idaho.

And what was worse, people who heard she came from Manhattan seemed simultaneously fascinated and disturbed. The people of northern Idaho didn't appear to hold warm and fuzzy thoughts for city folks—especially elite Manhattanites. When they thought of New York City, they thought of huge skyscrapers, Times Square, Wall Street, and crime.

Skyscrapers like the original Tower of Babel. The fallen city of Babylon itself, perhaps.

But when Lindsay thought of New York City, she thought of

skyscrapers, yes, but in a good way. Buildings that scraped the sky! Lights everywhere. The place where you'd never be alone, because there were always other people around. Any kind of cuisine you could ask for or think of, including types of foods you'd never've considered before. All sorts of culture and diversity. Museums of all kinds. Parks, especially Central Park. Anything you could want, you could find it in the Big Apple—twenty-four hours a day, seven days a week.

It was a big difference between New York and Bear Creek Saddle, Idaho.

Would she ever fit in here?

Was she just kidding herself?

Maybe it doesn't matter.

Idaho was where her only family was now. Idaho was where Megan and Zach were. Her husband, of course. Her mother-in-law; father-in-law. And her brother-in-law, and sister-in-law, and soon she'd have a new nephew born. She'd gone from having no family other than Megan and her father off in London…to being surrounded by family.

This was a blessing. And it was the perfect environment to raise a happy little boy.

No matter what, she was going to make this work—for her Little One.

Maybe someday, she'd feel like she fit in. A square peg in a town of round holes. Maybe after a while, her edges would wear off a bit, and she'd be able to settle into one of those round holes herself. A square didn't have to be square, if you took the corners off.

So which parts of her would have to go, before she could fit in?

* * *

Eric's chest tightened as he opened a window to let in the clear summer night air, and took a seat on the couch in their living room. Though they'd been blessed with good weather for Megan and Zach's wedding a few weeks ago, it had been getting warmer and warmer the last few days. He wanted to make a fire in the fireplace to set a romantic mood and put Lindsay at ease, but it was too hot.

The cheery glow of the flames would do little to brighten the topic Lindsay had broached, anyway.

She sat on the loveseat, catty-corner to where he sat on the couch. When he looked at her he saw everything beautiful and good. He saw his wife, and his child within her.

What if Grant took that away from him?

"Grant doesn't even know you never had the abortion," Eric said slowly. "He hasn't texted you or called you. You said it yourself—he doesn't care at all about how you're doing. So why even bother letting him know?"

"It's been over four months without a word from him or to him," Lindsay said. "We're married now, and we're having this child together. Grant needs to know that. It's his baby, too."

No.

It was *not* Grant's baby, too. It was Eric's own baby. He felt that in his gut, in his soul.

Grant should not have any part of that. All Grant had wanted was a dead baby. So why give him a chance at fatherhood now, when their son had a father who actually loved him and wanted him, in Eric?

But as much as Eric seethed, he couldn't find a way to put into words his jumbled emotions. He stared at Lindsay, his lips tightening into a grim line.

"We're going to need Grant to sign the adoption paperwork," she said, crossing her legs beneath her. "I looked into it, and you can't legally adopt a child until after he's born. But if we want that to happen on the day I give birth, we need to get everything set up ahead of time—including getting Grant to sign agreeing to that."

"But he doesn't even know," Eric said. "We're married. We could just put my name on the birth certificate. Nobody would question it. We're just a married couple, having a child together."

"I understand what you're getting at," Lindsay said. "And while it's true in spirit, it's not true *technically*."

"And then what happens when our son is born?" Eric couldn't sit still. He fought the urge to stand, to pace.

He rolled his hands into fists to keep himself from cracking his knuckles.

"Why don't we find out what other couples have done?" Eric asked. "I bet if we'd used a sperm donor, or if you had used an egg donor, for example—you wouldn't put the name of the donor on the birth certificate. Especially since they're usually all anonymous. It would be the intended parents' names on the birth certificate."

"But he's not anonymous, Eric. *We know who he is.* And at some point, if we're honest with our child about where he came from, he's going to have questions. He'll figure it out the moment he does any genetic testing service online. It's already becoming common—imagine how common it will be when our child is older."

She had a point.

But he didn't want Grant's name on their son's birth certificate. The same birth certificate that he'd need to get a Social Security number, or his passport—a birth certificate was something that they would have to save forever.

He didn't want Grant Bowland's name *defacing* it. Not after how he treated Lindsay. Not after what he wanted to do to his own child.

"What if we talk to Grant," Eric said, "and we asked him if he'd be okay with my name being on the birth certificate?"

Lindsay paused, as if she were unsure. "I–I guess that would be fine... I mean, if Grant is willing to sign away his parental rights, he'd probably be willing to not be a part of any aspect of our child's life. Including on the birth certificate. But he'll still need to sign the adoption papers."

The fist clenched inside Eric's chest relaxed slightly. Okay. That could work.

"It's not that I don't want our boy to know the truth, Linds. You're right...he'll find out at some point anyway, so he may as well grow up knowing. It'll just be a part of him, and not some big secret." Eric sighed. "But what if Grant has a change of heart? What if he wants our child in his life simply because it's his genetic offspring?"

Lindsay shook her head. "It's a risk we'll have to take. Ultimately, our son is ours. He'll grow up calling *you* Daddy, not Grant. And if and when he does meet Grant, he'll know that he's his biological father, but that you are his *real* dad. The dad who counts."

Eric smiled tentatively. Her words gave him hope. Hope that maybe everything would be okay. Just the thought of their baby growing, becoming a cute little toddler, one who lifted his chubby arms in the air and asked for his daddy...

Asked for *him*.

He swallowed hard around the lump forming in his throat.

Lindsay stood and took the few steps over to where he sat, and without hesitation, sat on his lap.

"Hi." He looked up at her face in surprise. She'd never sat on his lap before.

It was an intimate gesture—something a wife would do.

Maybe she was beginning to see herself as he saw her. As his wife. For real, and not just for the baby's sake.

"Hi," she said back softly.

And then, ever so gently… Lindsay pressed her lips against his own.

Her kiss took his breath away.

Yes—maybe things could be okay, after all.

All they needed was for Grant to get on board. To give up his parental rights to their child.

But what if he wouldn't? Would they have to take him to court?

How far was Eric willing to go to save his family?

Chapter Sixteen

LINDSAY WRAPPED HER cardigan around her. With summer coming to a close now, it was getting chillier out. Some of the trees were losing their leaves. The kids in town who weren't homeschooled would soon be getting back on yellow school busses every morning.

Summer had flown by, probably because there was so much to do on top of working on the business during haying season. The Kootenai County Fair had been awesome. Maybe when their son was older, he'd want to join the 4H club and raise a pig or a rooster to showcase at the fair like those other little kids had done.

Did they even have experiences like that for kids in Manhattan?

The more time she spent in Bear Creek Saddle, the firmer her conviction that she was doing the right thing by her baby when she'd committed to stay.

The trips to the river with Eric, her sister and Zach had been amazing, but as Lindsay's belly got bigger, she had less and less of a desire for adventure. Right now, she was in full-on nesting mode, doing everything she could to get the nursery ready, and even baby-proofing the house.

With a trembling hand, she took her phone off the counter where it was charging. Time was getting short—there was no way to keep putting this off.

She'd been dreading this moment since she first told the cab driver to go to the airport instead of the women's clinic, so many months ago.

Six months. Six months with no contact at all from Grant.

Was he even aware she hadn't gone through with the abortion?

What had he done with the few personal items she'd left at his apartment? Thrown them out?

One would think he would've texted her nonstop, waiting for her confirmation that she'd done the deed. Given him a Get-Out-Of-Jail-Free card on their massive mishap.

But he'd said nothing.

And neither had she.

How could she even begin to compose a text message to him, after all this time? And what if he didn't reply?

But he *had* to respond. This was his baby, too.

Lindsay left the "To" field empty, so she wouldn't send the message by accident before she was ready. And in the message field, she wrote:

"I'm sorry I did not reach out before, although to be fair… Neither did you." Half-frown emoji. *"I never had the abortion, so I figured I should tell you I'm having the baby."* Baby emoji.

No, that was like rubbing it in. She deleted the baby emoji. Was there a GIF she could add that would better suit her message?

No.

This wasn't going to work.

She couldn't text him. This was too much information for a simple text.

Lindsay deleted the text, unsent.

It would be more appropriate to call him. But would he even pick up the phone when he saw her number?

Only one way to find out. If Grant wouldn't answer the phone, she'd mail him a certified letter.

At least she knew where he lived.

The line was ringing. She didn't want him to pick up, but she did, too—speaking to him was the only way to get this whole thing over with.

"Grant Bowland." His voice came through clearly.

Why had he answered it like that, when he knew it was her calling? Or was she not even in his contacts list anymore?

"Hi Grant, it's me… Lindsay Moore. Sorry it's been a while."

"Lindsay!" He did sound surprised. He must've deleted her from his contacts after all.

That was weird… She would've thought he'd keep her in there, if only to be able to block her number for some reason. But to just delete her from his contacts, as if she was deleted from his life? Really?

"Yeah…" Grant said, once he'd found his composure. "I'm sorry I haven't been in touch. I should've called you and checked to see how you're doing after the…um…"

"Abortion?" she asked coldly.

"Yes." He paused, and cleared his throat. "Honestly, I'd thought you planned to come back to my place after and rest. You left your stuff here."

"I ended up going to my sister's house instead."

"I didn't even know you had a sister," he said, sounding confused.

"You met her at my birthday party a while back," Lindsay said.

As much as she wanted to dislike him for forgetting Megan even existed, she couldn't blame him. When you meet so many people at so many parties, the names and faces just blurred together after an hour or so. It had happened to her when she lived in Manhattan, too. You met people you'd never see again, like ships passing in the night.

It was different in Bear Creek Saddle. Her high school in New York had twice as many people as the population of the entire town. When she met someone here, she saw them again and again.

It was nice.

"If you could've stayed with your sister," Grant asked, "why were you staying with me to begin with?"

Lindsay sighed. "I've been asking myself that too. I guess I just wasn't ready to tell her I was essentially homeless. She's in Idaho, anyway. So… it was a long way to travel."

"You traveled all the way to Idaho right after having a surgical procedure?"

Well, at least he sounded concerned. Sort of.

"That's what I'm calling you about, Grant." She took a deep breath. Squared her shoulders. "I couldn't go through with it. I'm still pregnant, and I'm keeping the baby."

Silence on the other end of the phone.

"Grant? You still there?"

"I'm here."

"Say something." Every nerve in Lindsay's body was on edge. What on earth was going through Grant's mind right now?

"This is unfair, Lindsay. We made a deal." He paused, sighing heavily. "How do I even know if it's mine? I want a DNA test."

Unbelievable.

She'd been a virgin, and he *knew* that. He knew that for a fact. How could he ask her for a DNA test to prove it was his baby? She'd only ever slept with him.

"I'm not asking for you to take responsibility for a child you never wanted," she said finally. "I don't want child support. I don't want your money. I just want you to sign the contract giving up your parental rights so my husband can adopt this baby, and can be the father you don't want to be."

Lindsay covered her mouth with her fingertips. It was all out now. What if he said no? Why had she said it so rudely? She should have at least been nice, given it to him with a little sweetness, bit by bit. Instead she'd just thrown it all out there.

"Your—you have a husband?" he asked. "Since when?"

"I moved to Idaho, I met my brother-in-law's best friend, we hit it off... and we got married. And he wants to be my baby's father. He wants his name on the birth certificate; he wants to adopt him the moment he's born. But since I know the truth, that you are the biological father—"

"Wait—are you saying your husband doesn't know?"

"He definitely knows. I told him everything. There are no secrets. I know you don't want to send child support, or have custody of this baby... Right? That's not even an issue for you, right?"

Grant seemed to be thinking. Why was he taking so long?

"Grant... Are you still there?"

"Yes, Lindsay. I'm just... I'm not ready for a child. At some point... Yeah. At some point I'll get married, have kids. But not now. So—besides, aren't you living in Idaho?"

"Yes. North Idaho, not too far from Canada. It's a long way off from Manhattan."

"Well… I'm glad you found someone who wants to be with you. I really am." He breathed into the phone, sighing. "You're a sweet girl, Lindsay. I always liked you. Maybe if we hooked up when I was at a different place in my life, things would be different."

"I've already met someone who is in the stage of life I need my partner to be in. He's committed to me—we're married."

I am my beloved's and my beloved is mine.

"He wants this baby," she said softly. "Please—just say what we both know is true. You don't want this baby any more today than you did six months ago when you asked me to kill him."

"Don't say it like that," Grant snapped. "Six months ago, you just had like a… medical condition. A clump of cells—not even that. A pinpoint spot stuck to your uterus like a parasite. You can't compare a baby who's going to be born in a few months to you having a double pink line on a pee-stick."

Lord, give me the words to say, and don't let me ruin everything by cussing this jerk out.

"It's the same baby, Grant. The same person growing in my womb. To me, he was as real then as he is now and as he will be when he's born."

"Then why did you say yes?" Grant asked. "Why did you tell me you were going to the clinic to take care of it? Why'd you take my money and walk out that door? I thought you Christians aren't supposed to lie."

There were a lot of things she'd done that she wasn't supposed to do.

That's why I need You, Jesus.

"I didn't mean to lie when I told you I'd do it, Grant. I *thought* I was going to do it. I thought I could. Even though I didn't want to. I never wanted to kill this baby… I just felt so alone, and like I had no choice, and the way you were talking… Like everything could just go back to the way it was, as if it had never happened… I was scared, and selfish."

It felt good to say all that out loud. She'd prayed it to God, confessed it all to Him, but saying it out loud to another person made it feel all the more real.

Thank You for Your grace. She needed it.

"What changed?" Grant sounded annoyed, as if terminating her pregnancy was the sort of thing no one needed to think about twice. "Why didn't you call me in the cab and talk to me, if you weren't going to go through with it? At least let a guy know!"

"If I'd spoken to you, you'd talk me into doing it. And the only time I felt like I was being true to myself was when I made the decision *not* to go through with it after all."

Silence on the other end of the line. She could only hope he was still listening. That he could understand.

"I'd left God out of the decision entirely before," she said. "And once I talked to Him about it… I knew what I had to do. I know that doesn't make sense to you."

"You're right. Doesn't make sense."

Lindsay rubbed her fingers along the wooden countertop, feeling the ridge where the counter edged down and cut off. The varnish was shiny and smooth under her skin. "Grant…please. You don't want to be a father."

"No," he said softly. "Not now, I don't. But us men, we don't get a choice in the matter. It's always the woman's choice. Takes two to get pregnant, but only the woman has the decision power when it comes to whether or not to have the child. It's not fair."

"Is 'my body, my choice,' only a real choice if I intend to terminate the pregnancy? Is it not my choice to have the baby, considering it's my body?"

"It's not just you and your body," Grant argued. "That baby comes from both of us."

"I agree," she said. "And no one ever gave that baby a choice."

"I get it. You're keeping the baby, and I become a father whether I want to or not." Grant sounded so bitter. He seethed. "You get to hold me hostage for the next eighteen years. And it's not fair. That's all I'm saying."

"Well... in this case, it kind of *is* fair." She adopted a conciliatory tone. "You wanted me to not have the baby, but I am, and so I am relieving you of parental responsibility. I just need you to *make it official and legal.*"

"And what happens when this baby grows up? Is he going to come looking for me? Come knocking on my door at some point? Come ruin whatever life I've made for myself with a new wife and my *real* children?"

What did that even mean, *"real* children?" This child was real, too. It was as if Grant was having some sort of cognitive dissonance. As if before he'd picked up the phone, he wasn't going to be a father, but now suddenly he was.

And he didn't quite believe it yet.

"I I don't know," she admitted.

There was no way to say what her boy would do when he became a man. Everyone wanted to seek out where they came from. Would her child be any different?

"Not good enough," he said.

"As long as you're honest with whomever you end up marrying, I don't see how it would ruin anything if he wanted to meet you at some point, when he's older, I mean. You don't owe him anything. Won't you at least be curious, to see what sort of young man your own flesh and blood has become?"

He breathed heavily into the phone. "I can't believe this is happening to me."

She leaned back against the counter and closed her eyes. They were going in circles, and the conversation was devolving. She had to get off the phone before she turned him against her and the baby forever. The worst thing that could happen would be if Grant decided to be even more of a jerk about all of this.

What if he changed his mind about the baby completely, and sued for custody, just to get back at her?

"Grant. I'm sending you an email right now." Lindsay put her phone on speaker, so she could still hear it, and swiped to her inbox. She attached the document they'd had a lawyer draw up, a basic boilerplate, and clicked send.

"Check your email," she said. "You can print and sign it and just FedEx it back, okay? Then Eric can adopt the baby. Eric's name can be on the birth certificate. This will be Eric's baby and mine. Not yours. *Just like you want.*"

"But you still know who I am," Grant said. "Where I live. This child is going to find out at some point, and go searching for me."

"Why does that scare you so much?" she asked. "You don't need to worry about that now. Maybe in ten or fifteen years, you'll take the kid on a trip to a museum in the city or maybe you'll come out to Idaho. Maybe you'll have other kids by then, who'll want to meet their half-brother. Or maybe not. Maybe our son—"

Grant interrupted. "Don't call him 'our son.'"

"Actually, I was referring to me and my husband. *Our* son. Maybe our son won't care at all about who the sperm donor was who provided half his genetic material. He'll know that Eric is his real dad. And you won't have to worry about it."

"I'm going to have my lawyer look over this before I sign anything," Grant said. "I can't believe you did this to me—that you're *doing* this to me. I can't believe you told me you'd take care of it and you're still pregnant. I thought...I thought we were friends."

Her head ached just thinking about everything he said. "Please, Grant—please don't talk like that. We *were* friends. Colleagues. We screwed that up when we slept together."

Lindsay winced, half from the sudden headache that had come on, and half from what had just come out of her mouth. She hadn't meant to bring that up, ever again.

But she had a point to make.

"Doing that was our fault," she told Grant. "It takes two to tango, just like you said. But *none* of this is my child's fault. And he didn't deserve the death sentence for it."

"Next time you hear from me," Grant said, his voice devoid of emotion, "it will be through my lawyer."

Chapter Seventeen

THE INTERIOR OF Kootenai Hospital in Coeur d'Alene looked a lot nicer than the unintentionally-retro exterior. Lindsay didn't particularly care for its bluish-gray paint job. But inside, it was every bit the modern hospital.

There were four other couples taking the birthing class with them. All the moms had big pregnant bellies that rivaled Lindsay's own. Thank God she had Eric with her. It would've felt extra-awful to be in this class as the only single woman. Having Eric at her side at times like this, reinforced her decision to marry him.

She needed him for this—and she wasn't afraid to admit it to herself. If she wanted to have a natural, non-stressful birth experience, Lindsay needed him to be a huge support. Thankfully, Eric had been not only willing, but eager to attend with her.

"Having a game-plan for the birth is good," he said. "But you sure you don't want pain meds when it's time?"

"I'm pretty sure…" Lindsay glanced up at him. "I've read a lot of blog posts about home births, natural births, that sort of thing. They make it sound doable."

"Sounds to me like it's gonna hurt like all get-out."

One of the other women gave Eric a nervous look, and he grimaced.

"Our baby's birth is going to be one of the best, most exciting days in our lives," Lindsay said. "I don't want to miss even a moment of it by being in a haze."

"We'll remember it forever." Eric grinned at her, then turned his attention to the teacher, since their short break was over.

The childbirth educator lady who was teaching the class seemed nice, if a bit "woo-woo." Lots of talk about energy and deep breathing, that sort of thing.

Lindsay raised her hand.

"Mrs. Hunt."

Despite the many months she'd been a married woman, she was still getting used to being called Mrs. Hunt. But Lindsay had to admit…it felt good.

Like it was real.

"Are there any good positions or things we could do during labor to help with the pain?" Lindsay asked.

"It's like you read my mind." The instructor clasped her hands together. "*That's* what we're talking about next!"

She had a very calming cadence to her voice, and she kept emphasizing certain key words, and drawing them out.

"Okay, dads," the instructor continued, "I want you to sit on the floor with your *legs out*,"

Legs ouuuuuuut…

"…and let mom sit *between* your legs, *leaning* against your chest. Moms, put your *knees up*…let your *pelvis open*."

Pellllvis ooooopen… Lindsay giggled.

Eric sat on the ground as she'd instructed, his long denim-clad legs spread on the floor. He patted his muscular chest. "Bring it on in."

Okay. It was kind of an awkward position, but as soon as she sat with her back against his chest, she felt good.

Comfortable.

Partly because she wasn't actually in labor—she probably wouldn't be feeling comfortable when it was time to have the baby. Right now (especially since she'd never been in this position with him) it felt nice just to be so…close.

Eric's chest rose and fell, against her back, with each breath. She could barely hear what the instructor was saying over the pounding of her own heart.

"I'm going to give everyone a *birthing ball*, and moms…you'll *lean forward* against the birthing ball, and dads…you're going to provide *counter* pressure for the contractions by *massaging* mom's *lower back*." She demonstrated on a heavily pregnant blonde woman. "Okay, Dad," she said to the woman's husband. "You try."

Lindsay leaned against the big purple ball in front of her, and Eric's hands gently gripped her lower back.

"Tell me if I hurt you," Eric said in her ear.

"It feels good, actually. You could do more, even."

She hadn't even realized how tight her lower back was until Eric started massaging it. All the extra weight she was carrying on her front made a difference in how she carried her body, so it made sense that her back ached.

Eric's hands on her felt incredible. He moved with slow steady strokes, without hesitation, as if he'd given a million massages to pregnant women before. She sighed with contentment and relaxed further onto the birthing ball. She could definitely see this helping when it was time to have the baby.

She could see this helping any time.

As if he could read her thoughts, Eric said, "Just ask. We can do this whenever you want."

She might have to take him up on that offer. But—was it possible he was just doing it to get her more comfortable with having him touch her, so she'd sleep with him?

Probably. It was kind of how all men thought, wasn't it?

But could she blame him? He was her *husband*. There was definitely not one woman in this class who hadn't slept with her husband. Their bellies proved it. Why was she still so scared of taking that next step?

Had her experience with Grant scarred her so much?

"Okay, moms, birthing partners, now we're going to *stand*, and we're going to do some *standing positions* that will make *gravity* your friend. Gravity is your *friend* when you're having a baby, because it will help baby go *down into* your pelvis, into the *birthing canal*."

Eric helped her to her feet. She couldn't wait to be able to move around normally again.

"*Soooo*, moms…you're going to be standing and *dads*…you're going to put mom's hands on your *shoulders* like you're *dancing partners*, and *rock* back and forth, *rocking* that baby's head *down into* the pelvis. To support her balance, put your *hands* on her waist… That's right."

Eric's hands on her waist reminded her of dancing at Megan's wedding. They hadn't danced since.

"Now moms," the instructor said in that slow, soothing voice of hers, "*move* it on in, *step in* towards your partners, real close, there you go."

Lindsay stepped tentatively toward Eric. Her belly pressed against his.

"And dads, this is a perfect position to *wrap your hands* around her lower waist and hips and *massag*e that lower back. *Massage* the hips. This provides a great *counterweight* to labor, and when the baby's head is *pushing* against her and making her uncomfortable."

Eric's hands spanned her hips, and he pressed his fingers into her flesh. They rocked back and forth slowly, dancing to unheard music.

"I've missed dancing with you," Eric said softly in her ear.

"I was just thinking that, too." She laid her head against his chest, feeling his heartbeat.

Bah dum. Bah dum.

He was her husband. He wasn't going to leave her. At least, that's what he promised. What would it take for her to believe it in her heart? To not be afraid he would abandon her the way Grant had done?

The fact was, she couldn't be sure. Because if she wasn't having this baby, he would've never married her in the first place.

On her own, she wasn't enough for him to have proposed. Not without what she could offer him…a family.

Lindsay needed to know in her heart that Eric wanted *her*—and not just to fulfill his vision or as an antidote to his infertility. When would she be sure he wanted *her*, personally—Lindsay Moore? With or without a baby, with or without her business skills that she was utilizing at the ranch.

If he wanted *her*—that's what she needed to know. Lindsay needed him to be in love with her, even if she wasn't able to reciprocate yet, because of fear, or uncertainty. It was the only way.

They continued their silent dance in the brightly lit room.

"I'm so glad we're having this baby together," Eric murmured against her hair.

"Me too."

Because she couldn't do it on her own.

And Eric didn't want her on her own.

Would she ever be enough?

Chapter Eighteen

IT WAS THREE days later when she got the first text message from Grant.

"I've been thinking about our conversation. I feel awful. Can I call you?" the message read.

Lindsay looked down at her phone in shock. Whatever happened to the next time he spoke to her would be through a lawyer? Whatever happened to her being horrible for forcing him to have a biological child in the world?

She texted back: *"okay…"*

The phone rang a moment later.

"I have to admit, Grant…I'm surprised you're calling me."

"I apologize for how we ended that conversation." Grant exhaled into the phone. "The news that you're having our baby just took me by surprise, to be honest. I've spent the last six months thinking you'd had an abortion, and coming to terms with that."

"What do you mean, coming to terms with it? It was your idea. And then you never even checked on me."

"I just assumed you had it done, and didn't want to see me anymore. I'm sorry, Lindsay—for everything. We used to be friends…I've missed having you in my life."

He was sounding more like the Grant she knew. They had

worked together side-by-side for nearly five years. They never once dated, or saw each other in a romantic way...which was why she'd thought she could trust him when it came to needing a place to stay. But he'd taken it a step too far. A few steps too far, actually.

She looked down at her belly.

And here we are.

"I miss you at work," Grant said. "I was even thinking, maybe I should just pay off your debt so that you could get hired back. It's almost for selfish reasons, really," he said, with a little laugh. "My workday is much more boring without you."

Lindsay gripped the phone in her hand. This was the sort of thing he'd said when she'd gone to stay at his house. He promised her the moon and then completely abandoned her.

But Eric had promised her security, and delivered.

Whereas Grant was a betrayer, an abandoner...*Eric* was a provider, and protector.

"My husband sold his truck to resolve that debt."

Grant gave a low whistle. "That's devotion."

Yes...it was. More devotion than any other man had shown her before.

"How's that going—Idaho, married life?" Grant had the same tone he used to, when they were just talking as friends—back when he'd tell her about girls he was dating, and she'd ask questions and offer a female perspective.

"It's going great." She no longer trusted Grant enough to be his friend again, much less to know all the details.

"I have to admit," he said slowly. "I didn't expect you'd meet someone and fall in love enough to get married quite so fast."

"Stranger things have happened."

"Maybe," Grant conceded. "But not to you. You've always been much more guarded with your heart. Like you were with me."

"I don't think I was being guarded with my heart with you, Grant," she said. "I was being guarded with my virginity."

And look how that had turned out.

"But once you lost your virginity to me, it must've been easy to fall right into bed with Eric, huh? I was the icebreaker, I guess."

"I did no such thing," she said sharply. "Eric and I still haven't slept together."

Lindsay covered her mouth. How had he just gotten her to say that? She never should've told him she wasn't sleeping with her husband.

How could she have told him that?

"Wait—you haven't slept with your husband?" Grant echoed. "Did I hear that right?"

Lindsay sighed. "I care very deeply about Eric. And we wanted to get married. It takes time to develop the sort of relationship that would make me feel comfortable sleeping with him. We just haven't been together that long. I mean… I knew you for five years."

"Wow." Grant was silent on the other side of the phone. "Is Eric going to have to wait five years?"

Lindsay laughed. "You're funny. No. I just want to make sure we're both on the same page before we take that next step. It's a very big step to take. And it makes all sorts of bonding hormones get released and stuff."

"What do you mean?"

"Grant—I wasn't ready to sleep with you. But I did it, because I felt like a… like you deserved it, somehow. Because you were taking care of me. And once we did sleep together, I really did feel bonded to you. I think I could've fallen in love with you. Then I got pregnant—"

"You were falling in love with me?" Grant sounded completely surprised, as if he'd had no clue.

"That's what happens when you sleep with someone. You feel bonded to them whether you mean to or not. We've been friends for ages—you'd taken me in, we were sleeping together, and you were promising me everything under the sun, just as you did a moment ago, again."

"I'm sorry…"

But Lindsay wasn't done. It felt good to get it all off her chest, and to let Grant know. "If you hadn't sent me off to abort our child and then stopped contacting me, we'd be having a very different conversation."

"I can't believe I'm hearing this now," Grant said softly. "Why didn't you tell me?"

"I did." How had he missed that? "I told you that if I was pregnant, the best thing to do would be for us to get married, to live together. You said that's what you wanted…before I got pregnant, you were talking about wanting us to be together. But as soon as you got me pregnant, all you could say was how you weren't ready for a family, weren't ready for kids—you weren't ready for a wife. And then you wouldn't even come with me to the clinic."

Anger choked her. Hot tears burned her eyes. She was gripping the phone so hard her hand hurt. How could Grant be so uncaring? How could he not know what he'd done?

And worse—how could he be acting like he was changing his mind?

"I'm married," she repeated. "I married somebody who would

co-parent this child with me, because *you would not.*"

"You haven't slept with him," Grant said. "You haven't consummated the marriage... You could get it annulled. You could come back to New York, come back and live with me. We could raise our child together."

Oh, Grant, what are you doing to me?

"Why now? Why are you ready now for a wife and child, but when it mattered the most—when I first got pregnant—why did you toss me to the side like that? I was your friend. At least...I thought I was."

Grant was silent. Maybe he hung up.

"I don't have an answer," Grant finally said. "Maybe I was just scared. But after you called and told me you were keeping our child, that you wanted me to give up my parental rights... I don't know, that just hit a nerve. I don't know if I want some other man adopting my child."

"He's my husband, Grant. I want him to be the father of my baby."

"But...I'm the father. Don't you want the real father to be your baby's dad?"

Lord, what do I do? What is Your will?

It would have made far more sense to have a marriage of convenience, if she was going to have one anyway, with Grant—considering he was the biological father, and she'd be able to stay in Manhattan, where she'd grown up and was most comfortable. At least... she used to be most comfortable.

Bear Creek Saddle had grown on her. Idaho had grown on her.

And she loved being near Megan, and having new family with her brothers-in-law Zach and Ryan, and the men at the ranch, and their families.

Bear Creek Saddle Ranch was *home* now. And Eric was her husband. She didn't want to leave him.

"Grant, have you really thought about what you're saying to me?" she asked. "I mean, I know you don't believe in God. I know you don't pray."

"Is that really a deal breaker for you?" Grant asked. "You know I don't have any issue with you believing in God. That's your truth. I have my own truth. You say God brings you comfort, and that's cool. I just don't believe in a bearded sky-god who controls everything. We were able to be friends, even with that difference between us, weren't we?"

Yes. They were. Part of her was always hoping Grant would find Jesus. That God would show Himself to Grant, so he would know the truth.

The truth.

"I don't think there's such a thing as 'my truth' and 'your truth,'" Lindsay said. "Because if everything is true, that's really like saying that nothing is true. And if I believed that, then I wouldn't be a Christian."

Grant grunted. "I guess. I don't see why it has to be such a big deal. I mean, you were holding on to your virginity because you thought God didn't want you to have premarital sex, but you did and now you're having a baby and you seem pretty excited about it, so it all worked out."

"I really don't know what to say to that." Lindsay sighed. "God has a plan that we can't see, and He uses ordinary people to help achieve His plans. Somehow, God knew this baby was going to come into this world. This baby has a purpose. I don't know what it is, but God does."

"Forget God for a minute," Grant said.

Impossible.

"Let's think logically for a minute here," Grant continued. "You're living in the boondocks, out in the middle of nowhere. I honestly can't think of the difference between Idaho, Indiana, Iowa and whatever other states start with the letter 'I.' It all mixes together, because all those random flyover states are basically the same."

"There's so much wrong with that assumption, I'm not sure where to begin."

"Don't you miss Manhattan? You can come back and live with me. I'm offering you that, as your friend, and the father of your child."

"Honestly… I'm still, *still* not over what happened between us. I still feel like I was pressured into sleeping with you. I made bad decisions. I made bad choices. You weren't exactly helping the situation, either. But whenever I think of you now, Grant…all I can think of is how you handed me that money, called me a cab…and told me to *take care of it*."

"I was taking responsibility, Lindsay. I thought that was the right way to go about it. It's what everyone else does."

"I was so devastated." She ran her thumb over her wedding ring. "And you didn't even care enough about me to find out how it went—if I'd even gone through it at all—much less go with me. I know I'm supposed to forgive you, and I'm working on it. I really am. But I'm never going to be able to forget that you wanted our child dead, rather than to be his father."

The silence stretched out between them, as long and distant as the country that divided them.

"Just think on what I said, Linds," Grant said. "Do me a favor—don't sleep with Eric just yet. You might change your mind and want to annul the marriage. And I really just want you to think about us—how long we've been friends. How the baby inside of you shares my blood, my genes. How much you love Manhattan, and how much you love working at the bank. I could give you all of that in the blink of an eye. I have the money sitting in an easily-liquidated account right now. I could pay back Eric for paying off your debt, just like that."

She could hear him snapping his fingers to emphasize his point. Just like that. *Snap.*

He was promising her the moon again.

"I have to go," she whispered. Her voice broke, and she hung up the phone.

* * *

Lindsay stood in the kitchen, her still-wet hands on the varnished wooden countertop, staring out the window above the large farmhouse sink. The dishes were washed, but there was too much to think about to move. Too much to figure out.

Lord, what do I do?

There was nothing to be done, or was there? Why would Grant change his mind so drastically now, after not speaking with her for months, and then pull a complete one-eighty like he had?

And he wasn't a Christian. While that had never harmed their friendship or their working relationship, would she be able to be with somebody who made fun of her for praying? Or thought it was stupid?

At least with Eric, she didn't have to worry about that. With Eric, they would raise their child in the church.

But Grant was the biological father of her child. And she knew him… She knew him very well. There was always going to be the chance in the future that her son would want to meet his father—he'd want to go meet Grant. If Grant was telling her he wanted to raise the child with her, was it right for her to say no?

But Lord, I'm already married. I made a promise.

She couldn't just annul the marriage to Eric simply because Grant had changed his mind. The ring on her finger spoke of the promise she had made to him, and that he had made to her. That they would stick together through good times and bad.

The crazy thing was, less than seven months ago, if Grant had told her he wanted to be with her, that he wanted to marry her and live with her in his condo in New York on the Upper West Side, and raise their child together, she would've been over the moon ecstatic. Not because she loved him, necessarily. But because she would've been in the same place she was when she'd agreed to Eric's proposal. She would do anything for her child's sake. Anything. And marrying the father of her child just made sense, too.

But that wasn't what happened. She married a complete stranger—a man who was not a stranger any longer.

Eric was her husband. He wouldn't desert her. How could she desert him?

Heavenly Father, I need guidance. I'm pretty sure You're going to say I should stay married, because that's Biblical. It's not like Eric has cheated on me or abused me. So if we go with that assumption—

Lindsay paused, waiting for a gut check. Waiting for the Holy

Spirit to let her know she was on the right path, or if she was simply having ears for what she alone wanted to hear.

If I stay with Eric—because I will *stay with Eric, I mean… What does that mean for me and Grant? Is there even a "me and Grant"? Do you want Grant in this child's life, or is he just playing some sort of game because he doesn't want me to be with Eric? Is he just being territorial?*

But it was possible he had a complete heart change. Why did it have to happen so late?

No—his heart hadn't changed. How could it?

Snippets of their conversation stuck out in her mind. How even when Grant was being as persuasive as he could be, he still said little things that showed her he thought her opinion was not as good as his. In his tone, he made it seem like a relationship with God was the equivalent of hearing voices in her head and believing in a "bearded sky-god," as he'd said. She'd once heard him ask why she didn't believe in the "Flying Spaghetti Monster" instead.

It was rude. It was disrespectful. Grant wasn't on the same page with her about something that was integral to her identity and her life.

What did that mean for their baby?

God, am I supposed to be keeping my baby safe from Grant's influence? Would Grant be a negative figure in our child's life?

Maybe she couldn't be the one to make that decision. Certainly when their child was grown, she'd have no say in whether or not he had a relationship with Grant. Shouldn't she want him to, anyway? Wasn't it good—even if biological parents didn't remain together— for a child to have a healthy relationship with each parent?

But what if Eric can't adopt our baby? What if Grant won't give up his parental rights—and it sure sounds like he's not going to. Not with the way he was talking. Fix it, Lord, please fix it.

She took a deep breath and opened her eyes. She hadn't even noticed that she'd closed them, until she'd blinked and saw a moose standing not ten feet from her kitchen window in the front yard.

"Hi," she whispered. She didn't want to scare him away.

This was amazing. She'd never seen a moose this close before. Had she ever seen a moose, at all?

"So this is what you look like up close," she said softly.

The moose wasn't looking at her. He was munching on one of the bushes outside, his heavy rack on his head bowing down and up as he ate. He was huge. As big as a horse, and wider. That thick body on those thin legs. It would almost be silly looking, if she didn't know how dangerous they could be if they felt threatened.

Did Grant feel threatened?

Did Eric?

And how would that threaten their relationship with her, and with the baby?

Lindsay reached into her fleece pocket and pulled out her phone. She took a quick succession of pictures through the window of the moose.

Maybe she could go out the front door and get a better angle.

Lindsay went to the front door and slowly opened it, phone camera at the ready. She stood on the front porch and took some shots, but the moose hadn't noticed her yet.

It was so beautiful here. Imagine… a moose had just walked right up to her house! That never happencd in New York. Would she miss moments like this if she moved back to Manhattan?

She shook her head. Why was she even thinking about that?

There was no going back to Manhattan. For whatever reason,

Grant's suggestion that she annul the marriage with Eric and move back to New York to be with him had edged its way into her brain, setting a foothold there.

But why? She wasn't going to divorce her husband, or annul their marriage, or whatever it was that she'd be able to do.

It wouldn't be right.

And even though she'd known Grant for a long time, in the short time she and Eric had been together, they'd become friends.

More than friends.

She'd be lying if she didn't admit she was attracted to her husband. How could she not be? Eric was a beautiful man. And he certainly knew his way around the ranch.

He also knew how to kiss.

The baby kicked her, a tiny jab of an elbow or foot in her womb. Lindsay smiled and put her hand on her belly.

"Don't worry, Little One," she whispered. "God already knows what's going to happen and how it's going to work out, even if we don't."

At that moment, Boomer ran outside from the still-ajar front door, barking so loud and so fast at the moose, it became a howl.

"Boomer!"

Well, that did it. The moose definitely noticed her now that Boomer had ruined their cover. The moose ran off through the trees.

She looked at the dog, who seemed triumphant almost, as if pleased with how he'd protected the house from the beast.

"Good boy, Boomer," she said with a laugh. She patted him on his wiry head. "You sure showed him."

Well, at least she had the pictures. She couldn't wait to share them with Eric.

He would've loved to have seen that moose. Yeah, surely he'd seen moose a hundred times before, but it never seemed to grow old for him. Eric loved the land, the animals… he loved Idaho and the mountains so much it was contagious. Even though she always considered herself a city girl at heart, living with him on the ranch had given her a new-found appreciation for the simpler life.

She didn't even miss her designer clothes or bags.

She kinda missed the shoes. But they would've gotten muddy up here anyway.

Eric pulled up in the four-door sedan he'd picked up when he traded the truck in, the tires crunching on the gravel drive. He jumped out with a concerned expression.

"What's going on?" he asked. "Why are you waiting for me?"

Waiting for him?

"There was a moose." She pointed in the direction where it had gone. "I got pictures."

"Lindsay, that's dangerous. You shouldn't get so close to a moose." He took the phone she handed to him, and scrolled through the pictures. "These pictures look really close-up."

"I have the zoom on," she said. "I mean, it was pretty close, but not as close as the pictures make it look like."

As he was holding her phone, a new text message dinged. She could hear the sound, but he was holding the phone. She knew what he was seeing, though—incoming texts flashed on whatever screen she was on.

"That Megan?" She her hand out for her phone so she could respond. But he didn't give it to her.

"It's from Grant," he said. "I didn't know you were talking with

Grant. I thought you told me he hadn't been contacting you."

"He hadn't been," she said. "But then I called him because we need him to sign over his parental rights, so you can adopt our baby. I had to talk to him. I told you I had to talk to him."

Eric's expression was stony. He was still looking down at her phone. "I thought you were talking about... I dunno, something that we'd get a lawyer to do at some point, not that you were going to go ahead and call him on your own."

"Why shouldn't I call him on my own?" She crossed her arms. "I've known Grant for years. He's the father of my child. Why should I not call him, if I have to talk to him about something?"

Eric looked at her as if she'd just kicked him in the gut.

"You know what I mean," she said. The baby elbowed her again and she shifted uncomfortably. "I need to go lie on the couch. The baby's beating me up."

Eric nodded and walked ahead of her to the door, holding it open for her in stony silence.

She went inside and sat on the worn, brown leather couch. Boomer jumped up next to her and curled next to her side. He wasn't supposed to be on the couch, but she didn't have the strength to turn him away. She could use the comfort.

"I thought we were going to communicate about this stuff," Eric said. He sat on the arm of the couch opposite her and kicked off his muddy boots. A little too late, after he'd stomped through the house with them. "What happened when you called him? Were you ever even gonna tell me about that, or was that gonna be your little secret?"

She actually hadn't thought to tell Eric. No, that wasn't true...she'd thought about it, then made a decision *not* to. Because she didn't have any answers, and there was nothing Eric could do to change the situation.

It would've just worried him…and he already had enough worry on his plate about the ranch and the finances. She knew he missed his truck—the sedan he'd gotten as a family car to replace it just wasn't the same.

It didn't make sense to add more stress on top of that.

"We hadn't settled on anything yet, really. I was just telling him that I kept the baby, and I figured he should know."

"He don't deserve to know. He didn't want you or that baby."

Lindsay's chest tightened with unease. She had to tell him.

But Eric already seemed so on edge about not being their baby's biological father. Just bringing that up seemed to offend him. So how could she tell him that Grant had changed his mind?

Lord, give me the words. What am I supposed to say here?

Eric stood and walked over to the fireplace. He took a poker and rearranged a log. "We need more wood," he muttered.

"This all happened really recently."

"How many times have you spoken with him on the phone?" He wasn't looking at her. The flames danced off his face.

"Twice. Long conversations. We had a lot to talk about."

"Well then?" Eric asked. "How did you guys leave it?"

"We didn't, exactly. It's a complicated issue. He was really mad at me for not telling him from the beginning that I was keeping the baby. He said he'd spent all this time coming to terms with it, thinking I had the abortion, so the call was a big surprise. But then I guess he thought about it, because when he called today, he seemed like…a different person."

"Don't you remember what this man did to you?" Eric asked.

"You're a good woman, Lindsay. And I wish I could be half as forgiving as you are, because you're really walking the talk. You're a good Christian I guess. Maybe I'm not. Because I'm definitely having a hard time forgiving Grant for what he did."

"It's not like he raped me, Eric. I made a stupid choice, but it was my choice to sleep with him. And I'm glad I did, because if I hadn't, I'd never have this baby that I want with all my heart."

Eric winced as if she'd physically hurt him. "I get it."

Lindsay didn't know what to say. She'd just reminded her husband how he wasn't able to impregnate her. How she'd slept with someone else she wasn't married to, but wouldn't even sleep with him.

No wonder he hurt.

"This guy must really be something." Eric laughed, a harsh sound with no joy. "He got you knocked up, and God knows I can't do that. He managed to convince you to sleep with him, and I'm your doggone husband, and I can't even do that either. What do you want me for, anyway?"

"I want *you*—"

"You want a father for your child, I get it—but you're calling Grant the father. You're telling me he wants back into your life. So what is it I'm giving you, Linds? How am I holding up my end of the bargain? If I have nothing to offer you, *why would you stay?*"

Lindsay sat frozen on the couch.

Eric shook his head. "I can't give you museums and Broadway shows. I can't give you a high-rise apartment in New York City. I can't offer you a job in the bank, just one in the old farmhouse. Maybe Grant is right."

Lindsay stood, reaching for him, but Eric walked past her and pulled his boots on. He walked back out the front door without saying another word.

Lindsay looked at the arm of the couch where he'd been a moment before. Her phone lay there.

She gasped when she saw the text message that Eric had seen come up on her phone from Grant:

"Don't sleep with him, Linds. You can still get that sham of a marriage annulled and come back home with me. You, me, and our baby—we're the real family. And you know it. Love ya."

Chapter Nineteen

BACK AT THE ranch, Eric dropped Lindsay off at the farmhouse to work. He had to go over to Spokane and drum up some more business. Anything would help.

"See you later, Lindsay."

She sat behind his desk—now hers—touching her temple, and didn't look up to wave goodbye.

Instead, she winced, as if she were in pain.

"Hey—are you all right?"

Lindsay smiled weakly. "I'm fine. Just another stress headache, I think. This headache has been going on forever. Days."

"I want to take you home so you can rest." He walked back into the office, looking at her face carefully for signs of illness.

She seemed all right... But he wasn't a doctor.

Her face looked a little puffy maybe, but wasn't it normal to gain weight when you're having a baby? Maybe it just went to her face.

"While you're here," Lindsay said, "can you just get me that box over there? I just want to put my feet up."

He picked up a box filled with papers and set it at her feet. Gently, he lifted her foot by the ankle and set it on the box for her.

Whoa. "What's going on with your ankles?"

She looked down. "Wow…they're super swollen. I feel like I want to take my shoes off, but better not, or I'll never be able to get them back on."

Something didn't feel right.

He didn't know what it was. But something just wasn't right.

He stopped at the doorway once more and turned around. "You sure you're okay?"

"Okay as I could be with a belly this big." Lindsay laughed, but it wasn't her real laugh, he could tell.

What wasn't she telling him?

The silence hung between them heavily.

He didn't feel right about this. But he didn't even know what "this" was.

Probably just imagining things.

Eric turned again to go, but her voice stopped him before he was ten feet down the corridor.

"Eric?"

He immediately turned around and poked his head back into the office. "Let me take you home."

"Yeah—this headache isn't going away anytime soon, and I should probably have my legs up higher."

Something wasn't right.

"Lindsay, I'm gonna take you to see Dr. Peterson. You don't look good."

"You sure know how to make a girl feel special," she joked.

He shook his head. This wasn't a joking matter. He didn't normally get bad feelings, but if he did, he was gonna listen to it. She'd looked like the picture of health up until a couple days ago, and now she looked awful.

She was still beautiful, of course, but there was something off. Maybe it was the swelling. Maybe it was the pain around the corners of her eyes from her headache.

But he'd feel a lot better if Dr. Peterson gave her the all clear.

"Let's go," he said firmly. "No arguments. Doctor's office. Now."

To his surprise, she didn't argue.

That was even scarier. Lindsay usually called him out for being "bossy" when he went into take-charge mode. Instead, she mutely acquiesced.

What if something really was wrong?

* * *

At Dr. Peterson's office in town, Lindsay did everything she usually did at the doctors'—had her temperature and blood pressure taken, gave a urine sample, and let the nurse know what was bothering her—today, just the headache and the swelling.

Five minutes later, Dr. Peterson walked in. His usually cheery demeanor was different today.

"Mrs. Hunt, how are you feeling?"

"Not great, to be honest," she said. "Eric wanted me to get checked out, just in case."

"I'm glad you came in. My nurse got a really high blood pressure reading, but it was so elevated, I'm thinking it might be wrong…so I'm going to check it myself manually."

He wrapped the blood pressure cuff around her arm, a different cuff than the one that had buttons on it to automatically tighten and read-out the results—and pumped it up by squeezing the black rubber bulb in his hand.

The cuff squeezed her arm. *Ow.* The doctor listened with a stethoscope, his eyes closed as if to further concentrate on what he was hearing. Slowly he let the air out of the cuff.

"The good news is I've got a smart nurse. The bad news is, your blood pressure really is *two-hundred over one-ten.*"

Eric frowned. "What should it be?"

"I like it to be one-ten, one-twenty over seventy or eighty. Definitely want it to be under one-forty over ninety. This though, this is way, way too high. It's odd, you've had good blood pressures all along till now." He touched her ankles, pressing his thumb against them. "You're all swollen."

Dr. Peterson paused, his mouth scrunched up, staring off in the distance, as if he was thinking.

"I'll be right back."

As he was walking out the door, he barked something about needing to see her urinalysis immediately.

"What's going on?" Eric asked.

Lindsay shook her head and shrugged. "I guess the high blood pressure explains the headaches. Maybe he'll give me some blood pressure medicine or something."

"That look he has on his face…" Eric shook his head. "It was the same look he had on his face when he diagnosed me with azoospermia."

"Well, at least we know I'm not infertile," she said, chuckling. But Eric wasn't smiling. "Sorry. I didn't mean to joke about that."

"It's fine," Eric said. "I just want to know what's going on with you—with your health."

Dr. Peterson came back in, not bothering to knock like he usually did.

"Okay," he said. "You're spilling protein into your urine. That's not good—it means you're having a problem with your kidneys. That would explain all this extra swelling. You're probably holding on to a lot of extra water that your kidneys aren't able to process."

"Okay," Lindsay said slowly, echoing him.

What did that mean for the baby?

"We're going to have Eric drive you down to the hospital. I'm going to follow. I need you evaluated over there. I think you have preeclampsia, and we have to take it seriously."

Eric jumped up from his perch next to her on the exam table. "Is she gonna be all right? Is the baby gonna be all right?"

"Here's the thing about preeclampsia—if we don't treat it, it can lead to seizures, and those seizures can be fatal for mom or baby."

"I've never had seizures before." Lindsay patted Eric's arm. Maybe she could reassure him with that.

"All right, so how do we treat this?" Eric asked.

"We get her on some IV medication, try to slow everything down, get her blood pressure down, get some of this extra water off of her. We're going to have to give her some steroid injections that will help the baby's lungs develop."

"What's wrong with my baby's lungs?" Her breath caught in her throat.

"They're not fully developed yet," Dr. Peterson said softly. "The steroids help the baby's lungs develop faster. The sooner we can do that, the better, so let's get in the cars and go."

Eric helped Lindsay up from the table, and put his arm around her, as if she might fall over.

"The only cure for severe preeclampsia is delivery of the baby.

You're thirty-five weeks pregnant, which isn't too early for a good outcome, but hopefully we'll be able to hold off on delivering for as long as we can. But at the very least, you'll have to stay at the hospital on bed rest until the baby's delivered."

Did he say *delivering* the baby?

She wasn't due for another month. Five more weeks, to be exact. There was no way she was delivering now.

And bed rest? She was fine.

Some headaches, some swelling—just give her a Tylenol and she'd be good to go. She wasn't flirting with death like he made it sound.

This was getting out of hand.

"I haven't even written out my whole birth plan, though. We've got so much happening right now, Doctor, you have no idea—everything that's going on with the ranch, and we're still not even ready for the baby with the nursery at—"

Eric cut her off. "Your job is not to worry about any of that," he said sternly. "I'll take care of everything."

"I don't even have a change of clothes," she snapped. "I'm certainly not going to just lie in a hospital bed for the next five weeks."

Maybe it was fear making her irritable, or maybe it was the headache, but she didn't like how all of a sudden everything was out of her control, and she was being bossed around as if she had no say.

"Focus on helping our baby," Eric said. "You need to be healthy. And you have to stay in the hospital as long as the doctor says you need to."

This can't be happening, God.

Dr. Peterson grabbed his coat and stethoscope, draped it around his neck, and quickly washed his hands in the sink. "I have a feeling you're not going to be staying in the hospital too long. We might need to deliver that baby sooner than you think."

* * *

Eric struggled to keep his hands on the wheel at ten and two, and his eyes on the road. All he wanted to do was keep looking over at his wife and make sure she was okay.

He'd never been this terrified in his life, not even when his mom was diagnosed with breast cancer years back.

He hadn't been this terrified even when he thought he might have cancer too, and it turned out to be scar tissue…the same scar tissue that kept him from having children.

They pulled up to the emergency room entrance, and Eric handed his keys to the valet. Dr. Peterson had already called ahead, and he was right behind them.

They sat Lindsay in a wheelchair. She looked more terrified than sick. But not all illnesses could be seen on the outside. Eric knew that better than most.

"I don't need a wheelchair, I'm perfectly capable of walking," Lindsay insisted.

She started to stand, but Eric put his hand on her shoulder.

"Just let them do it their way, Linds. This isn't something to play around with."

Maybe she could see the concern in his face, because she didn't argue further.

He texted his parents, and everyone at the ranch.

"We're at the hospital. Preeclampsia. Please pray."

It all happened so fast. They got her into a bed, hooked up to an IV, and within minutes she was slurring her words.

"Why is she talking like that?" he demanded.

"It's the mag-sulfate," Dr. Peterson said. "We don't want her to have a seizure, so we're slowing down the synapses in her brain so they don't over-fire. When you slow all that down, it makes it hard to speak and think clearly."

Two different ER doctors and a nurse were looking at a big monitor attached to the wires they'd stuck onto his wife. The monitor was filled with lights and numbers that constantly changed and beeped.

"If she keeps this up," the other doctor said quietly to the nurse, "she's going to stroke out." He tapped a red, flashing number on the monitor: 210/100. "Let's try hydralazine."

Eric didn't think he was supposed to overhear what the doctors were murmuring, but he couldn't help it. Everything was so confusing, and he needed as much information as he could get.

None of what he'd heard sounded okay. *Stroke out?* Even more drugs on top of whatever was making her slur her words and act like a zombie?

"Sir, is your wife allergic to any medications?" The nurse tapped Eric's shoulder.

Was she?

"I don't know." Eric should know this sort of thing about his own wife, and the fact that he didn't tore him up. "She's never told me about any medical issues or anything."

Lindsay was way too out of it from the meds to answer for herself. She had to depend on him to be her advocate.

Lord, help us.

How did this happen so fast?

Dr. Peterson walked over to Eric as he sat at Lindsay's bedside in the emergency room. "I'm going to pass this case on to the high-risk OB/GYN, and a neonatologist who can look out for the little one. You're in good hands here. I'll be praying for you guys."

Eric put his hand out to shake the doctor's hand, but Dr. Peterson surprised him with a hug. Tears formed in Eric's eyes, and he blinked them away hard.

There was no time to get emotional. He had to be strong for Lindsay.

Lord, whatever You do, don't take her away from me. I need her.

A young female doctor arrived and went over some notes with the nurses before coming over to see them.

"Lindsay, I'm Dr. Sorin," the woman said. "I'm going to get you admitted into the maternity ward, and we're going to deliver this baby. You already had your first shot of the steroids, and I don't think we have time to do another round, unfortunately."

"Why?" Lindsay's eyes looked bleary from the medication.

"Your blood pressure just keeps getting higher. This is severe preeclampsia, and if you have a seizure it could suffocate the baby. We need to get the baby out now."

"No," she whispered, "I need more time."

"I'm going to give you more medicine that will induce delivery, and some pain medicine as well. Your platelets look good, so I think we can do an epidural, if we can get one in fast."

"It's too early," Lindsay said. "I'm only thirty-five weeks, I'm not due for another month."

"We don't have a choice, Mrs. Hunt." Dr. Sorin frowned sympathetically.

"I wanted a natural birth." Lindsay struggled to meet Eric's eyes, as if she couldn't quite get them to focus. "Why is this happening? It's not what we planned."

Eric put his hand on her shoulder. "We have to do whatever we can. He said you could have a seizure or a stroke if this keeps up. Delivering the baby is the only way, early or not."

Chapter Twenty

T HE ROOM WAS closing in around Eric. The beige walls of the maternity ward room where they had taken Lindsay may as well have been black.

Eric couldn't take his eyes off of her. Something might happen if he blinked, if he moved. Something bad.

Lindsay lay in the hospital bed, an IV running into her arm, her eyes closed. She had fetal monitoring on her belly, and monitors checking her blood pressure, heart rate, all sorts of things. They wouldn't let him put the TV on for background noise, something to take her mind off of what was going on, because the flickering lights might give her a seizure.

A seizure. That was crazy. How had his healthy-as-a-horse wife crashed so hard, so fast?

Someone had just come in and done an ultrasound on her belly, then walked out just as quickly.

"How are you doing?" Normally, she'd get annoyed that he was asking every two minutes, but whatever medicine they had her on to keep her from seizing made her slow, her words slurred.

She didn't seem to remember from one minute to the next anything at all. The nurse said her neurons were firing extra-slowly because of the magnesium they'd given her, or something like that.

"It's too hot in here," she said for the eighth or ninth time.

They had the air conditioner on, it was at fifty-five degrees Fahrenheit. He was wearing two sweaters, one borrowed from another dad whose wife was, fortunately, not experiencing overheating.

Eric looked at Lindsay impotently. The cool washcloth the nurse had laid on her forehead turned warm the moment it hit her skin. She'd already tossed off her blanket and sheet. She wore nothing but the thin hospital gown. He'd already moved her hair off of her neck and up onto the pillow. They didn't have any fans.

And he wasn't supposed to give her anything to drink or eat, just in case they had to do surgery.

Lord, heal her. Please.

Her blood pressure wasn't going down. Zach pulled a chair up to the edge of her bedside and sat close to her. He held her hand. She was sweating. She really was burning up, despite how cold he was. Another side effect from the medicine.

"What are we going to name the baby?" he asked.

She seemed so miserable, he wanted to get her to think of something good. The ultimate result of all this pain—their child.

Lindsay opened her eyes and looked at him, but her eyes were blurred. There was no way she could answer coherently. She was so completely disoriented, and getting more so by the minute.

At that moment, the doctor walked in.

"We're going to deliver the baby," Dr. Sorin said. "At thirty-five weeks gestation, I feel confident we'll have a good outcome. Obviously it'd be better to be completely full-term, but we've had preemies born much, much earlier who've done well. This is really what we call a 'late-stage' preemie."

"Today?" Eric asked. "I thought she was gonna be on bed rest."

Dr. Sorin shook her head. "*If* she were responding to the medication. She's not. If anything, despite the anti-hypertensives we have her on, she's degrading. I'm hesitant to give her Pitocin to induce labor, because I don't want her to have a stroke, or seize."

Dear Lord. "Tell me what we have to do."

"We're going to do an emergency C-section right now," Dr. Sorin said. "Unfortunately, I cannot have you in the operating room, even though normally we like to have dad there during the delivery. There's just way too much medically going on. It'd be better for you to wait out here." She paused, tapping her chin with her pen. "Mr. Hunt...do you have anyone you can call, to be with you here?"

That didn't sound good. Someone to be with him... It almost sounded like she was preparing him to have family nearby in case something terrible happened.

Was that what was going on?

"She's gonna be okay, right?" He hated the desperation in his voice. It only served to fuel his fear.

"That's what we're working toward." Dr. Sorin flipped some pages on her clipboard and handed it to him with her pen. "I need you to sign this consent form, for her to have the surgery right away."

Eric took the pen, but hesitated. "This says *death* is a possible outcome. Massive blood loss..." He scanned over the form, every word making him sick to his stomach.

What would Lindsay say, if she could speak for herself?

"She wanted a natural birth," Eric said as he read the paperwork. "She didn't want any of this."

The doctor looked up at him with great seriousness. "The only treatment for severe preeclampsia is delivery. Your wife is very, very sick. But she's not in labor. She's too unstable medically to do it on her own, and certainly not naturally."

Eric looked down at his wife. Her eyes were closed, a sheen of perspiration covering her face.

"It'll be all right, Linds." He wiped Lindsay's forehead with the damp washcloth again. "Sometimes plans have to change, okay?"

"Noo," she moaned. It looked like she wanted to say something else, but she didn't—or couldn't.

What do I do, Lord?

Dr. Sorin sighed impatiently. "She's in no shape to make an informed consent decision for herself. Your wife doesn't even know what she's saying 'no' to."

"She was saying 'no' pretty clearly not too long ago, actually."

"That's because *she's getting worse*," the doctor snapped.

Eric's heart clenched. *Heal her, Lord.*

"I'm going to be very clear with you, Mr. Hunt." Dr. Sorin tapped the clipboard where his signature needed to go. "Either we get that baby out of her now, or she *will* die, and the baby will die with her. Their *only* chance is immediate surgical delivery. That's your baby's only chance, as well. He's safer outside the womb than inside, at this point. I understand you want to honor her earlier wishes, but if she understood what I just told you now—"

"I'll sign it." Eric scrawled his signature and handed the clipboard back to the doctor. Lindsay could be mad at him all she wanted. He just had to make sure she lived to get the opportunity to be mad at him, first.

"Call somebody," Dr. Sorin ordered. "You shouldn't go

through this alone."

He nodded, surrendered. "I can call my parents, and her sister."

And he should really call Grant. As much as it pained him, if Grant really wanted to be a part of Lindsay's life, or rather, their child's life—

Eric didn't want Grant to take his wife and child from him, but if something went terribly wrong today, would he spend the rest of his life feeling guilty for not letting Grant know his baby was being born early?

It's my *baby. Me and Lindsay's.*

But it was also Grant's. He'd at least let him know…and Grant could do what he wanted with that information.

Nurses came in, checked Lindsay's hospital band twice, and wheeled her off to surgery. She was so out of it, she didn't even protest.

The wait was interminable.

Megan and Zach had arrived as soon as they heard, and sat with him in the privacy of the single-bed maternity room, for women who were in active labor and delivery.

Eric's parents were there as well, although his mom wouldn't sit on the folding chair they'd brought in for her. She paced, which was what Eric was doing right then too. He must've gotten that from his mom.

What characteristics would their baby have from Lindsay?

Lord—if it's Your will, please let her be okay. Let the baby be okay.

Quietly, in the very darkest, deepest recesses of his heart, he added a half-formed negotiation, a concession to God:

Lord, if You have to choose just one to save, save Lindsay. Please. I love her, Lord. I know I married her because I wanted to have a child, and Lord

You know I still do, but if somebody has to go be with You today—Lord—don't let it be Lindsay. I need her more than I need my own child's life.

A cry escaped his throat as the thought bubbled up to the surface of his brain and he realized what he'd been harboring inside. What sort of terrible negotiation was he making? He couldn't make deals with God. God had a plan already, and Eric had no idea what it was.

Of course he loved that baby, even though they had never met. He wanted their baby. But he loved Lindsay... and Lindsay was the only one of the two who he knew.

God willing, someday he'd know that child better than anyone else he knew in the world—but right now, their baby was someone he didn't know yet, other than as an idea.

A tiny foot poking Lindsay in the ribs.

A quick heartbeat heard through a monitor.

An ultrasound of the teeny-tiny hand, their baby, sucking his thumb in her womb.

A tear rolled down his cheek. *God, save my baby too. I want them both to live...please Lord if it's Your will, let it be so.*

Why did it feel like death had to claim someone today?

Was it the sterile, oppressive atmosphere of being in a room with somebody in such critical condition? Was it the smell of the disinfectants and rubbing alcohol?

Maybe You could take me, Lord. But let Lindsay and the baby be fine. Grant will take care of them, and I'll know she'll be okay. They both will. If someone has to die today, You could always let it be me.

His mom came up behind him and gently touched his shoulder.

Eric turned around, and let her wrap her arms around him the way she did when he was a boy and had skinned his knee and needed comforting.

"Oh honey," his mom said softly. "I know you're scared. But she's far along in the pregnancy, and those doctors are really good at what they do. It's really rare to have bad outcomes. I think you're gonna be just fine. That's what the doctor said. High confidence."

"Getting preeclampsia was supposed to be rare too." Eric shook his head. His mother was only trying to help, and she was probably also scared. "Yeah. I suppose you're right."

"Remember your vision? You told me God showed you with Lindsay and the baby together. So far, God's given you Lindsay. Her having a baby, and you all being together, that completes the picture. He's not done yet with you guys."

Eric pulled back from her embrace and looked at her in amazement.

She was right.

He'd thought God had given him the vision to get him to propose to Lindsay, but maybe it was to get him through this very moment as well. Knowing that there was another side, that they would come through this as a family.

"Thank you, Mom." He squeezed her. "That's exactly what I needed to hear."

Thank You God too, that everything is going to be all right. Thank You that Lindsay and the baby are going to come home with me.

That no one has to die today.

Thank You for giving me that knowledge ahead of time, for letting me know.

I'm sorry I forgot.

I'm sorry I was weak and so scared.

But it's all in Your hands.

There was a knock on the door to the room. Everyone jumped to their feet.

Was there an update?

* * *

"How is she?" Eric stepped forward toward Dr. Sorin, desperate for answers. "Is she okay?"

"She will be—yes. Your wife lost some blood. We had to give her two blood transfusions on the table. But her body accepted the new blood well, and she's stabilizing. We didn't have time to give her an epidural, unfortunately…she was just going downhill too fast. We had to give her general anesthesia."

Blood transfusions and general anesthesia? That was about as far from a natural birth as a cow was from a chicken. He just hoped Lindsay understood that they'd had no other choice.

It didn't matter how many plans they made if God had other ones in mind.

"We'll be wheeling her back in here shortly, after she wakes up from the anesthesia. She'll need that IV to prevent seizures for another twenty-four hours, to be safe, though fortunately her blood pressure is already starting to drop toward less dangerous levels."

"Thank you, Dr. Sorin."

But she hadn't mentioned the baby.

His stomach twisted—then he saw the picture in his head once more.

Him, Lindsay, and their baby. Together. Happy.

"How's my baby boy?"

"He was having some trouble breathing," Dr. Sorin said carefully. "We had to bring him to the NICU—"

His mom interrupted. "Nick-you?"

"Neonatal ICU. It's the intensive care unit for newborns," Dr. Sorin told her.

Eric's heart thudded in his chest. Could they hear it the way he did, pounding in his ears?

"They put him on a CPAP machine," the doctor continued, "which helps push air into his lungs. It's less invasive than a ventilator, but provides more help than just putting oxygen on him. He's had some episodes of his oxygen saturation dropping, but the CPAP will help with that, and I'm hoping to wean him off of it as soon as he can."

"Are we talking hours, days, weeks?" his mom asked.

"That's up to your grandson." Dr. Sorin smiled and looked at Eric. "Dad—you can go see him now if you'd like."

He was Dad. And he could see his son.

Eric's heart leapt into his throat. "Yes."

"Now, because mom's got lots of different medicines going, we didn't want the drugs in her breast milk to go into the baby. So we had to give him some formula. Fortunately, he's got the 'suck, swallow, breathe' combination down right. It doesn't always work out that way with preemies. But he seems to be doing just great with the bottle."

Preemies.

"You can hold him, and feed him. After that, we have to put him back in the incubator, under the bilirubin lights, because he has some jaundice. We'll cover his eyes to protect them."

All of the medical talk swirled in his head. He wasn't sure what was important and what wasn't, what he should worry about and what he shouldn't.

None of it.

He wasn't going to worry about any of it. Because he was already praising God for getting his baby through it. He already knew the outcome.

"He's going to be okay," Eric said.

It wasn't a question—he was informing the doctor.

She put her hand on his. "Yes, he will be."

Over in the NICU, Eric sat anxiously in a rocking chair at the side of the incubator. The nurse handed him his little baby boy, wearing a device on his face that went into his nostrils, and had a big thick tube attached to the machine.

His son.

Eric didn't want to move the wrong way and mess up all the wires and monitoring stickers on him, much less the breathing device.

"I don't want to hurt him."

Was he even qualified to hold something so tiny and fragile?

* * *

Lindsay woke up in a hospital bed, a stabbing, aching pain across her lower abdomen. Her body seemed unnaturally empty. What was going on?

A blue balloon attached by a string of ribbon to the foot of her hospital bed floated into her blurry line of sight. It said: IT'S A BOY!

It's a boy.

She had the baby? When did that happen?

How could she miss that?

This was supposed to be one of the most important moments in her life, and it was completely missing from her memory.

She looked around the darkened room in confusion. Her sister was in the chair next to her bedside, her head back, eyes closed.

"Meg?" Lindsay's voice sounded completely unlike her own. Creaky and rusty.

Megan's eyes opened and she leaned down, peering into her face. "Thank God," she whispered. "You're going to be okay. So is the baby. He's in the NICU right now with Eric."

"What happened?"

A nurse came in, and washed her hands. "You're awake!" the nurse said cheerily. "You gave us a scare, didn't you?"

Lindsay looked at Megan in confusion. What on earth had happened?

"How's your pain level?" the nurse asked. "I brought you some medicine."

Lindsay tried to sit up, but her abdominal muscles wouldn't work. She sank back against the hospital bed mattress, panting from the effort.

"Yeah, you're gonna need that medicine." The nurse handed Lindsay two horse-sized pills.

How was she supposed to take those?

More water. Right. She swallowed, fighting the urge to gag as they went down her swollen throat.

There was that blue helium balloon. *It's a boy.*

The nurse followed her gaze. "You like that? Your hubby brought it in for you when you were still conked out." She smiled knowingly. "That one's a keeper, lemme tell you. You've got a good one there."

"What's happening?" Lindsay asked.

What was wrong with her voice? And whatever medicine cocktail they had her on was making her memory even fuzzier.

The nurse looked her over sympathetically. "Your poor throat.

That's from the airway protector. We had to move quick, so your throat's irritated, but it'll be back to normal soon."

She didn't care about her voice. "I don't remember having my baby."

"Mrs. Hunt, they had to do an emergency C-section, and there was no time for the epidural, for you to be awake. The doctor put you under general anesthesia, and you had some bleeding. They had to give you a blood transfusion—two, actually—while you were under."

Lindsay looked over at her sister again. Did all that happen, for real? And somehow…Lindsay had missed it.

Megan smiled reassuringly. "You'll be okay," she said. "The doctor came out and told us you were bleeding, that you needed a transfusion…"

It must've been so scary for them. And Eric—he'd probably been so afraid of losing the baby.

"You scared me, Linds," her sister whispered. "You scared all of us. Eric's parents are here—they're getting coffee with Zach, but they'll be back soon."

"Why can't I remember having my baby?"

"You're still kinda slurring your words a bit." Megan's brow furrowed in concentration. "Don't you remember what the nurse said, just a moment ago?"

Did she? Lindsay focused, trying to clear the fog clouding her brain. "They put me under."

"Yeah." Megan looked so worried for her.

"I'm okay," Lindsay reassured her. "At least, I will be once they get this stupid IV out of me."

She let her head fall back against the pillow. The stabbing pain in her abdomen started to subside, and a feeling of warmth spread to her cheeks. The pain medicine the nurse gave her must've kicked in.

Maybe she'd refuse it the next time if she could.

Anything to be able to think clearly again.

At least the way she felt now was a million times better than before they delivered the baby.

She was a mother.

A mother!

She hadn't even met her baby yet, but she ached for him.

* * *

In the NICU, Eric cradled their baby, when something on the large monitor blinked red, and alarmed.

Beep-Beep-Beep-Beep-Beep-Beep—

"I'm right here." The nurse came up to them, and rearranged one of the stickers holding a wire onto the baby's chest.

The alarm stopped.

"He's fine, he's fine," the nurse assured him. "Always look at the baby first, not the monitor. He's nice and pink, see? And I'm keeping an eye on everything on the monitors, too, so if anything changes, I can run right over, just like that."

"I didn't hurt him, did I?" Eric looked up at her from the rocking chair with concern.

"He's fine, daddy. It's actually quite helpful for the baby to be held. It's good for him. You're helping."

His baby opened his little eyes, and seemed to stare right into Eric's own.

"Hey there," Eric said softly.

Yes, he was qualified to hold his son—he could feel it now.

He would do anything to keep this boy safe. "Welcome to the world, Little One."

His baby.

Any fear he'd had earlier about not being able to bond with a child that wasn't his own DNA instantly washed away when he stared at that little fragile body, and held him in his arms.

His tiny chest rose up and down. There was a card on his incubator that read: BABY BOY HUNT 5LBS, 4OZ.

"I'm your daddy," Eric said softly to his son. "Do you know my voice? You're gonna be okay. So is Mommy. You'll meet her as soon as she's feeling better."

Little baby fingers wrapped tightly around Eric's thumb. Every bit of him was small and precious.

"You're my baby," Eric whispered, holding his boy against his chest. "I love you." The words fell so easily from his lips.

And when he saw Lindsay, he would get to tell her, too.

Because he did. He loved her.

It didn't matter that he'd felt like less of a man because of his infertility. None of his fears mattered, like that he couldn't provide for her and the child—even though they were still concerns—he was just going to have to figure something out to make sure the ranch would flourish instead of fail.

But holding his baby in his arms, it was suddenly crystal-clear to him.

Eric still had value to offer, even if he were broke and living in a tent. He would die to protect her and their child. God had shown him that.

It was something he hadn't even known about himself—he

thought he was simply providing a home, and going to be a father to her baby.

But Eric would do anything for them.

Tackle any obstacle.

Die a thousand deaths to protect them.

And he was *not* less of a man, after all.

* * *

Lindsay woke again, in pain. Early-morning light filtered through the hospital-room window. How long had she been out? Was it tomorrow already?

A nurse wearing blue gloves was unhooking the IV in Lindsay's arm. "Doctor says you're out of the woods now, so I can disconnect this mag-sulfate. That should make you feel better."

Thank God.

Then she woke, again. Had she passed out? The sunlight in the room had changed. Closer to noon, now?

This whole experience was insane. None of this was what she'd hoped for when she'd imagined the experience of becoming a mother.

Despite the brave face she'd put on for Megan, Lindsay had been scared, too. She'd thought she was going to die.

Coming out on the other side of an experience like that…it put everything into sudden, stark perspective.

When she'd been lying there, seeing everything all blurry and double around her and unable to even know what was going on, surrendering to oblivion had felt like the best choice—her only choice.

Every single thought she had tried to conjure up slogged

through layers of thick mud in her mind. With her body flushed and hot as well, it had been obvious even in her diminished mental state that she hadn't been doing well.

Even the fact that she'd been so adamant against having an emergency cesarean-section when she so clearly had needed it, just went to show how altered her state of mind had been.

Lindsay took stock of how she felt now, compared to before time had been put on pause, fast forwarded, and restarted.

She no longer felt overheated. Her head wasn't pounding anymore, thank God.

As for the rest of her, it was as if someone had popped her like a water balloon. She'd been deflated, from her puffy face to her much-less-swollen ankles. Breathing was easier now, too. Like the fluid was off her lungs.

Her big pregnant belly had been replaced with a much-flattened version, minus the baby but with the addition of a row of ugly staples.

Had she really gotten blood transfusions on the operating room table?

Just how close had she been to meeting Jesus?

And to think... Jesus had literally died for her, so she could live forever with Him. And while she'd always known that, maybe she'd only known it on an intellectual level.

She'd never thought about what it actually meant, to have someone lay down their life so that she could live. She was that valuable to Him—that important.

She wasn't valuable because of what she could do or provide. She wasn't valuable because of how well or how poorly she filled her roles in this world as an employee, rancher, wife, or mother.

She was valuable simply because *God valued her.*

And that was enough.

Was it enough for her husband, too?

Eric had stood by her through all of this. He'd been her rock, and had become her best friend.

She didn't want to be with Grant, even though he was the biological father of her child. She didn't want to be with anyone but Eric.

Any thoughts she'd had about how she'd "settled" for a marriage of convenience for her baby's sake—well, that may have been true in the beginning, but it was no longer true now.

She loved him. She loved Eric with all her heart.

And he was the *real* father of her baby. She wanted to be his wife, his partner, his best friend, and yes…his lover. She no longer had to be afraid of that aspect of marriage.

Grant may have abandoned her when she needed him most, but Eric had proven he never would.

Her sister was still at her bedside, reading a book. Lindsay had a fuzzy memory of Eric having been there too—had that been last night?

"Where's Eric?" Her voice was so rough. "How long have I been here?"

Megan pressed the call button on a remote near the hospital bed, and handed her a cup of water.

"You've been in and out all day, all night," Megan said. "I think you wake up every time the pain medicine wears off. I called the nurse."

Lindsay tentatively took a sip. The cool water soothed her ragged throat. "Can I see my baby?"

"Look who's awake again!" the nurse said from the doorway.

"Where's Eric?" Lindsay looked at her sister. "My baby?"

"Your husband's been going back an' forth, between visiting you and the NICU. I can't bring your baby in here," the nurse said, "'cause we need to keep him under the bili-lights for at least the rest of today and monitored in the NICU, and then the doctor'll reevaluate him again."

She smiled, smoothing her pink-and-blue scrubs, and took the water cup from Lindsay.

"But you can definitely have some time to hold him and feed him, if you feel up to it. I can wheel you over there."

"Please. Yes." Lindsay pushed herself up to sitting with her arms, since her stomach muscles were completely useless. "Don't need a wheelchair, though. I can walk."

The nurse laughed. "That's the spirit. But it's hospital policy. So we're gonna have you use the wheelchair for now, to make sure you get to the NICU nice and safe, 'kay?"

Lindsay didn't have the strength to argue. She just wanted to see her family.

Her family... Her husband and her son.

Thank You, God.

For everything.

Chapter Twenty-One

LINDSAY HELD A pillow against her lap to support her C-section incision, her slippered feet on the foot pedals of the wheelchair. The nurse wheeled her, with Megan, Zach and her in-laws by her side.

But when they got to the entrance to the NICU, the nurse there put her hand up. "Only three people are allowed at a time in the NICU per baby," she said sternly. "And there's already two in there with your son. So it's just going to be you coming in, mom."

Two people?

Eric, of course… and who else?

The nurse rolled her in, and Lindsay's heart clenched at the sight of Eric holding their Little One. It was a combination of joy at seeing them together, and fear. Her baby was covered in wires and something on his face, and his nostrils.

How was she going to take care of him now?

"Will he be okay?" she asked, her voice catching in her throat.

"Absolutely," the NICU nurse said. "In fact, his 02 sats have been so good while he's been sitting here with dad, that we're ready to take him off the CPAP and try just a regular nasal cannula for oxygen."

Lindsay's own breath caught at the thought of her child not

getting enough air. "Will he be able to breathe?"

"Absolutely. We'll keep monitoring him, so we'll know how well his oxygen saturation is doing." The nurse pointed to a number on the monitor.

Carefully, the nurse removed the CPAP off of her baby's face. That face! He was beautiful.

"Eric," she whispered, meeting her husband's eyes. "Our baby."

Eric handed her the baby, his eyes glistening with unshed tears. "He's a tough kid."

Lindsay nodded, cradling their baby. The nurse placed a pillow on her lap so she could rest her arms against it, as if she already knew how weak every muscle in her body felt at the moment.

"You look way better than you did the last time I saw you," Eric said. "How do you feel?"

"The cobwebs are clearing. Pain medicine seems to be working, though I don't know how I'll feel when it wears off. I've literally got staples in my abdomen."

Eric winced. "You're the tough one. I don't know if I could handle everything that you just went through."

"That's why God made it so only women would have the babies," she pointed out.

Eric laughed in response. "You'll have a well-earned battle scar, Linds. Wear it with pride."

She smiled. And yes, she would happily wear her battle scars. Holding her baby now, it was all worth it. Anything would've been worth it.

"The nurse said there were two people in here visiting. Who's with you? Because your parents were with me—they're in the waiting room."

"He walked off the moment the door to the NICU opened," Eric said. "Said he wanted to give you some time with the baby, first."

Who?

Eric nodded over toward the nurses' station.

Grant Bowland.

Live and in the flesh, standing uncomfortably off to the side, looking completely out of his comfort zone.

"Hi, there." Grant waved from across the room. "I figured I'd give you guys some privacy."

Lindsay raised her eyebrows in surprise. "Wow…I mean, how did you even get here so fast?"

"Wasn't that fast…you've been asleep for a while." He walked over, nodding respectfully toward Eric. "When I heard from Eric, I caught a flight out."

Eric had contacted him? The same Eric who'd spent the past six months consumed by fear that she'd choose Grant over him?

She glanced at her husband and gave him a mental high-five. He smiled back at her.

"He's got your chin, Grant," Lindsay pointed out. "Don't you think?"

Grant smiled and nodded. "I'm not usually a baby-person, but he really is cute. He actually looks a lot like you, Linds." Grant studied their faces, first hers, then the baby's. "What are you naming him?"

"Eric?" she asked, turning to her husband. "What would you like to name our baby?"

In the periphery of her vision, she kept an eye on Grant, to see if his expression changed, or if he stiffened with irritation at her calling their baby "ours."

But Grant seemed unruffled.

Was he really fine with all of this? She wouldn't blame him if he still harbored some animosity. This was such a complicated situation.

At least she was starting to be able to think more clearly now that she was away from the IV pole in her room.

But with Grant standing there, how could she tell Eric, for the very first time...that she loved him?

Eric knelt at her side, so that he was face-to-face with her and their baby. "I was thinking Paul, after your mom."

Paula Moore had to be looking down from heaven and smiling at that.

Lindsay nodded. "I love it. Paul Hunt. It's a strong name."

Next to her, standing a foot away, Grant cleared his throat. "I came down here because I wanted to, you know... Meet the baby and all. And see you one last time."

"Last time?"

"Well... You guys are a family. I can see that. Any fool can tell you guys belong together. That you're madly in love. I don't want to mess that up for you. I'm happy for you, Linds. I really am." Grant took a deep breath. "Maybe at some point in the future, Paul will want to meet me, and I'd be happy to do that. Maybe I could send him birthday presents or something."

Lindsay looked up at him. Grant was finally starting to sound like the old friend and colleague she'd grown to know, before she'd made the mistake of crashing at his apartment.

"I've been thinking about this the whole plane ride here." Grant exhaled heavily. "I was—I was wrong when I asked you to have the abortion, Lindsay. I'm really sorry that I did that. And that I didn't even offer to go with you, or support you and your decision."

He paused. "That was wrong, and I hope someday you can forgive me for all that. But…I was right about the fact that I'm just not ready for a kid. I'm willing to sign away my parental rights, so that Eric can officially adopt him. He deserves to be more than a stepfather in the eyes of the law. Your husband should be his real dad. Just watching him, I can see…he already is."

Praise God!

Lindsay held baby Paul against her chest and put out one arm toward Grant. He leaned in and gently hugged her before stepping back.

Eric put his hand out to Grant. "Thank you," Eric said, his voice filled with emotion. "That's very honorable of you. And we are so grateful. I promise I'll do right by him. By both of them."

"I know you will," Grant said.

They shook on it.

Grant picked up his jacket. "I'm in the Coeur d'Alene Hotel. My plane's not leaving until tonight, so you can have your lawyer contact me and I'll stop by his office and sign whatever you need before I head back to New York."

"Can we get a picture of you holding Paul?" Lindsay asked. "He might want to see it one day. You will be part of his birth story. We don't want any secrets with him." She looked at Eric, and he nodded in agreement.

Eric took his phone out and took a picture of Grant gingerly cradling Paul in his arms, his jacket slung over his shoulder, as if he already had one foot out the door.

Grant gave the baby one last look, handed him over to Eric, and left.

As soon as Grant was out of the room, Lindsay took a deep breath, as if she'd been holding it the entire time. "Thank you, Jesus."

Eric wrapped his arm around her shoulder, and put his head down against her hers. They sat like this, her in the wheelchair, their heads bent over their baby, him kneeling in front of her, for a good solid moment.

"He could see it, did you notice that?" Eric looked up and smiled at her. "He said any fool could tell we're madly in love. I must be that fool, because I'm so in love with you, Lindsay, and I only realized it when…when I thought you were going to die."

His voice broke on that last word, and his eyes welled with tears.

She'd never seen him cry before today.

Lindsay squeezed his hand. "I love you too, Eric. I love you so much."

"I promise you, Linds, I'm going to take care of you both. I have a meeting next week set up—could be a huge new beef contract. It would get us out of the red and into the black. We're going to keep the ranch going. We'll get it all taken care of."

Lindsay shook her head. "That's what I realized, though—it doesn't matter what you can give me, not anymore. Because all I need from you… is you. That's all I want. My husband."

"I feel the same way about you." He gently laid his hand on Paul's head. "Heavenly Father, thank You for this baby, thank You for getting Lindsay and Paul through this. Thank You for softening Grant's heart toward us. Please heal Lindsay and Paul completely, so I can take them home. We pray in Jesus' name, Amen."

"Amen," Lindsay said.

"Amen," the nurse standing several feet away said. She smiled shyly. "Sorry—couldn't help but overhear. You're just...you're such a beautiful family."

Eric looked up at Lindsay. "How long do you need to plan the wedding of your dreams? Because I want to marry you all over again."

Epilogue

Six months later...

LINDSAY STOOD UNDER the gazebo in a long white wedding dress. Eric stood beside her, looking amazing in a black suit and cowboy hat. The yellow flowers at their feet danced in the spring breeze.

Lindsay looked out at their friends and family. Megan held baby Paul on her lap, who was smiling at her. Lindsay waved. She was so happy her father had decided to fly out from London to see them, and to meet his very first grandchild. He was going to be staying a few weeks in the guest cabin behind Megan and Zach's home, so they'd have plenty of time to see him and reconnect. Grandpa was overjoyed with baby Paul—and he loved his name.

Not only had Eric gotten the new contract he'd promised would save the ranch, but Zach, Chris, and Jay had each been thinking the same thing—that they needed to figure out a way to increase their income at the ranch.

Zach had organized to sell timber from some back acres that needed to be cleared anyway. Jay had rented out some unused land to nearby residents who didn't own enough land for crops, so they could grow corn and beans.

Chris had gone out and gotten another huge contract for the ranch. So not only were they back in the black, they were doing great.

Eric was even able to get himself a new black pickup truck…this time, with a quad-cab that could accommodate a car seat in the back. They upgraded her used sedan to a four-wheel-drive SUV, perfect for Idaho winters.

And while Lindsay had taken the first few months off just to be at home with the baby, now she was back to work at the farmhouse, and they even set up a room with a baby monitor as a second nursery so she could have Paul with her, with a play-space taking up half of her office.

It was perfect.

He was too little to do much just yet, but they both enjoyed her holding him against her in a wrap as she worked.

With Lindsay handling the business side of things, Eric and the guys were free to do what they truly loved—ranching. They were back in their area of expertise, where they thrived.

"And now," Pastor Jim said, "Eric and Lindsay will exchange their rings."

Eric took out a beautiful gold band with three diamonds, and held it in his hands.

She covered her mouth in surprise.

It was an amazing, gorgeous ring. And this was the first time Lindsay was seeing it.

Eric smiled at her. "Lindsay, this ring has three stones, for our past, our present, and our future together. I also like that three is the number of our family: you, me, and our son. Most importantly, three represents the threads that, when combined, are not easily broken. You, me, and God. It's only because of God our relationship is a strong as it is today."

He smiled and took a breath. "I love you so much, and I'm so grateful you agreed to be my wife and married me on faith. I vow to be that man who justifies your faith in me, so it never fades. I vow to be with you, Lindsay, for richer or poorer, through sickness and health, through good times and bad, for as long as we both shall live."

Lindsay held out her trembling left hand.

Carefully, Eric slid the ring onto her ring finger. It fit perfectly, and it looked amazing. The ring they had originally married with would go on her right hand now.

Lindsay turned, looked at her friends and family and smiled. "I also have a ring for him that he hasn't seen yet."

The congregation tittered. Lindsay looked back at her husband.

"When you first proposed to me, so soon after we met, I knew then that it was going to take a leap of faith to say yes. I'm so glad that I took that leap, and landed squarely in your arms. Since we first got married, we've grown closer every day, and you have become my very best friend in the whole world. I love you so much, Eric."

She held up the ring. "It's in Hebrew." She pointed out the Hebrew lettering to Eric, who stared at the engraved brushed-steel ring in fascination. "You read it from right to left."

אֲנִי לְדוֹדִי וְדוֹדִי לִי

Lindsay recited the words in Hebrew carefully. "A*nee* l'doh-*dee*, v'doh-*dee*, lee."

Some people clapped at her attempt, and she blushed, glancing over at their friends.

"It means, 'I am my beloved's and my beloved is mine.' Song of Solomon. It's also engraved on the wedding band Eric originally gave me when we first eloped."

Out on the lawn, her father turned to Megan and said in what he probably thought was his quiet voice, but was actually loud enough for everyone to hear, "That's what I gave Mom on our honeymoon."

Yup.

And that's what made it so perfect.

"With this ring," she continued, "I renew my vow to be with you—through richer or poorer, through sickness and health, through good times and bad, for better or worse, for as long as we both shall live."

Pastor Jim clasped his hands together. "By the power vested in me by God and the great state of Idaho, I pronounce you are *still* Mr. and Mrs. Hunt, husband and wife—now, with a renewed strength and love in your marriage. Eric, you may kiss your beautiful bride."

Eric leaned in close, ever-so-gently cupping her cheek, and kissed her full on her mouth.

Everyone clapped.

"I am my beloved's," he whispered against her lips.

She kissed him back. "And my beloved is mine."

* * *

After dancing all night, and baby Paul sleeping over at Aunt Megan and Uncle Zach's house just for the one night, it was finally time. Eric lifted Lindsay in his arms, her beautiful white dress silky against his hands.

"I gotta carry you over the threshold again, I think." Eric grinned at her.

"Yes, those are definitely the rules."

"Well…we can't break the rules." Eric held her in his arms and gently carried her over the threshold.

He had no intention of setting her down in the front hall like he had the first time, however. Holding her close to his chest, he kept walking with her, carrying her straight into the master bedroom.

With a laugh, Lindsay pushed their bedroom door shut behind them.

The End

Sign up for <u>Shoshanna Gabriel's newsletter</u>
<u>ShoshannaGabriel.com/subscribe</u>
to know when
the next BEAR CREEK SADDLE Series book releases!

Acknowledgements

FIRST AND FOREMOST, I would like to give the glory to God for making me a storyteller, for which I am forever grateful! Thank You for sending us Your Son.

Thank you to my readers. Without you, I would be writing into the abyss. And a special shout-out goes to the Shoshanna Street Team—thank you for your support, and for spreading the word!

Thank you to the inspirational Christian authors who have encouraged me to write the stories I feel called to write, and for my readers for joining me on this journey with my new name as Shoshanna Gabriel, and my new genre. I'm so excited about the Bear Creek Saddle Series.

Thank you to Karen Solem of SpencerHill Associates, for your support.

Thank you to my beta-readers.

Thank you to Therese Marie of ChristianProofreaders.com, for editing this book. Any errors or omissions are my own.

Thank you to my cover artist, Rob Sturtz, from SelfPubBookCovers.com for my cover. I co-founded SelfPubBookCovers.com with Rob to help fulfill my dream of having quality covers at an affordable price available to all indie authors, instantly. If you're a writer, too, you might want to check out the amazing artists we have on board!

Last on the list but not in my heart: thank you, Dear Husband, for being awesome and for being my soulmate, and to my children, for going to bed so sweetly every night, so Mommy can write while the household sleeps. I love you!

About Shoshanna Gabriel

SHOSHANNA GABRIEL WAS previously known as Shoshanna Evers, a *New York Times* and *USA Today* bestselling author who wrote over twenty-plus secular romance novels and novellas, and published with big New York publishers, small presses, and through indie-publishing. After much thought and prayer, she decided to **change her life and career path to be for God's glory**. Shoshanna Gabriel is currently writing Christian inspirational romance novels. For a detailed explanation of this big change, read her blog post "Saying Goodbye to Erotic Romance" (http://bit.ly/GoodbyeErotica).

While published as Shoshanna Evers, Amazon had listed her as one of the "Most Popular Authors in Romance," as well as one of the "Most Popular Authors in Contemporary Romance." Reviewers have said Shoshanna has "…**beautiful writing**, and a **truly imaginative** and wonderfully descriptive storyline" (Night Owl Reviews) with stories where "the plot is fresh and the pacing excellent, **the emotions…real and poignant**." (The Romance Studio) She hopes to bring her gift of storytelling to her new inspirational books written under the Gabriel name.

Shoshanna used to work as a syndicated advice columnist in NY and a registered nurse, but now she's a full-time author and a homeschooling mom of a son and boy/girl twins. She is also **the co-founder of SelfPubBookCovers.com**, the world's largest selection of high-quality, affordable book covers for indie authors, available instantly. She lives with her family and three big dogs in northern Idaho, and loves to connect with readers on social media.

Faithfully Ever After...
ShoshannaGabriel.com

Want to know when my next book comes out?
Sign up for my newsletter to hear about new releases first, and read excerpts you won't find in the sample pages!
ShoshannaGabriel.com/subscribe

Visit ShoshannaGabriel.com/contests for monthly giveaways of different inspirational romance novels!

Let's be BFFs!

@ShoshnnaGabriel (Twitter.com/ShoshnnaGabriel)
@ShoshannaEvers (Twitter.com/ShoshannaEvers)
Facebook (faccbook.com/ShoshannaGabriel)

To my readers:

If you enjoyed this book, I'd love if you could **leave an honest review,** *because your opinion matters*!

Reviews are so important; thank you for taking the time—I really appreciate it!

Pick up a book and visit
Bear Creek Saddle, Idaho, anytime—
you're always welcome HOME.

www.ingramcontent.com/pod-product-compliance
Lightning Source LLC
Chambersburg PA
CBHW030644260626
47157CB00007B/2482